About the Author

Jo Jackson King is the author of the award-winning and best-selling *Station at Austin Downs*. An occupational therapist, she works with remote communities in the outback. A gifted writer with extensive rural women's networks, Jo is a School of the Air mother and veteran of late-night talkfests between women where the conversation veers away from school and land care and becomes about love.

Love in a SUNBURNT COUNTRY

JO JACKSON KING

HARLEQUIN®

First published June 2016 by Harlequin Nonfiction
An imprint of Harlequin Enterprises (Australia) Pty Ltd.
Level 13, 201 Elizabeth St
SYDNEY NSW 2000
AUSTRALIA

ISBN 978 176037199 9

Cataloguing-in-Publication details are available from the National Library of Australia www.librariesaustralia.nla.gov.au

Cover design by Christa Moffitt, Christabella Designs
Cover photographs © Shutterstock
Printed and bound in Australia by Griffin Press, South Australia

FSC www.fsc.org MIX Paper from responsible sources FSC® C009448

Wishing you love
And on your land a flourishing garden
Our loves and our gardens are all different
And all the same.

Contents

Setting Out

At the beginning of 2015 I set off on a journey to find and tell some of remote Australia's best love stories and to paint a portrait of not just the lovers, but the endless pattern of how the land transforms those who live on it and how those who live on it transform the land.

I am an outback dweller myself, and I have young children, so I am a School of the Air mother. Parents teach the children a curriculum supplied by the school, and once a day the children speak to their teacher and classmates 'over the air'—this was once done via radio but now involves virtual classrooms on computer screens. Every so often there is a camp. We drive our children hundreds, sometimes thousands, of kilometres for these gatherings. These are necessary for the children and for teachers, but also, as you might imagine, for mothers. We talk and talk. Late at night, when the children are hopefully sleeping (or, at the least, settled!) we tell the stories of how we came to live where we do. And so often these stories are ones of life-derailing and transformative love. In this book, from all around Australia, are the kind of stories that I hear late at night and into the early morning on School of the Air camps. The outback setting forces couples to rely on each other far more than usual as there is often no-one else—it strengthens marriages or breaks them. And within each love story I wanted to share the other aspects of living remotely—both the smaller and larger stories of our lives, the dangers and comforts, the history and the possible futures we see. I didn't want the love stories to have just a romantic beginning. I wanted to find people with lives about which my readers and listeners would say 'you couldn't make that stuff up'.

Initially I thought the hardest part of this book would be finding stories from all around Australia. And it was tricky. For example, the first story was found by friends of friends through the bush telegraph that still operates across regional Australia. One of the numbers I was given to call was that of South Australian artist Marie Parsons, mother of another well-known artist Ally Parsons.

I rang Marie. As I spoke the words aloud I could hear for the first time what a very strange request I was making. 'Even if a love story comes to mind in a few weeks' time, perhaps you could call me ...'

'Oh, no,' she said warmly. 'A story has come to mind straight away. One of my daughter Ally's governesses from when Ally owned a station. Her name is Frances. Frances and Luke fell in love ... well, that took a bit longer ... but they met when Frances was working for Ally as her governess, and Luke came to the property to shear sheep. Now they're restoring the historical buildings on the station belonging to Frances's family and the ABC has just made a TV show about what they've done. The story I heard about their meeting was that Luke went shearing in a suit, tie and jacket and all, and that's what caught Frances's eye.' So that became the first story in this book.

But, in fact, finding the stories was the easiest part of writing. When you begin to write a book it feels a great deal as if you are packing for a long, exciting and arduous journey. You hope to have most of what you will need in your suitcase. On first setting out I felt confident I was uniquely qualified to write this book. I was in the midst of the first story when I began to suspect I was missing something vital—something I had not even known I needed to pack. To write this book I needed to understand love, and it had never occurred to me before that I didn't understand how love works and what it is.

My home is in remote Western Australia on a pastoral property with my husband, my parents and my three sons—and together we are regenerating it. We have lived there for sixteen years and Austin Downs is well and truly halfway back to life. I know how land degrades and how it can heal. My family's adventures on Austin Downs are the subject of my first book.

Healing land must be rested. This means less stock. Sometimes it means no stock, and therefore no earnings. But you must still live! All the adults in our business work off the property—my husband and father in mining and making fences, solar arrays and monitoring systems, my mother and I as occupational therapists. We don't work in clinics, but out in the communities themselves, and our favourite work is with children. And so my second book was on human development. It lays bare the interconnections between generations and shows how the way love is expressed travels down between generations. It tells the stories of how the forces in wider society shape the interactions between parent and child and how we all transform each other, all the time: bodies, minds, hearts and relationships.

My work as an occupational therapist often brings me close to people during the most painful parts of their lives. So what do I read to recover from vicariously experiencing that pain, to be able to be present with a full heart on the next day? Apart from research about how to do my job better (I am a research junkie, as you will see), I read romance. I read a lot of romance. I am particularly fond of Regency romance. I had assumed that this, combined with my own happy experience of love and marriage, added up to a natural understanding of romantic love. There is a book called *Everything I Know About Love I Learned From Romance Novels*—but, I was to discover, reading romances had apparently not taught me enough.

I was astonished to discover that some people who were falling in love had no idea what was happening to them. In fact, when I heard this from the first couple I talked to, Frances and Luke from Holowiliena Station, I didn't believe them. In our long discussion of this intimate, extraordinary part of their lives I actually argued with them about their feelings and the sequence of events in their own love story. I am mortified when I think about it now. At the time I just couldn't help myself.

The next interview was with Robina Meehan ('outback gypsy') who said: 'Limerence, that patch when you are off your head, that didn't happen with me and Aaron. It was better and deeper than that.'

Then, on the plane journey back from Lightning Ridge to Western Australia, I fell into conversation with Lachlan Gatti, who was in his second year of a Bachelor of Arts and Teaching. At Lachlan's college an expert had been brought in to talk about love and so Lachlan knew all about limerence and he also told me it had another name: PEA Brain.

Back to the research I went, but by now I was becoming aware of how very much I didn't know about love. Talking to each of the couples in this book resulted in me returning to the library to learn more of the neurology, the psychology and the philosophy of love. And I was on another journey too: to better understand the land.

Driving through the Flinders Ranges to meet Luke and Frances, the uncovered hills have me wondering if they have always been so picturesquely, so revealingly bare, or if this is a result of early overgrazing. Once I would unhesitatingly have thought 'most certainly', but now, I'm learning this is not necessarily the case. Aboriginal people kept the 'woody weeds' that cover much of Australia to a minimum by use of fire. The 'parkland cleared' landscape that early painters replicated faithfully in the 18th century was not the original Australian landscape, but the landscape created deliberately by the Aboriginal people. The Australian 'natural' (not farmed or grazed) landscape of later centuries—dense scrub, forests, woodland plains—is therefore one created by human intervention too, in this case the cessation of the Aboriginal people's efforts.

In fact, the question of whether a landscape is natural or not is similar to that of whether nature or nurture shapes a child. Both questions are based on flawed assumptions: firstly, that 'nature' is inanimate and static rather than dynamic, responsive and creative; secondly, that change is always human-led; and, finally, that we ourselves aren't part of nature. The truth is that the land and all that live on it, below it and above it are always changing—innovating, responding, adapting—and the idea of an unchanged virgin landscape is nonsense.

How land changes people and how love changes land is the context for this book and to write it I've had to come to a better understanding of what love is, and what land is, and of how they both work, and how love and land work together to create us.

Didn't Know I Was Looking For Love

Frances and Luke Frahn, Holowiliena Station, Flinders Ranges, South Australia

It is evening and early winter, and my father Tom and I have just reached the twisting gravel road that will take us through the Flinders to Holowiliena, one of South Australia's most remote and historic sheep stations. Holowiliena has been in the hands of the Warwick family for 160 years. This long association of family and land is rare, and becoming rarer with every year that passes.

It is a lonely road. For some unknown reason I expected to see the same messily rounded shrubs and short trees and willowy grasses that are found around our own station, but I see nothing of the kind. In this part of the Flinders Ranges the hills are covered in low grasses and small rocks. The complex and self-contradicting form of the land is instantly apparent: soft beginnings, sudden scarps, deep incisions where the water runs, and gently rounding crests. The hill shapes echo each other, travelling further and further back, until I am no longer sure what is range and what is cloud on the far horizon.

But there are trees here, creek bed and valley dwellers, river red gum and native pine. Few trees combine solidity and grace like these river gums: where they touch the sky they are delicate, each twig carefully placed so it doesn't crowd another, maximising light onto leaf, and yet they pour out of the earth with such power held in their massive trunks and low branches. The native pine is a very humble, prosaic tree in comparison, with stubbled bark, trunks of even width, and closely hung dark leaf clusters.

There are well-fed grey-and-black kangaroos at every creek bed. I've been counting them, trying to get a sense of how many there are on the property, but there are too many. In fact the number of roos on the road here has me rattled and I'm finding it hard to concentrate on what Dad, who has been talking for the past few kilometres, has to say. He is braking and swerving intermittently, and glancing at me to check that I am listening. I am silent, braced against everything available to brace against and with my teeth locked together. I cannot help wishing he would simply concentrate on driving and I am relieved and delighted when we find the edge of the shearing-shed yards and turn in to the homestead. We are here to meet Luke and Frances Frahn, who have a story that is one worth telling.

We are met by the family dogs, welcoming and smiling all over their black-and-tan faces. Luke Frahn strolls towards us, gently sending his five-year-old son Todd, who has come out in his dressing gown to meet us, back to finish his dinner. I am curious about Luke. He is a shearer, and the story I have been told is that he does this work dressed in a suit and tie. But tonight he is dressed for visitors and the cold in a plain navy woollen jumper and neat jeans.

In fact, almost all the photographs I've seen of Luke show him costumed for an ABC television episode showcasing the building restorations on Holowiliena. In the photos he looks remarkably comfortable in the kind of clothes that have not been worn in Australia for over a century: high-necked shirt, high-waisted button pants, vest, hat—clothes that even predate those worn by the men in Tom Roberts's iconic painting *The Shearers*. I look for signs of the flamboyance I've more than half-expected. But it is quickly clear that I have misunderstood Luke's character. He is not at all flamboyant or eccentric. He has a rather austere face for such a young man. He looks approachable but not persuadable: clean-shaven, conservatively dressed, thoughtful. (I am soon to realise Luke looked comfortable in the clothes of over a century ago simply because he is at home in his body. A shearer, after all, is a professional athlete. Physical and emotional balance, the skills to reassure a stressed animal or colleague, rhythm, patience, love of craft, learning by doing, team-thinking, enjoying the moment and the work—these are the gifts of the good shearer and Luke, as it turns out, is one of Australia's best.)

In the warm kitchen-dining room, with overloaded bookshelves and an efficient potbelly stove, Todd and three-year-old Stella, Luke and Frances's daughter, gaze up at us speculatively from their dinner. My dad is grandfather to twelve children, many of whom have perfected the art of extending dinner in order to avoid going to bed. 'It would have been better if we'd been an hour later!' he says apologetically to Frances Frahn.

Frances has remarkable eyes, which are large and lovely. I have read about eyes like these. They are the 'well-opened eyes' with which Georgette Heyer endowed her heroines, who were of a selfless and giving disposition. She flashes us a glance of warm gratitude and relief. It is a terrible time for us to have arrived. There is no doubt that schemes to suspend bedtime are being hatched and refined, in Stella's mind at least. Her fine hair is bunched into a pigtail, and it shines sparkly gold under the bright light. She is warmly bundled up in a soft dressing gown of greys and pinks made by Janne, Frances's mother. No child could look sweeter. She is smiling at us, but her eyes are alight with plans rather than welcome. I smile back, trying to do so in a way that conveys that I am not to be considered a fellow conspirator. Stella immediately returns my smile with a significant look and slips from the table, leaving her dinner uneaten.

The children's governess, Miss Mikaela, dark-haired, dimpled and from a Queensland bush family, comes in to sort out weekend arrangements. Todd is debating a range of pudding options.

Stella returns holding what I think is a sheep—it can be hard to identify species with some stuffed toys—in all the shades of the rainbow.

'This is Daddy's,' she explains. 'When he goes shearing, I look after him until Daddy comes home again.'

'He *was* Daddy's,' Todd clarifies for me. 'From when Daddy was little.'

Luke will be away all of next month, and Stella is getting herself ready to bear it. Luke's earnings from shearing still assist the family budget. This includes his prize money from shearing competitions which is considerable—and about which Luke will say very little, changing the subject instantly to the gentleman who taught him to shear, John Hutchinson. (Luke considers John an important mentor. 'If I could please him, then I was happy,' Luke says. And he did not just mentor Luke. John was Australia's champion shearer for six years, but found time to work with troubled young people and was eventually awarded an Order of Australia for this.)

Then Luke is finalising dessert plans with Todd, talking to Stella about putting away the rainbow sheep again, prompting her to have her hair brushed before bedtime and explaining to us Frances's role in local government. Frances is on the phone, cooking our dinner and finding Todd's read-aloud book. Children's bedtime is not the time for me to be asking questions—or, indeed, for observing what drew Frances and Luke to each other: because it is their story I am here to explore.

And shortly afterwards it is time for me to go to bed too. I fall asleep still wondering why Luke wears a suit when he is shearing.

By morning, I have developed a new working theory about the suit.

Frances and Luke are serious in all their shared undertakings: within the wool industry (where they've been offered leadership and training roles), in terms of land and animal management, in curating and restoring Holowiliena (for which they've also been well recognised), and in parenting, which is so manifestly their top priority. Luke grew up on a farm, where his parents still farm, and he knew from very early on that he wanted to shear and to farm. Then there is Luke's precision and work ethic, both of which are in tune with his German Lutheran heritage. Luke says grace before meals too, which I take as a demonstration of a pious but also a serious and thoughtful attitude to life. Perhaps, said my ridiculous theory, Luke is such a serious person that he habitually wears a suit to indicate he is a professional shearer?

After breakfast Frances and Luke tell me that they have planned to use the daylight hours for Dad and me to become acquainted with Holowiliena, however, they have set aside this evening to tell us how they met and fell in love. So whatever the story is behind the suit, I know that I am soon to hear it. (The story of all we learned in the daylight hours is told in the next section.)

'Frances and I love our story,' Luke tells me during the afternoon, accurately reading my sudden qualms about being intrusive and wanting to reassure me.

All through the day it has grown warmer, the sky cloudier, and now it is raining sweetly and steadily outside as inside Dad and I listen.

'I grew up with a strong farming influence and struggles, much like Frances's family. It's made us similar people. We both know how to do without,' says Luke.

Luke's mother steered her son out of school and into paid work early as his restlessness in the classroom began to distract other students. At eighteen, with his body developed well enough for the long days of hard work, he was finally able to enrol in shearing school as he'd wanted to do for so long. There, in addition to learning to shear, he discovered that there was a world-wide demand for shearing skills.

'I started as a rouseabout, then I picked up the handpiece. I had an instructor—a very respected person in my life, he was like a father figure—who pulled me aside, helped me out. By my third and fourth years, I was off, travelling and shearing. I'd been away for seven months, came home, and then I was asked if I'd shear at this station. And there was a governess there, and that was Frances.'

Frances too has a passion for wool and sheep, and like Luke she was a traveller.

'I didn't want to be a governess again, I wanted to do a wool-classing course, but Ally and Miles talked me into working for them for just six weeks—and I ended up working for them for eighteen months.'

Being a governess is a difficult job in a School of the Air family: you are paid by the family and you must work to their satisfaction, but you must also work to the satisfaction of the School of the Air teachers who provide the learning program.

As with any teacher, much of a governess's time is spent preparing work so that the day flows smoothly: she must be familiar with what will be covered and have everything ready for every activity, whether it be a science experiment such as making volcanoes with tomato sauce, bicarbonate of soda and vinegar, or playing a maths game which needs counters and dice.

Frances's room was at the shearers' quarters: a nice room with a carpet, well set up. It was April 2004.

'I rocked up with another guy. We were both footloose, we arrived at the shearers' quarters and we did the lap around—like a male dog marking his territory,' says Luke, his voice full of lazy humour. 'There was a light on, and we looked through the window and there was Frances in a lounge room, lying on the floor doing some bookwork.'

On the same evening the shearers arrived Frances walked out of her room to find everyone sitting in the dark (in order to avoid attracting insects) and she went along and shook hands with everyone politely, and chatted, politely.

'Was there only four of you? It seemed like hundreds,' she says, deadpan.

There's a playfulness to these exchanges, which I had missed earlier.

The next day, they say, Luke turned up to go shearing in a suit, tie and white shirt. Finally, I am going to learn just why Luke shears in a suit and tie. 'Now, was this standard practice?' I ask earnestly.

Luke and Frances stare at me, as well they might. I did, after all, grow up on a wool-producing property. 'No, absolutely not,' they say.

'Was it standard practice, though, for you, Luke?' I clarify, still wondering if Luke might have worn a suit as a way of demonstrating his professionalism.

'No!' says Luke, baffled. 'The weekend before I had been to a gourmet weekend at Clare with friends. It was a themed weekend—we had to wear a school uniform, and I'd gone into an op shop and picked up a suit, pants, tie and white shirt. I still had it with me and I didn't plan to ever wear it again. And on Monday morning I thought, "Why not? I'll go to work in my ... suit."'

Even now it makes them both chuckle, and I laugh too.

'Instantly,' says Frances, 'the story is that he's doing this to impress the governess.'

It is not clear to me if Luke did or did not wear the suit partly for the purpose of catching Frances's attention. They are still teasing each other about this, but they agree that the real connection between them begins in a conversation some days later.

'Isn't it funny,' says Frances, suddenly serious, 'how sometimes something seemingly unimportant at that time and in that moment and in that headspace turns out to be the most massive moment in your life.'

'So, there's all this small talk around the table, everyone's making jokes, winding down, and here I am, showing Frances some photos—'

'—showing ... off,' says Frances, giggling and then apologising.

'And I say to her, "You don't speak any German do you?", as if she's going to say, "Yes." I was waiting for her to ask, "Why?" and I was going to say, "Oh I've just got a contract written in German here for my next job in Switzerland." But she said, "As a matter of fact I do."'

Luke pulls for me the confounded look that must have appeared on his face all those years ago.

'I'd just spent two years in Europe and I'd learnt German to go and study at a German university,' says Frances.

'So I got my contract out and she checked it. That really broke the ice between us.'

This was the moment when these two adventurers worked out that they just might have found a kindred spirit. Frances, who by this stage was helping the shearers' cook, as she dislikes sitting down when someone else is working, embarked on a gentle tease. To rub in her unexpected knowledge of German, she wrote on Luke's cling-wrapped bowl of breakfast cereal little notes in that language for Luke to attempt to translate.

Their sudden enjoyment of each other's company was not missed, as the property owners and the rest of the shearing team turned matchmaker.

'I was sharing a room with a terrific gentleman in his forties, and at the end of the first week he said to me, "What are you doing for the weekend?"'

Luke had nothing planned.

'He says, "The Hawker Races are on." And I say, "Oh are they?" and he says, "The governess is from Hawker."

"Ah," I say.'

The next evening Luke asked what Frances was doing the following weekend. She wasn't doing anything. And Luke casually mentioned that he was going to Hawker—and Frances immediately (as he intended her to do) asked if she could catch a ride with him as she lived at Hawker.

'Oh, do you?' said Luke, gently surprised.

This is all delightful listening and, after my lack of insight into the business with the suit, I'm pleased that this part of the story is at least much as I'd expected. As we talk, Frances is putting together dinner and glancing flirtatiously at Luke from time to time. I am now confidently waiting to hear of a mutual recognition that this was the right person or something of that nature.

'Now, I didn't have any sense of any romance coming out of this,' says Frances.

'Oh come on,' I say indignantly. 'You must have.'

'We liked each other—' says Luke, '—but we were living our own lives, having our own adventures.

'The second week we had to knock off early because of rain and I'd gone home to shear sheep at a stud close to home. So I said to Frances, "I'll pick you up and take you back to Redcliffe, and I'll bring a meal." So I purchased pork cutlets with bacon wrapped around them, some strawberries, chocolate sauce, some red and white wine and then, for a joke, I went down to the supermarket and bought the cheapest brand ham and pineapple pizza so I could say "Here's tea" and throw the pizza down. And I did.

'Frances just looked at the pizza and she said "I'm allergic to pork", because she is. And what was my other option? Pork cutlets.'

Luke also brought a posy of daffodils for Frances, picked from a family garden ... but both insist that neither of them saw the other in a romantic light until much later: Frances didn't want a boyfriend or Luke a girlfriend.

'I kept a diary at the time, and I know when it first dawned on me that we might be seeing more of each other in the future—I wrote that I wasn't sure that this was a good idea, because Luke was going to be away for big blocks of time, and it isn't much fun for the person left behind waiting.'

Over the next three years, with Luke away so much and Frances having done most of the travelling she wanted to do in earlier years, they kept in touch by letter and seeing each other just for a weekend here and there, making an effort to attend the same functions. Luke wrote to Frances from wherever he was working, sending her beautifully detailed descriptions of the parts of the world he was seeing. Frances shows me a photograph that Luke sent her before leaving on one of these trips, and on the back is written: 'To a special person, thinking of you while in my travels, love Luke'.

On reading that I decide then—disregarding anything Luke and Frances go on to say—that deep in the subconscious of each was something like a holding paddock or special shelf for found treasures. The time wasn't yet right, but each, in the hidden depths of their mind, was considering the other for when it was.

On one of these infrequent meet-ups the penny finally dropped for Luke. They were driving back from a party with a friend, and the ute hit and killed a roo. The young men were about to drive on, when Frances said, horrified at the waste and thinking of the family dogs, 'Aren't you going to cut its legs off?' Luke could see the merit of this. But his coordination was somewhat impaired and, to his stunned admiration, Frances, in high heels and pretty dress, took the knife from him and swiftly had both legs neatly severed. 'This girl,' he thought, 'is a keeper.'

In 2007 Luke went on a shearing trip to the Falklands, and he asked Frances if she would like to come with him. And Frances, who had mortified herself by crying her eyes out when Luke had left the country on a previous occasion, said yes.

At this point they considered the other person their official romantic interest but no-one, they say, would have been able to predict if they would stay together after this. A working holiday like this is often make or break for a new couple. This one made Frances and Luke—but it went well beyond that, showing them what kind of life they wanted to share. They wanted to live in Australia, but they wanted it to remain a journeying life: for it to offer, as travel does, a never-ending, life-enhancing supply of challenge, stimulation and learning. On their return the safe and financially sensible choice was for Luke to keep shearing and Frances to keep classing wool, but that wasn't the decision they made.

'We didn't want to be stuck in that environment—it doesn't lead to anywhere but another shearing shed. And I wanted a life on the land but, as I said to Frances, I didn't know how to fix a flat tyre.'

'The manager at Teetulpa Station, who knew what sort of person Luke was and knew what he needed to learn outside the wool industry, offered him a role as overseer,' says Frances. 'So Luke went from a shearing wage to an ordinary jackeroo wage, which was hard—but the manager taught him how to kill a sheep, to fix a tyre. It was a perfect apprenticeship.'

Luke worked and learned the basics of land management at Teetulpa. Frances worked as a contract cook, coming and going from Teetulpa. When she was there she brought her experience of the land to help Luke out where she could.

'We were there for twelve months, and we'd still be there if Richard [Richard Warwick, Frances's father] hadn't asked us to come back to Holowiliena,' says Luke. 'He was going through a hard patch after having a motorbike accident.'

It is now time to eat, and Frances and Luke quite deliberately stop the story at the start of dinner.

'We've got to tell you about the wedding,' says Frances, her face lit by mischief. 'It's a surprise.'

Having been surprised by the explanation for the suit and the progression of their relationship, I don't really know that I want to be surprised again. Then I think, well, I read a lot of romance and I watch romantic comedies. I decide that I am unlikely to be surprised by their wedding.

We finish eating, and Luke, leaning back from the table and smiling at Dad and me, picks up the tale. There is nothing austere about Luke's face tonight—as he said to me earlier, he loves their story.

A year into living together Luke made up his mind that he wanted to marry Frances and commenced planning. He had obtained and measured Frances's favourite ring and, with the assistance of a good friend who was a jeweller, had the engagement ring ready to go. Next on the list was asking Richard.

'We were driving out to fix the windmill. And I said to Richard—we're talking about the weather and the sheep, it was a quiet moment—"Do you mind if I marry Frances?" He reached over and shook my hand and said, "Uh, uh … I'd be delighted." Richard couldn't concentrate for the rest of that day, but nothing more was said.'

Nothing more was said for another month, as it turned out. Then, on the weekend before Luke left for a seven-week shearing contract, he and Frances had gone down to the Clare Valley for a birthday luncheon for Frances's sister.

'It wasn't very romantic the way I asked her to marry me, waiting for the taxi, sitting out on the lawn. I was a bit nervous about it. I said, "Frances, will you marry me and be the mother of my children?" And she said …'

Dad and I are riveted.

'She said … "No."'

Luke pauses, while peals of laughter come from Frances.

'"No, you're not asking me like that!" She wanted me down on my knee and not sitting on the lawn. I got down on my knee real quick and gave her the ring.

'The following day Richard and Janne came down, and Richard's sort of looking at me. We were probably looking pretty happy, but we didn't tell them …'

'We wanted to tell all our parents together. We knew everyone from both families would be together at Christmas and we decided to tell them then,' adds Frances.

'So I was away shearing and she was away on a mining camp cooking. We weren't really able to be in contact with each other, but we were thinking of each other. The moment I'd finished I was keen to get to the mining camp and see her.'

'We knew we were spending the rest of our lives together by then,' says Frances.

In this beautiful, close time after weeks apart, at the remote mining camp on Mulyungarie station, they talked about their lives, beginning with getting married. The date was the tenth of December, and Frances was inspired with the idea that they should marry on Christmas Day.

Why not? Both families would be together on that day and attending a service at Luke's family church in a group. Frances's sister was going away from Australia for a year immediately afterwards. Luke's brother was back only for Christmas. Almost everyone important was already going to be present.

I think this idea is delightful. After all, Christmas Day is a wonderful foundation for a wedding! The right food for a celebration is already planned and to hand. Houses are already swept through and made their most beautiful and trees are decked in red, green, silver, gold and fairy lights. People slow down to sing, talk and reflect together and to properly feel the emotions to which we pay scant attention in our daily lives: ethereal joy, belly-deep merriness, the ringing of ritual through the soul. Such days stand out in our lives like polished, lustrous, remarkable jewels—and they are strung on a different kind of thread to the kind we use to link the days making up the rest of our lives. The meanings threaded through a wedding day and Christmas Day are so very much the same—celebrating new life, announcing transformation and connecting with the world.

'Lovely,' says Dad. I can see he is not surprised by this choice either.

Luke called Pastor Tim, the pastor at his family church, to see if it was possible for them to marry after the Christmas Day service. Sadly it was impossible, said Pastor Tim—well, impossible without a special dispensation from the Registrar of Births, Deaths and Marriages, as thirty days must elapse between application to marry and the wedding itself. But Pastor Tim, who knew them well, offered to write a special letter of support to the Registrar. Frances and Luke (still on Mulyungarie station) needed to collect supporting paperwork: her sister's visa, his brother's plane tickets.

They did this—and they did it all covertly. This was because their other idea was that no-one (except Pastor Tim and Frances's grandfather, who was too unwell to attend but loved to keep the secret) would know.

'What!' say Dad and I together. We are dumbfounded. We can't imagine a wedding without every close family member pitching in on the cleaning and decorating, without misunderstandings and sortings out, without photographers, music, flowers, special outfits, people flying in, ensuring parking ...

'We didn't want the fuss and bother,' says Luke. 'We just wanted the day to be celebrated for what it was, the joining of two people.'

Frances's contract finished, and they returned to Holowiliena on 19 December. On the twenty-third they had an interview with the Registrar of Births, Deaths and Marriages in Adelaide.

'We left Holowiliena for Adelaide not knowing if we could be married or not,' says Frances.

'We go up to Level Six. The Registrar walks out, and she looks just like a school principal: glasses on her face, severe expression. We think: "This doesn't look good." And she says, "What are your reasons for getting married?" And we go through them all: the brother, the sister, the no fuss—and then she says, "Why have you left it this late? It's the twenty-third and you want to get married on Christmas Day." We really thought we'd no chance.

'And I said, "Well, Luke's been away shearing for two months, and I've been cooking at a mining camp at Mulyungarie."

'And the Registrar blinks, her face lights up and she says, "Mulyungarie! I know Mulyungarie! My son worked there as a jackeroo. He was having some trouble and he went up there, he had the best time and he loved it."' Frances transforms her voice to show the passion and gratitude with which the Registrar spoke.

In that moment they've won her heart. She attempts a return to her previous stern demeanour but she can't quite recapture it: she is too softened by the mention of Mulyungarie and station life, and the time and space they offered for her teenage child to sort himself out. I feel she must have been softened too by the season, the circumstances and the rightness of this pair of lovers.

'She felt she owed something to Mulyungarie and the bush, and we benefitted. She said: "Well, I'll grant permission—but don't do this again,"' says Luke.

They thank the Registrar profusely and leave with all speed. After all, the clock is ticking. They have less than forty-eight hours until Pastor Tim is to marry them, and every second of this time is going to be needed to pull together their still-secret wedding.

In Adelaide, at the very height of festive season shopping, Frances tries on beautiful wedding dresses from boutiques, but they aren't right. In a cheap little dress shop, for an unnamed amount under a hundred dollars, she finds a cool white frock—perfect. To that she adds a cheap-as-chips tiara. Luke spends rather more on a new pair of jeans, a shirt, a haircut and a twenty-dollar ring. From Adelaide they travel to Luke's home town of Monarto, and continue preparing.

'People don't notice if you're sneaking around at Christmas time,' says Frances. 'We'd say, "We've just got to duck out for a couple of hours," and no-one batted an eyelid.'

'Our tradition is German,' says Luke. 'On Christmas Eve we go to church, and open our presents after church. Prior to going to the church I said, "We've got something to tell you. Frances and I are engaged." And everyone was expecting it. We'd been together for a couple of years. They just said, "Oh yes, yes, congratulations."'

'We had planned to say "We're engaged and we're planning to get married in the morning," it was our full intention, but we just realised—' says Frances.

'—it wasn't going to work,' says Luke.

'If we tell them tonight, there's going to be a fuss ... everyone would be too excited to sleep. I was worried my mum would be down at 24-hour shopping in Adelaide buying a dress to wear. There'd be questions ...'

'It would put stress into it and take away from Christmas.'

At church they tell family friends they are engaged. It's a small church with a mostly farming congregation, half of them related to Luke.

After a nice family evening the rest of the family goes to sleep—Luke and Frances are sending last-minute text messages to other family and friends apprising them of the wedding tomorrow—with the cat still in the bag.

The next morning over a seven-thirty breakfast—with both sets of parents and Luke's grandmother sitting at the table, everyone relaxed and in pyjamas, and Luke and Frances standing together by the sink, they (finally) seize the moment.

'We've got something to tell you. You know how last night we said we were engaged?' Luke says to them, 'Well, no-one has asked us when we're getting married.'

Frances's mother Janne looks up at him and says, reasonably, as any practical woman would: 'We'll get Christmas out of the way first.'

'No, we won't,' says Luke, also in a reasonable tone. 'We're getting married at nine o'clock.'

Silence. For at least five seconds no-one says a word. Frances's father Richard's mouth is hanging open. Eventually Luke's father says: 'Don't you need permission for that?'

'That's all organised,' says Luke.

Joy follows pandemonium as family realise that Luke and Frances are quite serious: handshakes, hugs and tears—drama about clothes, the order of events, cars …

'Frances and Richard went to church in the Monaro that we'd used for my brother's wedding. I grabbed a shotgun and let off a few shells as they drove off,' says Luke.

'Pastor Tim went right through the Christmas service without saying anything, and then right at the end he said: "And now Luke and Frances are to be married, and if you'd like to stay, you are invited." Everybody stayed.'

No photographer had been organised, but a congregation member and old friend had raced home for his camera, determined that the family would have pictures of this precious, unexpected day. On the family pin-up board, next to drawings by Todd and Stella, is pinned one of his photographs from six years ago—Frances and Luke, their fair hair shining, eyes starry, faces incandescent at their Christmas Day wedding.

*

The previous day ...

After breakfast the day before my father and I wander in and around the treasured old buildings of Holowiliena. Holowiliena dates back to the 1850s: the old stone homestead is the heart of the property, but it is surrounded by historic outbuildings, some restored, some not. Some of these restorations were completed as part of the ABC's Restoration Australia program, filmed in 2013 and 2014, but Luke and Frances had begun on this work before the series and will continue it into the future. Frances believes that restoration and preservation is the job for her generation of Warwicks. To restore the buildings will take both time and money, and Frances and Luke are now venturing into tourism in order to 'make the history pay for itself'.

'Being asked to be part of Restoration Australia was wonderful luck,' Frances had told me.

It was wonderful luck for the producer of Restoration Australia too. Holowiliena is among the few pastoral properties where the family who took up the lease still runs the property. Add to this the family's passion for sharing, their deep tradition of hospitality and their ability to bring to life family members who are long gone—I imagine the producer was overcome with relief and pleasure.

Rather than charging for accommodation and food, Holowiliena provided it gratis to the ABC production team—and that money saved, Luke tells me, went straight into producing high-quality television on their episode, the seventh and last of the series, which screened in October 2015. Frances and Luke value good craft in the same way they value time spent talking, interacting and eating with guests: it is a good thing in and of itself. They are delighted that the production team crafted a beautiful opening for their episode and pleased to have played such a big part in enabling them to give of their best.

The opening sequence shows the Warwicks arriving at Holowiliena in 1852. Frances plays her own great-great-grandmother, and Luke is William Warwick. With them they brought their ten children and they were to have two more.

Those children grew up in and cooperatively ran Holowiliena when, after sixteen years of life there, William and his wife left to live closer to Adelaide. The youngest child was left behind for the oldest sister to care for. In the end, only three of William Warwick's children married, and only one of the married men had children of his own.

The things these people made and used are all around me, and Frances had talked about her departed family members as if they were just over the next hill repairing a fence; as a result, time here feels less as if it flows and more as if it is draped in layers over the land. In a closed section of shed, behind wire, are wagons with wooden-spoked wheels with metal rims. The skills that were used to make these wheels—to curve the wood, place the spokes, shrink the metal around the wheel, ensure all wheels match and balance—were once commonplace. Every station and small settlement would have had a blacksmith's shop with a forge where this work was done. At the time of colonisation blacksmiths had a place equivalent to today's software and hardware developers, as toolmakers in a high-status profession taken up by those of good intellect, design skills, physical prowess and business sense.

Behind a tractor is hooked an arched contraption with a seat and a long blade beneath. 'This is still in use!' my father exclaims. He is astonished because this arched contraption is a hand-operated grader which on most properties would have been retired decades ago.

Behind the main shed we find a well-rusted Model-T Ford. Over it grows a vine with a woolly, herbaceous, pastel leaf and white clusters of flowers. I've never seen this plant before.

'It's horehound,' Luke says, appearing around the shed corner, explaining that it was brought into Australia for flavouring in brewing and has become a weed in South Australia. He shows us the way to the storeroom where Frances and her father Richard are waiting. Richard's hair is dark and the worry lines that financial struggle usually carves aren't apparent on his face. I have difficulty believing he is over seventy years old. Richard bought Holowiliena from his uncle in the 1980s. Janne and Richard, just married, had to go massively into debt to purchase the homestead. The wool boom was over, and that came at the end of a run of dry years. It would have been enormously difficult to repay a debt that big and under those conditions, but Holowiliena had been in the family for four generations, and Richard and Janne wished to hand it over to the next generation.

The storeroom roof was once thatched and now it is tin, but under the pole rafters and lathed purlins, running perpendicular to the rafters, little else has changed. The floor is river-bed stone. The bookkeeper would have stood behind the substantial angled desk and recorded wages drawn, allowances taken in stores and advanced allowances debited. The shelving of local wood held everything needed in the way of stores and more besides: flour, sugar, salt, cigarettes, coffee, boots.

Now the long, high shelves overflow with things that have lost their place in time elsewhere. One of Janne and Richard's first management decisions was to return this building to its original role—it was in use as a shed—and put in it all the someone-might-find-interesting or might-be-useful-again items from houses and sheds. The light and the colours in here are soft, sepia-tinted, and the fine apricot dust of Holowiliena coats everything.

There is a hip bath, roasting covers and many bottles. Some bottles are iridescent, some pearlised, brown or blue or green, dusty from the ground in which they were found, standing like old friends together despite huge discrepancies in age and origin. A hand-held seed and fertiliser distributer, tiny, but with a huge gear ratio to blast out the seed: all done with the minimum of working parts. Cow bells, sheep bells, some still striking a clear early-morning note. A bee smoker, horse castrator, butter paddles, an icing syringe of metal and wood and a perplexing item which turns out to be a homemade fly zapper. The biggest gravy bowl I've ever seen, and the very biggest bread box, testament to just how many had to be fed at every meal—full-time gardeners, transient workers, a tutor, cowboys, shepherds, bookkeepers, people passing through, and family. A bunch of white tin mugs is strung like a bunch of grapes in the foreground. The smell of age rises from the saddlery, held above on the raft mezzanine, and from the hessian bags, which contain leather strapping for cart horses, complete with blinkers.

In the corner waits an ancient vacuum cleaner, still working. We trundle it across the floor and it whirrs and the old fabric bag obligingly inflates, no electricity required. Near it is propped a shepherd's crook in a pale wood of some bush timber, reinforced to support the hook and lovingly polished. This is a family that loves their wood and their metal. Tools have been forged here, wooden handles shaped and polished. There are scales everywhere, but they are not measuring time or, if they are, it is only very gently.

'There's a family story for everything that is here—why it was made or how it arrived,' says Luke.

A commercial knife, the handle of which must have broken, has been re-handled in local wood, beautiful to hold and detailed with a wheat-head pattern: quite possibly some of Frank Warwick's work. Frank was a great-great-uncle to

Frances. In 1908 he was rounding up horses on foot when a rabbit warren collapsed under him and he fell into the dusty hole, breaking both legs. He had the ill luck to see a drunken doctor, who set both broken legs poorly. A shepherd re-broke and reset them, to better effect, but afterwards Frank was never without pain—or, it seems, without his woodwork. His well-used woodworking tools are touchingly kept next to his crutches. Hanging from a rafter is a double-sided pistol holster.

'This fitted over the neck of the horse—here is where you put your shells. I suspect my father sewed this together himself,' says Richard, going on to explain that his father used gunfire in much the way the sound of a motorbike or helicopter is used now: 'He used to use a firearm as a means of mustering. If he found scrub he couldn't ride through, he'd shoot to start them out.'

As there are just two of us visiting, the family decide to show us the office, which was built in 1856. 'To me this is the heart of Holowiliena here,' Frances says. 'We generally don't show it to people because I can't resist handing them the diaries, the catalogues—and it is all too fragile to stand much of that.' These treasures of ink on paper, Frances says, need climate control and they need to be digitised. She is a passionate curator and researcher as well as an archaeologist. In this special room two of Frances's strongest instincts are set at odds: her sense of hospitality versus her passion for preservation.

The opportunity to be hospitable has come to be seen by Frances and Luke as a priceless one.

'You see a lot of people who say, "Oh, we are too busy to have visitors," but Richard will drop everything, sometimes to the detriment of the work that needs to be done. He'll drop everything to spend time with people. At first when we came here it would drive us crazy,' says Frances.

'We'd just moved here ready to make a difference and get in and do some work, but it would be time to pull up and talk to people,' says Luke.

'Have another cup of tea ...'

'It was wearing on us, but now—'

'—now we see why.'

'Richard always spoke to people on the road and said, "Pull in, have a cup of tea with us." One cup of tea on the road,' says Luke, 'and we've got lifelong friends out of it, people who have been coming here for thirty or forty years.'

'Do you know Trove?' says Frances, referring to the National Library of Australia's online archives. 'I use it quite a bit for my research and it is easy, because Holowiliena is such a unique name. From the late 1800s and early 1900s reporters wrote about the hospitality of the people at Holowiliena.'

In the office are family portraits. One handsome gentleman stares vaguely down from the wall—I think it is William, the son of the original William—and it is not possible to miss the family resemblance. William in the portrait, Richard and Frances all have the same beautifully modelled, patrician nose.

There is a medicine cupboard here, testament to the isolation, with old syringes and ointment jars to hold chemical concoctions including opium.

Frances holds a station supplies catalogue. 'As far as I can tell it dates from around the turn of the century because you can see the camel train on the cover there.'

'You could set up a whole station with this,' says Luke. Like Frances, he handles the catalogue with tenderness and pride.

'I desperately want to republish it—it's a good collector's edition, a good reference for what was available—but I want it printed on paper like this, not generic paper. People need to see what books were like at the time.'

The paper is thin and shiny and the fine black line drawings of stoves, saddlery, rat traps, lamps, firearms, Fowler's bottling equipment, wool presses and hundreds of other items shine off the page. The catalogue is comprehensive and fascinating and I have no difficulty believing it would find a market.

'I can see a Holowiliena collection of books … one day, one day. I have a lot of "one day" projects. The children's books we have here—with really gorgeous plates—I'd like to see them republished too,' says Frances, her voice by turns self-deprecating, wistful and determined.

Closest to Frances's heart are the diaries, the books that hold the minds and the memories of her kin. I suspect she sometimes feels them beside her as she polishes the wood they've carved or reads the words they've written in exquisite, measured copperplate script. In the work of restoring she has found herself effectively conversing with them: trying to answer the questions of why and how from these diaries.

'The beautiful thing about the records we have here is that sometimes you think they are just records and history—there, but not useful—but through this project, so many times, we've come back to the diaries and looked things up. We could go back to my grandfather in the 1940s when everyone had gone off to war and there wasn't much concrete available and he wrote about burning limestone for mortar again and his phrase was, "They used to do it in the old days and I don't see why we can't do it now." And it is the same for us, exactly what grandpa said—there's no reason not to do it.'

'The rocks are still there,' says Luke.

'The rocks are still there and we could see in the diaries just what they put into the kiln, how long it was in there, which day they bagged it up. It meant we could create the same product.'

Luke has used mortar made to the family's traditional recipe and local stone to add a kitchen to the original homestead, where it fits seamlessly into the house. He used the same techniques in restoring the cellar in the wall of the creek.

Luke's first piece of restoration was the blacksmith's shop: now a beautifully rendered white rectangular low-roofed building, done before Frances had rediscovered the mortar recipe.

'Up until four years ago this building was fairly wrecked. You could see daylight through it, the pines were all exposed and their bottoms rotting off,' he says. 'We had a guy on the shearing team who was a fully qualified concrete renderer and he came back over winter and helped me, and it saved the building. Although it wasn't done in the correct way, it is still restored and useable again.'

Luke opens the door and we see that one half of the blacksmith's shop is the forge and the other a store for miscellaneous metal objects. Cataloguing these is another of Frances's 'one day' projects. There is a glass-topped, hand-operated fuel bowser. Copper wire glows from among the soft rust. Huge scythes for hand-harvesting crops are hung like bats from a wire alongside harvester fingers and rabbit traps.

We step further into the room and my eyes are instantly drawn past the forge and into a cut-out inlet. There crouches a set of bellows, twice the size of a garden wheelbarrow, reminding me irresistibly of a little leathery-winged dragon. It has been carefully mended by a friend of Frances who, like her, has inherited his great-grandfather's business: in his case, upholstery. I am enchanted and astonished, both by their size and the fact that they are still here and because Luke has not just restored the blacksmith's shop, he's returned it to life. Visitors can watch Luke draw out iron and then beat, twist and twirl until it becomes a poker or a candlestick.

'You want a high steady heat—no sparks!' Luke says. 'Frances's great-great-grandfather William Warwick was a master blacksmith and his father-in-law was too. So it ties into the history. But I can only do relatively simple, decorative things at this stage.'

We come to another restoration, this one using the original pug and pine. This method required minimal materials, time and effort at the outset, but needed constant renewal: more pug, more pine to fill in the cracks created by the contracting cold and expanding heat.

'When we looked back through the history we found these old notebooks by Alexander Goyder. In there he called it "Scalp Hut" but we don't know why. We do know that Holowiliena was a depot for wild dog scalps. People travelled to bring the scalps here and collect their government bounty. The family here was responsible for destroying the scalps so they couldn't be bought back to claim another bounty.'

In looking at the restorations we are seeing too the steady progress in Luke's skill. Next on the list is the cellar which, like Scalp Hut, was filmed as part of the ABC production. Rock and mortar are set in the deep creek wall, and a wooden frame is fitted into the rock, wooden door precisely fitting into the frame—inside are river red gum beams and shelving, and on the shelves are bottled fruit and preserves. There are bottled grapes, cauliflower (which looks good but apparently tastes precisely as one would expect cauliflower and vinegar to taste), plums, peaches, pears and apricots, jams, marmalades and relishes—all made by Frances. The jars, the bottles and the red gum, all in the rich subdued colours of Rubens and Titian, glow against the walls of grey creek stone.

The two pieces of work that Luke is most pleased with are his most recent: the pizza oven (near the cellar in the creek bank, and designed to cook with ambient temperature: the fire is lit the day before the pizza or roast is cooked) and Janne's new kitchen. We gather there for tea and coffee with Janne and Richard, to learn more and to see some more of the family treasures. One of these is written and the others are worked in wood and metal.

Luke hands us a beautifully finished wooden chain with swivel and turnbuckle, at the end of which is the bark-clad stick from which it was carved. This is some of Uncle Frank's work.

'Uncle Frank also tried to carve chain out of matches,' says Richard. I find both ambition and attempt hard to credit, but perhaps Frank was inspired by a family-held curiosity of unknown origin: so minute and finely made that it looks like fairy work.

In a tiny transparent box, nested in cotton wool, sit a carved peach stone, plum stone and cherry stone, each with a tiny neat plug. Richard pulls out the miniscule plug from the delicate cherry stone and carefully tips the mouth over a sheet of white paper. Tiny identical metal shapes spill out.

'Don't anyone sneeze,' says Frances.

Careful not to breathe, I lean closer. The tiny shapes are teaspoons, their shallow bowls and their handles plain against the white paper.

How are these tiny spoons to be returned to their cherry stone? With the dexterity and grace which is surely one of the chief family gifts, Richard touches his work-roughened index finger to a spoon and then to the mouth of the tiny vessel. We fall silent watching him until every spoon is out of sight and the plug back in.

The written treasure is a letter of proposal.

'It's from my great-grandfather Robert, who was 52, to his 31-year-old next-door neighbour, Edith Davies,' says Frances.

The letter has been lovingly typed out for modern eyes, including the original misspellings, but the Warwicks have (of course) also preserved the original.

25 May 1860

My Dear Miss Davies

I am about to give you one of the greatest and I hope most agreeable surprises you ever get in your life. I can assure you I have thought this all over for a much longer time than you will think and have now made up my mind to know my fate right off and it all ends in this. Will you be my wife. I know you are far too good for me and have waited longer than I should have done to ask you this partly because I have always been afraid your answer might be no and partly to see if any one else was going to step in and be the lucky one. Now I think you know enough about me and all connected with me to be able to decide for your self. You know the life I like and am likely to lead is in the bush. Now I want you to think this all over by your dear little self and decide whether you think you could be happy with me and make your home with me where ever that may be. You must remember this is not a matter to rush into without thought. (For my part I have done nothing but think about it for a long time past) as it is for the remainder of our lives and it means that we must be happy or miserable together for the rest of our time.

I may tell you that you are the first and only girl I have asked to be my wife and you are going to be the last. If there is anything you want to know write and ask and I will tell you and I can only say no matter what I have gone through in the past it will be gone and done with and it is what I am going to be to you and this will be what every husband should be to his wife. A faithful and loving husband.

Now I don't know how you will take this. When I started to write I thought I could put things in a much better form but I find I can only blurt out what is in my mind and anctiously wait for your reply to make me one of the Happiest or most miserable men on earth. You must remember I want you to consider your own feelings above all things and if your answer is to be no I would rather that you will say so right away and never mind me.

You might think it strange that I did not tell you all this when last we met. I did not because I thought if it was to be no it would be easier for you to write it than say it and it would be much easier for me to take no on paper than from voice.

Now My Dear Girl I don't know whither you will laugh at all this or have a good cry but if the latter I hope it will not be through saying no. Above all things I would ask you to give me an answer as soon as you can and let me know my fate as soon as possible. Will you consult your Father and Mother about this before you give me your answer. I would rather you gave me your answer before consulting anyone, then I might know that you told me before anyone knew of it and afterwards you could tell them, but this I leave to you. If I am to be disappointed and you think for any reason this should not to be, do not hesitate, but wire and say so and I will pull through and no one need to be any the wiser or sadder but my self.

My only excuse for all this paper is that this is the first letter I have ever written on this point and I don't know hardly how to say what I want to. I did not know till I came to write how hard it is to tell you what I want to on paper and I am sure I would make a greater mess of it if I tried to tell you all I would like to. If I only knew what your answer will be I could get on ever so much better, but this I will have to wait for so long. I cant hear from you by letter before Friday 3rd June or wire via Pooncarie on Wednesday the 1st June this now seems ages to wait.

Sometimes I think I have been a coward not to have told you all this long before now or at any rate before I came away. Then again I think it is better when I'm away with the uncertainty than have to have draped all the way back with your refusal and the home coming was bad enough with out that to make it ten thousand times worse and if it had been as I wished I might not have been home yet. I have tried to tell you all that you want to know and trust that you will know from this that your answer will mean every thing to me if you decide to share your lot with me I can only say that I will be or try to be as good and loving husband to you as should one give well to a wife and that you are and will be the only woman in the world to me.

I hope and trust that you will never regret having taken the step I am asking you to, but at same time you want to be quite sure what ever you do will be for your own happiness, as once you are bound down it is for life and there is no get away from it, and you are far better off as you are than it find out you have made a mistake when it is too late, or to even wish you could undo what you have done.

As I write this I wonder whither this will be my last letter to you, and an end to my first and only attempt to settle down in life and if this fails I will never wish for another. What ever happens you can always depend on my being

Your ever Loving and Faithfull Robert Warwick

P.S. If it is to be No Could you simply wire me No and this will Condemn me to all the misery I deserve, and if we are to become engaged write me a long yes R.W.

The script in the original letter shows the anxiety and feeling of the writer. It is not written in the almost mechanically neat copperplate of the station diaries; the loops are heavier and the words seem spilled onto the pages rather than measured out perfectly. You hear of such letters being drafted and redrafted, but I believe Robert simply wrote his heart out on the page just once.

Phrases like 'You know the life I like and am likely to lead is in the bush' make sense. Edith needed to love the life as well as the man. Little has changed in all the years since Robert penned this letter. The person marrying into an outback life is taking on far more than just a partner.

Robert's letter brims with his desire that Edith will be happy. This is the very essence of love and as I read and reread it, I understand why she chose to marry him, even while knowing just how hard a life it would be. A photograph of Edith shows a woman with a delicate frame and a fine-featured, gentle face: her expression holds a quiet self-confidence in her wisdom and competence. The daughter of a doctor and one of his few children to have survived, I imagine her to have been clever, and as familiar with loss and suffering as the much older Robert.

The rightness of Edith and Robert's marriage is part of the foundations of what we see today. The property is still in the family. The business remains viable—Richard and Janne have paid off the debt. Not just that; under their management the condition of the land has improved.

The debt is gone, but the maintenance of the buildings is now overdue, says Frances. That, she says, is part of the work for her and Luke.

'Tourism works for us because Dad has done it [informally] for years,' Frances says, 'but we are not trying to change the world and make a big business out of it. We just want the history to pay for itself.'

While the history tourism is only to pay for the restoration and maintenance work, the station must do a great deal more than pay its own way, and this is the biggest challenge facing Luke and Frances. Despite the pressure of a repayment schedule, Richard and Janne took great care not to overstock the property. This is now visible in the good condition of Holowiliena and the abundance of feed.

'If you love the land, it loves you back,' says Frances. 'You know the saying, "The country is in good heart"? Holowiliena is always in good heart.'

We go up to the top of the highest nearby hill to look down at the Holowiliena homestead as the sun sets: houses, gardens, outbuildings, shearing shed, shearers' quarters, yards, sheds and wells. Hills encircle the homestead and the gently undulating land around it, and there are hills past the hills, and then yet more hills further back. It is like standing on an outer petal of a rose and looking into its deep heart.

The Holowiliena family refers to this as 'Woolshed Hill'. On its very top is a shepherd's cairn. At shearing time, in the days before two-way radio, the shepherd waiting patiently with the next mob to be brought through for shearing would keep his eyes both on the flock and the shepherd's cairn. When he saw a flag of a particular colour appear atop the cairn he would know that it said 'Bring 'em up, Fred' and he would bring the sheep those last few kilometres into the yards to be shorn.

Out in the cold evening air, a little down the hillside from me, Frances is standing holding her latest find, a tiny piece of apricot-coloured ceramic. Her neat cameo profile is pale against the homestead in the darkening valley far below. 'Look, *more* porcelain pipe,' says Frances to Luke, holding up the pale fragment. He is instantly intrigued.

'So, what's that, sixteen pieces so far? We hadn't found any until a few months ago,' he adds in an aside to my father. Archaeology has become part of everyday life here. With her children, Frances is constantly digging up, sorting and storing pottery pieces, bottles, tools and wire. Three-year-old Stella, says her father, is like a bower bird, always spotting and then tugging at mostly-buried treasures from the earth, and taking them home to wash and store.

Like so many people on a quest Frances has a sense she's 'being helped' to find certain things or particular information: the timeliness of a find, the way details suddenly connect. It has been too serendipitous and has occurred too frequently for coincidence. She and Luke are clearly both waiting for an explanation for the use of porcelain pipe to emerge.

It's twilight now. We drive back down from Woolshed Hill to where Frances and Luke's house has settled itself, between the deep creeks that run through the Holowiliena homestead in South Australia's Flinders Ranges.

It's been a week since we left Holowiliena, driving back out along the windy road in the rain. Frances has written to tell me that Todd was digging near the schoolroom and found a much larger piece of pale porcelain pipe. Naturally, Frances, eaten up with curiosity and hopeful of finally discovering what this pipe was used for, stopped everything to dig alongside him. Next from the earth was the item in its entirety—stem and bowl, a pipe for smoking tobacco! Now, of course, she is wondering just whose pipes they were, and what stories could be told by the smoker.

And I left Holowiliena with a number of mysteries of my own to think about. The first of these resulted from something that happened on our first night there, just before the children's bedtime. Luke and Frances had together moved their children through all the bedtime rituals. It was time for saying good-night when suddenly Todd made an announcement. Tonight was the night for Lamba to be put away. I saw Frances and Luke's eyes meet and a shared decision instantaneously made.

'Tom, Jo, I'm really sorry, but this has to happen now,' said Frances, turning to us. 'He's been talking about doing this for weeks and if tonight's the night he's chosen, well, we have to go with it. Nothing is more important.'

Lamba was another sheep teddy—not the rainbow sheep teddy with which Stella planned to console herself in Luke's absence, but a rather frail teddy, with a gentle sheep-face and worn-away patches in his woolly coat. Lamba belongs to Todd: and it is Lamba that he has always slept with and particularly loved. Luke brought out a video camera to record this moment. Into this camera Todd, with Lamba clasped to his chest, told the story of their shared life together and explained just why Lamba needed to be put away. His face shone with intensity and conviction as he spoke: if Lamba isn't put away he will just fall apart and then Todd wouldn't have him at all. With ceremony, with grief, Todd placed Lamba in a white box. There are friends for Lamba in the box, other toys that are being kept safe forever and can be taken out for brief careful plays and loves.

The following morning Frances reported that Todd's first night without Lamba was very hard. Like me, she has wondered just what triggered Todd's decision to act on that particular night. It was certainly not a tactic for avoiding bedtime, or in order to out-compete the guests in the house. With Frances I puzzled over it while I was at Holowiliena, and I have continued to turn it over in my mind ever since.

Now that I have written it all down I can see on the page the moment that crystallised Todd's thinking. It was the moment when Stella showed Dad and me the rainbow sheep. I believe that in that moment Todd's mind flicked ahead through time to a place when he needed to leave a child of his own with someone special to love and hold. Lamba was clearly the very best candidate for the role and so Todd needed to act, to make sure that Lamba would still be in good-enough condition to take the job on when the time came.

Todd, like everyone in his family, empathises not just with the family he lives with now, but the family who lived here before now, and also with family members who are yet to come. This was the same impulse that moved Richard and Janne to turn the storeroom into a museum, and the same impulse that motivates Frances and Luke to restore the old buildings of Holowiliena. And this sense of an empathic connection through time is not something the Warwicks extend just to family. They often tell stories of people whose lives have been touched by Holowiliena in some way: Frances calls them 'the Holowiliena alumni'. I realise now that Todd's putting away of Lamba is yet another illustration of this family's ability to see their possessions not as theirs alone, but as a shared heritage that it's their responsibility and honour to preserve.

The other mystery I've been thinking about is just where the heart of a property like Holowiliena is located, and how love, even more than rain, is responsible for 'land being in good heart'. My first thought, encouraged by the topology of Holowiliena, was that the homestead is the heart. But for Frances it is the old office, where many of the keys to understanding, stewarding and living with the land have been recorded. Alongside these two possibilities I am now wondering about a third.

Holowiliena has always been in good heart because it has always been loved. That ability to love the land and connect deeply to a place is part of the human condition—a trait that is stronger in some people than others, but as much a part of being human as making things from wood or writing poetry. It flourishes when people have time, when they are content, when they are not fighting to survive—and when they are in deep engagement with the land. For every generation of Warwicks to have loved Holowiliena so well, they needed first a deep contentment and ease in their relationships.

Is the heart of Holowiliena, then, not in a place at all? Is the land's heart inextricably connected with the hearts of the people of Holowiliena? I think so. Care for land springs from the same well as care for children, for the traditions of welcome-back and welcome-in, for the history of the place—from the strength of the loving bonds of the people living there. The heart of Holowiliena dwells in those relationships: in marriages, between parent and child, grandparent and child, and even in relationships across time. When all is well with those, the land receives the best of care and is, of course, quite literally, in 'good heart'.

Anything But Mine

Robina and Aaron Meehan,
Outback Gypsies

Waterholes are the churches of the outback; everybody's place, and sacred. Often we picture these pools as small and deep and round. They are not. Long and curving, they traverse miles of country and seem to love human company: the cool mud is comforting, laughs echo down the water and up into the trees, and the fish hunt around your toes. They are the deepest part of a creek, holding water months after rain has gone, with lines of trees screening them from the outside dry. It was to the waterhole at Epenarra, a pastoral property in the Northern Territory, that Robina Hergenhan came at the end of a long shift. It was 2004 and she was on the last placement of her nursing degree.

She wasn't quite sure nursing fully satisfied her, but no other calling had appealed just yet. She could feel that disenchantment and cynicism were close but these weren't the feelings that she wanted: she wanted to live unconstrained, adventurously and with hope. She couldn't quite see how to get free to feel those things and, instead, her days ran to the rhythm of her work ethic and determination to do the right thing.

On the love front she's closed her heart down to make repairs.

There is an Aboriginal community as well as a nursing post at Epenarra. The nursing post is staffed with just one other nurse for anywhere between 250 and 400 people living in the community. In addition to running cattle, the pastoralists on Epenarra also run an outback store, as most station properties once did throughout Australia. Epenarra is managed by Aaron Meehan, who left his home farm at just sixteen to see what he could do in the world. This has occupied his attention to such a degree that there hasn't been time for girls, but, like so many people who work with stock, he is a great reader of body language.

A good stockman, for example, can be driving up to the yards and from that distance discern the flighty, twitchy heifer with a huge flight zone (even if you are two or three hundred metres away from her, she'll panic) from the ebullient, confident animal who will allow you to stand close to her and happily explore a new terrain to see what it offers. From outside the yard this kind of stockman can see the leaders and the animals who will always look for a lead from another. His job is to make every animal feel safe enough to explore happily: and he does this by watching what they say with their ears and heads, how fast they are moving and how quickly they respond to whatever he does.

Robina had told the nurse who dropped her off at the waterhole that she would walk back, as it was only three kilometres.

'I was in a string bikini and enjoying the water and sun on my skin when I heard a vehicle coming. I got out, got dressed because the nurse had told me that the local Aboriginal people didn't like to see too much skin, but it was Aaron coming down, and he'd heard there was a young nurse at the camp, and he'd seen the ambulance dropping me off. He told me he was just checking cattle. It took me twelve months of living and working there to realise that there were no cattle down there and there never would be cattle down there to check.

'We just chatted. People say he doesn't talk. That's just how people perceive him. They say things like "how did Aaron even know what to say to a girl?" But our conversation just came so easily.'

On that day at the waterhole, with the sun on her skin slowly seeping through to her chilled heart, Robina was only months out of a difficult relationship.

'That relationship should only have lasted twelve months, but with infidelities and separation and trying again, it lasted five years,' she says. 'And he knew how to talk to me, how to win me back in.'

As a result Robina could not face the thought of having a boyfriend ever again. She was comfortable with lust and friendship, but never again would she walk the high rope of crazy early love with no safety net.

Aaron didn't know this, of course, but he was able to apply the skills he'd gained from years of handling stock. He saw quickly that Robina, just like a skittish heifer, would take flight with any kind of pressure. He applied none at all.

During the week Robina continued her nursing placement at the Epenarra Community Clinic, but the rest of the time was spent having fun with Aaron.

'So we met at the waterhole on a Saturday, and he invited me to come on a bore run on the Sunday, just to look around. And then we just spent the rest of my spare time, my weekends in the Northern Territory, together. We went to the rodeo at

Tennant Creek, got five flat tyres on the truck and had to go to Mt Isa to get new tyres ...'

It was only when Robina found herself taking risks and flying high on the adventure of doing so that she realised that in Aaron's steady, competent presence she felt safe. She'd not felt that way in a very long time.

'At the rodeo I was drinking fire-engines—normally I don't drink.'

On the way back from Mt Isa Robina drove the ute while Aaron slept.

'I sped up and up, until I was driving at 130 kilometres an hour and the feeling was amazing.

'Every afternoon he'd pick me up to go down to the waterhole ... and every afternoon the same song would come on the stereo.'

The song, 'Anything But Mine', is a country song about a just-for-now romance. Robina didn't expect anything else of her friendship with Aaron. When her placement was over she even rewrote the words to the song for Aaron, to celebrate their friendship and to thank him for their shared time. It was her way of saying goodbye.

But Aaron had been quick to perceive what Robina had not—how very much they had in common. Robina had been raised on a dairy farm on the south New South Wales coast, Aaron on a cattle property on the north coast. Both came from tight-knit families of strong people who were quick to see what needed to be done and to do it without complaint.

Aaron had left the family farm to make his own way in the world at just sixteen. His family had felt both dismay and pride. He would have been a great asset in the family business, and yet they could not help admiring his calm dedication to the future he wanted. This was not to have a farm, but to have a pastoral business. The skills required are not quite the same and he had understood that at sixteen. And he'd also understood that to find the right property he needed to have the skills and the dollars ready to go, but also be in the right place at the right time. Aaron believed that meant he needed to be living and working in the station country.

Robina was awed by Aaron's unswerving drive towards a future he had visualised in his teens; after all, she was yet to visualise her own. Aaron was far ahead of her, and not just in imagining his own future. He was already imagining a future for the two of them together.

'I thought what happened in the Territory stayed in the Territory. But when he dropped me off at the Wauchope Hotel near the Devils Marbles to catch the bus back home he said: "Can I call you when I come to New South Wales?"'

Aaron did call, and soon they were talking regularly. When Robina failed a final paper and had to postpone completing her nursing degree, he promptly offered her work on Epenarra. This was a platonic arrangement at the outset, but did not remain so for long—although Robina was extremely uncomfortable with the word 'girlfriend' and Aaron could see that earning her trust was a long-haul job.

Some of this was to do with Robina's past experience of what she now refers to as 'limerence' in relationships.

Limerence is the nutty, yearning, frenzied, obsessive and unrealistic rush of early love; it's a separate state from either lust or love. Psychologists say that limerence has little to do with real love, and neurologists use another name for it entirely. They call it PEA Brain. The P, E and A refer to the phenylalanine that is the neurotransmitter responsible for the 'high' of new love: PEA is surging, stewing, vaporising and condensing throughout our bodies.

Love of this kind is the ultimate mind-messing drug. You will think obsessively about the beloved, agonise over their feelings and pine in their absence. In their presence your heart races, soars, aches and somersaults. When they reciprocate, you are euphoric. When they don't, you're despondent. Frequently you swing between the two. Under its influence you will find it hard to focus on anything else, leading generally to poor judgment and impaired memory. Shortness of breath, sweating, stuttering and clumsiness and general anxiety can also be expected.

Writers often use love potions to show the absolute absurdity that limerence induces. Think of *A Midsummer Night's Dream* in which Puck mischievously uses a potion to have each young man reallocate his affections. There can be no clearer statement that this kind of love actually blinds us to the object of our affections.

As just about every authority is quick to tell you, a powerful experience of limerence is a very poor basis for marriage. In fact, some authorities believe that strong limerence is somewhat of a red flag in terms of the long-term health of a relationship. Limerence lasts from anywhere between nine months to two years—although times away from each other will prolong this. The best-case scenario for limerence is that the PEA Brain hormones gently decay, either setting the scene for a separation or for the next set of hormones to kick in to take the lovers into the next stage. This is the deep, quiet attachment of long-lasting love, and the hormone involved here is oxytocin—as it is between new parents and their baby. The worst-case scenario is for limerence to deepen existing wounds in your psyche, or to open up new ones in a previously healthy person.

Sometimes limerence is triggered less by your admiration or desire for the other person than by your own vulnerabilities. These vulnerabilities may stem from difficult relationships in your family of origin or another psychological crisis in your life. Generally, at the times in our life that we don't really feel lovable in our heart of hearts we are at greater risk of limerence—it can be easier to fix on someone else as the cure for our hurts than to heal ourselves. If that person then goes on to hurt us in some way, that hurt compounds our earlier hurts. We desperately seek to re-engage with that person—or, if all hope is gone, we might look for someone else to love us. In this way the limerent person can become more and more emotionally dependent.

Not every couple experiences limerence. There are many reasons for this. For example, a young woman hurt by years in a messy, limerent relationship, such as Robina, might do everything she could to avoid that feeling again. Robina was determined to avoid limerent love, but she missed entirely the significance of the scaffold of fun, friendship and utter dependability that Aaron had constructed beneath her. Limerence is not the only pathway into deep love. Lust coupled with liking also works just fine.

'He was my boss for twelve months and he taught me so many things, and I learnt so much more about him like that.'

She learned that Aaron could communicate clearly and deliberately without words by watching him work alongside Aboriginal stockmen who have another language of sign, expression and posture. It is a fast and fluent language that conveys volumes to the people who know it, but which the rest of us simply don't see. She saw that peer pressure didn't touch him. She came to admire his work ethic and his competence deeply. She learned that while Aaron isn't traditionally romantic he could make a corned-meat sandwich shared on the back of a Toyota feel romantic.

'After nine months together he said: "Can we say you're my girlfriend now?"—he'd just waited for me to own it.' Robina hadn't seen love coming for her, but there was no doubt in her mind now that it was love that she was feeling.

And it was in this same year that Robina met for the first time what she refers to as a 'shape-changing demon'.

Robina first experienced this demon as perfectionism. She was determined to be the 'perfect station wife'. She wanted to be competent on the property and simultaneously totally in control on the home front.

'It was as if I thought this would be appealing. I wanted to show him,' she says, mystified at herself all these years later. 'I'd seen his nana do this, do the men's work and the other stuff as well, so I thought I could totally slip into this.'

She was up at dawn to leave the homestead, and when they returned from the day's work after dark, Robina cooked the evening meal, as well as the breakfast, smoko and lunch for the following day.

'One day in the yard I was drafting. I was on a five-way gate, Aaron was yelling from the back of the race which way the gate needed to go. I was very new to this work, and there were heaps of blokes in the yard. And I let a cow that needed to go back out to pasture in with the cattle to go to market. And Aaron yelled at me, and he swore at me. He's normally very even-tempered, so I was a wreck by smoko. I'd packed things for smoko and things for lunch, and he asked me which I was going to get out, and I told him, but then I took out the other one. And Aaron said: "What are you doing?"—quite nicely, but that was it. I had to get away, I just cried and cried. And he had no idea how to deal with that with all the men around. And then when we got home I went into the shower.'

In the shower she cried some more. Aaron came and awkwardly apologised for yelling and swearing at her. Long days working with stock roughens tempers and tongues and forgiveness all round is the only way to be able to work together the following day. Robina and Aaron did forgive each other and kept on forgiving each other and learning about each other through what was mostly a beautiful year. At the end of it, Robina had not just learned a great many practical skills but had also completed her nursing degree. The next step for her was a graduate nursing program and Aaron suggested that she apply for the program run out of Alice Springs. She did this, and from there spent three years working around the Territory.

'I used to work night shift, then I'd finish that, go back to my unit, shower, and drive out to the station. Once I was there I'd find Aaron wherever he was on the station and I'd go blow for blow with him, whatever he was doing—thinking I was such a hero. When we got home I'd get dinner ready and he'd just put his feet up. And I'd get cranky at him.'

Very slowly Robina realised that her own expectations—that she should, in addition to her own work, help Aaron on the station and also provide him with house-cleaning and cooking services—were not Aaron's expectations.

'I was putting it on myself. It was a really screwed-up perception. When I dropped those expectations of myself—surprisingly and unsurprisingly—everything became easy between us.'

It was the first time, although it had been hiding in plain sight, that Robina had caught a glimpse of her demon. She didn't have a name for it yet but she knew that she would sometimes shut away who she truly was in the endeavour to be someone else, another Robina, who would be more acceptable to the critic within.

She hadn't realised yet that this one victory in loosening the grip of her own expectations around what a woman on a rural property does, of asking, 'who says that?' and 'is that even remotely reasonable?', was only the first battle she would need to fight. She didn't realise she was travelling through life with 'should' sitting on one shoulder and 'must' sitting on the other, each looking for an opportunity to whisper in her ear a message that would unleash anger and resentment within her, and then an inevitable self-hatred for harbouring these feelings. Why she was listening to the 'shoulds' and 'musts' was the real question, and one she would not think to ask for many years.

Aaron continued to manage Epenarra and Robina continued to work as a nurse, always returning to Aaron on the station as she could. She loved nursing.

'The remote experience is so good because you have to make do with what you have. I imagined, when I became a nurse, that I could fly around solo delivering nursing care in an ultralight to remote people.'

She was to realise that this was what the Royal Flying Doctor Service did—but that dream of taking journeys to remotely located clients would never quite leave her. She loved the physical aspects of nursing, the suturing and the bandaging, but most fascinating of all to her was care of mothers.

'I had done a double shift at Tennant Creek and a young girl in labour came in. She was seventeen and this wasn't her first child. The ambulance had brought her from the post office, but she'd walked from the other side of the town to reach the post office. She was too far gone to get her to Alice and she was on her own. I played the role of father, I stood up at her head and she was reefing at me—pulling me in towards her with each contraction. I was just on a high. It was as if the oxytocin high of delivery overflowed into me as well, it was incredible. The girl delivered the baby safely and then we transferred her to Alice Springs.

'I learnt a lot about mothering and breastfeeding from the Aboriginal people. The children I saw were "on" their people all the time. I remember on night shift seeing one lady in bed with three children—one sleeping on one breast, another who had just come off, and one more further down the bed. They were all just sound asleep, loving each other.'

However, Robina's contact with the Aboriginal people she was living alongside was mainly limited to her nursing role.

'I missed out on those people—being on the station there was some divide. I never pursued those relationships and I regret that,' she says.

In their enforced long separations—Robina at some far-flung nursing post and Aaron managing the station—they kept talking. The great secret of long-distance romance is that sometimes it strengthens relationships as, with conversation as the only point of contact, you do really learn to communicate. It can be easy to rely on touch and action alone—particularly when you are by nature a doer, a fixer and maker, which is what both Robina and Aaron are. It was in these long conversations that the subject of marriage finally surfaced. Then Robina's much-loved grandfather became very ill. As was usual at that time, there were many kilometres between them—Aaron at Epenarra and Robina in Alice Springs. Robina rang Aaron to share the news and to say, 'I really want Pop to know that I'm going to be married.'

'So after I told Aaron he said, "Just hang on, I'll ring you back,"' says Robina. 'And then he rang Dad straightaway. Dad was visiting Pop, he was at the bedside. Aaron said, "Can I marry her?"

'Then Aaron rang me back and said, "Do you want to get married?"'

They were longing to see each other, but it was simply not possible. In the end, Robina was to see Aaron's parents before she saw him.

'His parents were coming to visit us, and they were arriving in Alice Springs that day. I just hung out with his mum and dad for two days. Then he called up and we put the phone on speaker and he said, "Did Robina tell you yet?" and his mum said, "Tell us what?" She was tickled pink.'

In March 2009 Aaron and Robina were married. Aaron's face was clean-shaven, perhaps for the last time, and Robina's hair was long. The photographs show her looking delicate and at peace. Certainty had been slow to emerge for Robina but knowing Aaron is her man feels like an inspiration from God rather than simply a personal conviction, and that's what she's taken to church this day. Aaron looks handsome and happy. There's an elegant country-and-western look to them both. Robina is in embossed cowboy boots and lace. With his natty morning suit Aaron wears a leather belt made by Robina. The wedding rings are both made from gold found by a prospecting friend on and near Epenarra, and celebrate the land on which they met.

Their wedding day had been one of quiet commitment in a small church, wrapped in her family and his. But the months following were full of drama: by August, Robina was pregnant, and Aaron had been kicked by a bull and had to be flown out by the Royal Flying Doctor Service due to a number of broken ribs and the fear that he was bleeding internally.

Aaron healed, then went back to work, and Robina spent her days on a friend's neighbouring property. Much of the time she basked in the sun at a waterhole reminiscent of the one at which she'd met Aaron, her attention on the son growing inside her.

'We did it,' she said to Darcy as she nursed him for the very first time. As she'd hoped and expected of herself, mothering her beautiful little son came easily to her. He was so very like his easy-going, steady-natured, certain-hearted Dad, not at all like Robina herself. Robina felt confident, she felt enough, and out of that her mothering flowed. But that flow seemed to dry up in the months after her second son Tully was born nearly two-and-a-half years later.

'Something about becoming a mother to two children ...' she says. Somehow, this once more opened the gateway to 'must' and 'should', of feeling not enough, not good enough, of needing to do a whole galaxy of things that she didn't believe in, but having to do them anyway and becoming angrier, more bitter, more resentful. Robina found herself raging at the children, frightening them with her sudden descents into hostility, then breaking her heart over the fact that she was hurting the ones she loved most of all.

'I was teaching my babies terrible things,' she says. 'I was a lovely mummy on the surface, but underneath was all this anger. There were words inside me, all this rot and chaos and I didn't know how to still it. I was really disconnected from my essence and eventually it was out of control. Aaron was walking on eggshells. He never knew what he'd be coming home to.'

She has insights and solutions now, but at the time, and for quite a long while, she simply felt guilty and isolated. The shame and the ugliness of it all made it too difficult for her to share until the day she realised that preserving her secret would only continue to hurt her sons. She needed help. It was at this point she saw a course on the Gold Coast that seemed to have been written just for her. This course aimed to help women start their relationship with themselves and their history afresh, and in being at peace with themselves, from there create truly loving relationships.

Aaron's family had welcomed her with open arms years before, even in the days when she and Aaron were 'just friends'. Now Aaron's mother took a week off from her work to look after the little boys on the Gold Coast so Robina could attend every day, secure in the knowledge that her boys were in loving hands, and could still breastfeed Tully at night.

The course was directed at healing all that might lie beneath Robina's unhappiness. And it worked. It reconnected Robina with the easiness she had felt in mothering in Darcy's early years. She came to understand that she had shut down that loving flow and joyful engagement with the world, that welling-up of soul from deep within the landscape of her being, all by herself. The demon she'd glimpsed, the one who had placed on her the heavy burdens of 'must' and 'should' and 'prove' under which she'd faltered and raged, was simply an aspect of Robina herself.

'For years I dismissed and minimised myself, until I didn't know what was okay about me and what wasn't. And, of course, it is all okay.'

For the first time Robina confronted the fact that in believing that she was not 'okay, enough, sufficient' as she was, she'd dethroned her true self. She'd placed in charge another aspect, an ignorant and misguided self, who saw threats where there were none—in the unwitting defiance of a small child, for example—and missed the real threat to family wellbeing: Robina's disconnection from herself.

Robina had arrived at the course almost silent under the weight of her sorrow, hidden beneath her long hair.

'I knew Aaron liked girls with long hair, so I grew it and I grew a big fringe,' she says. Robina herself liked her own hair short but she had felt that a good wife should suppress such preferences to make her husband happy. She emerged from the five days of intensive therapy totally made over: a change Aaron seems to have taken in his stride.

'The course took away the rage and the sadness and the anger. The only thing that was left was my hair, and three women there cut my hair. I realised, even if he does like long hair, he still loves me, long hair or not,' she says.

Her hair was cut to within millimetres of her scalp but the real makeover occurred deep within, and this Aaron welcomed even more. There's that old saying, 'if Momma ain't happy, ain't nobody happy', and Robina's rediscovered joy in life was a gift not just to herself but to Aaron and the two boys.

Robina had been taught as a child: 'There's right and wrong, you only do right. It doesn't matter how you feel, you do it; first with your head and then with your heart.' These words from generations ago are out of step with today's knowledge about the risks of teaching children to ignore their feelings. Of course, in some ways we learn to raise children when we are still children ourselves, by watching how our own parents raise us—at a time when perhaps we aren't able to evaluate how useful a particular parenting practice or belief is. When our own children arrive it is hard not to simply reproduce all that we were taught—not just in what we say, but in our expressions and our actions. This can be positive, but equally it can be negative. Something about the birth of Tully triggered in Robina feelings of being burdened, not coping and not being enough—in thinking about this, Robina discovered that far more people and stories lived in her heart than she had imagined.

'Aaron had always been okay with me, but I hadn't been,' says Robina. She had judged herself too harshly. She would no longer do that. And in accepting herself she found that the dry creek beds of her inner landscapes were once more flowing and that she had energy for her children, for Aaron and for everything else that mattered to her.

*

On the day I meet Robina she is making and delivering her Number 45 Curry Paste to sell at markets all over Australia. Robina makes this secret heirloom recipe mostly traditionally ... but not quite. Her hair is extremely short and this reveals the delicate bones of her oval face—at the same time she has perched on her distinctive, sculpted nose the largest, owliest pair of spectacles I've ever seen. I suspect Robina has the attractive person's ambivalence about her appearance. Good looks (like good bank accounts) can get in the way of people seeing and coming to know a person. And Robina wants people to know her, to connect to her, particularly women who are like the woman she once was. Having been helped to heal herself, all Robina wants to do is to see other women heal too. She added to this her particular focus on working with mothers of young children, and also her old dream of taking journeys out to the remote places in which some people live and working with them there.

So Robina and Aaron made a decision. They purchased a caravan, hung out a virtual shingle (featuring Aaron's ability to weld, mend, bodgie, work and handle, and Robina's emotional renovations for women), enrolled five-year-old Darcy at Alice Springs School of the Air (Tully is still too little for school) and metamorphosed into the most modern of gypsies.

'I had to be free of all those layers of things that don't matter,' she says. 'And when I experienced this, I realised this was my gig. Nursing is not all my heart, but this is. You can be you at a core level—it's a real place, and that's what I want to bring to other women.'

Robina now uses the method that helped her to help other women, particularly those who live in the outback. 'Those environments are so remote and the pressure on women can become so heightened,' says Robina. 'I've had women hiding under the office desk doing this work with me just so they can have some space.' Aaron needs this mobility too. He is earning money on his way to buying his own station in Queensland or the Northern Territory one day, but it needs to be work in the bush. He cannot handle more than two weeks in a town or city.

It seems to me the most elegant of solutions to the nature of working in the outback—where work is intermittent, seasonal or once-off—and it provides far more time together for families than fly-in, fly-out living arrangements. Whoever is not working looks after the children. More often than not it is Robina, but Aaron is very comfortable with hands-on fathering.

'I never really thought I'd have kids—not that I wouldn't have them, but I never thought about it. I didn't expect them to be this much fun.'

Robina and Aaron are now modern gypsies. In their caravan with their two little boys they travel the Australian outback. Aaron's fascination is with the land. Robina's is with the human heart. Each of them is exploring a different terrain. They observe, they reflect, they deduce. Robina's heart is an occupied one. Not only occupied by the people she's known and knows, but occupied by the stories left from the lives of people she would never meet. The story behind Robina's Number 45 Curry Paste business is this kind of legacy. Some years before she and Aaron purchased their caravan Robina had begun making curry paste, which she was beginning to sell in remote parts of Australia. Number 45 Curry Paste was almost her own personal scholarship fund: among other things, she used the profits to pay for professional and personal development. Robina inherited the recipe from her great-grandparents, and with the recipe comes the story behind it, which is another kind of legacy entirely.

Robina's great-grandparents were Anglo-Indians living in Bangalore. They had five children and then came the Depression.

'They actually couldn't afford to keep all of their children, to feed them all. Three of them had to go to an orphanage. Can you imagine,' says Robina, 'what that would have felt like? How much it would hurt your heart?'

The desperation to have all their children back with them again drove her great-grandparents into entrepreneurship. They began to make and sell different condiments, including the one Robina makes. It began as 'meals on wheels'. In her kitchen Robina's great-granny made meals that her great-grandfather delivered on his bicycle. Then her great-grandmother began making condiments from spices she'd ground up herself. The enterprise grew and eventually they established a factory, and then one day all the children could come home again.

Robina believes that perhaps the legacy of this family trauma contributed to her unexpected feelings of being unable to cope with a second child.

In fact, stories like these are known to travel down generations, rather less in words than in shared unspoken feelings, in our most subtle micro expressions and in unspoken family rules. Such stories act like a virus infecting our vision, or a ghost standing between our loved ones and ourselves, and they shape how we respond to a situation without us ever seeing their influence upon us. In psychological literature this is called intergenerational transfer: the author of *Anne of Green Gables*, LM Montgomery, wrote that 'no one can be free who has a thousand ancestors', a phrase that speaks directly to this. These subtle influences often do not bother women and men until we have children of our own, and then reveal themselves when we behave in ways we don't want to and don't understand. For example, we may refuse to console a child while knowing that our actions would look heartless to someone else—because a family ghost is whispering that 'he needs to stand on his own two feet to be safe in this life' and we are unknowingly listening to that voice rather than the despair of our child. Robina has busted these ghosts, she's brought these family stories and rules out into the warm light of day and examined them to see if they are true and kept only the stories that help her. She's happier; the whole family is happier. The caravan has become the Meehan family's magic carpet. They travel the red roads of Australia's vast interior—whether dust-devilled or sodden and treacherous—and peer down together at the view flowing past. When they see an adventure to take or an opportunity to earn they can stop where they are and explore it all together. The Meehan family climb hills together, together they paddle in puddles. The little boys are buzzed by the rush and bustle of cattle loading onto Dad's truck; later they are calmed by the silence of desert on a winter's night. The next day might bring school in a classroom or school high in their bunks under Mum's eye as she cooks dinner in the nifty, tightly organised caravan kitchen. The next day might bring home their trucking dad, or see their mum out-the-door on one of her solo working voyages: every day they are watching their parents returning from and setting out on adventures, and every day the boys are encouraged to take their own adventures.

'I love living in the caravan,' says Robina. 'It beautifully blends family unity and freedom.' She likes the combination of a limit on 'stuff' with a limitless view. Not only is it the life Robina has always wanted—unconstrained, adventurous and full of family camaraderie—and what Aaron has always wanted—in the bush, independent and physical—but perhaps the best part of this life is that it lets both Robina and Aaron show Darcy and Tully that such adventurous lives are still possible in the twenty-first century.

My Love Is Your Love

Cathy and David Jones, Boogardie Station, Mt Magnet, Western Australia

Cathy Ponton grew up in the Melbourne suburbs, in a family that lacked the money for such things as Girl Guides, but was rich in siblings and friends. Cathy is the third of eight children, and next door were the O'Neils with their seven children. The fence dividing the O'Neil and Ponton backyards (and children) was soon pulled down and never put up again. Cathy's family was Catholic. They were not great church attenders and the saying of grace was for formal occasions rather than everyday practice, but Cathy's mother had a deep faith. Her faith was shared from early on with her children, because Mary had the gift of engaging fully with her children in every way. Mary did not leave her children to play by themselves, as many women did at that time. She played games with her children and chatted to them about all kinds of things. Faith was one of these things, and Cathy's own faith was a living thing in her life from as early as she can remember.

At the end of her street was the neighbourhood church. At a quarter to seven every morning Cathy got up early, dressed, raced down the street to morning mass, raced home for breakfast and then went to her Catholic primary school—and the same pattern held true for her high-school years at a Catholic school run by the Good Samaritans of St Benedict. She was the only one in her family to go to church every day.

She trained as a teacher and went promptly to work in Catholic schools—her faith deepening all the time.

Faith was the most important thing in her life. Like any other gift, it didn't come free. Every gift comes with the cost of being different to most other people. So gifts make life rich, give you a sense of purpose, but they can also make life lonely. Like many people born with a gift Cathy longed to develop that gift further, to be mentored, to work within a community that valued and supported her faith and, surrounded by like minds, to lose that loneliness. In one of the quick, clear, untroubled insights that characterise her, Cathy realised that she needed to enter religious life.

'When I entered in the late 1970s, that was a big decision and it was a bit ... counter-cultural. Young women were not really going into religious life. People said to me, "But isn't religion dying?" and "Don't you want to get married and have kids?" And I loved kids, so yes! But I felt called—compelled, but not in a bad way—to religious life. I made the decision and I told my parents. My parents were wonderful people. They would just say to us, "If that's what you want to do, just sort it out." So I did. I went and sorted it out. I went to the local convent, the Good Samaritans, and said I thought I'd like to enter. The person to speak to was my old high-school principal and she said: "Well, here is what you have to do." I had to do a psychology test and a medical and then go for a couple of interviews. And then they accepted me.'

The commitment to join a religious order embraces all parts of life. Your earnings are shared, your costs are borne and possessions are minimal. Together you work, eat and pray on a daily and weekly timetable. All of that helps you develop another discipline—accepting that everyone is different and letting that be so, day in and day out. Religious life placed Cathy where she could give and surrounded her with others of faith with whom she could grow.

'Life in an intentional shared community is all about the quality of relationships you can achieve. Liking someone, disliking someone ... it all becomes rather more important in a situation where you are at close quarters and where everyone is trying hard to act with love.

'I had a novice mistress, Sister Elizabeth, with whom I didn't get on very well. Not Elizabeth's fault, not my fault, just our two personalities didn't gel. I really loved going to the seminary. There were very good lecturers there, very good courses. I enjoyed talking to the other students. But then someone (and I am sure it wasn't one of the students) went to Sister Elizabeth and told her he thought I was a flirt. So she called me in to her office. And I thought, "I don't know that I've been flirting, but I know that I am in really big trouble because nuns are not meant to flirt." I was so embarrassed! I couldn't believe it. And Sister Elizabeth said to me, "You are going red—you are going very red!"'

Cathy's pale face is filling with colour: this is a story she is telling with humour but she is clearly still mortified by the accusation all these years later. The accusation of behaving inappropriately was a blow to her confidence. Elizabeth's words had the potential to destroy not just Cathy's pleasure in being at the seminary but also her confidence in working with men. That this did not happen was due to Sister Joan.

'Joan was in charge of the congregation of sisters that lived in the professed house (where the sisters who had taken their vows lived). She did some work with us as novices one morning a week, about reflecting on life, getting to know yourself and using scripture to inspire you, to find out what touches you. I related really well to Joan. She was the person who really helped me grow as a person, and in the Christian sense too, for the two years I was there. So I went to see Sister Joan at the professed house, and explained that Elizabeth had said to me that a man at the seminary (because Elizabeth had stressed to me that it was a 'he') had said that I was a flirt. And I remember Joan saying to me: "So what if you are?" I said, "I'm a nun!" and Joan said, "It's nothing, what are you worried about it for?"'

Sister Elizabeth was one of those religious women who felt that Eve needed to take full responsibility for the business with the snake and the apple. Joan clearly was not.

Cathy had encountered one of the everyday ways that the schisms in belief among religious people are brought to life—in this case, who carries the responsibility for the sexual desire felt by a man? And for Cathy it was vital to hear that some religious leaders felt it was okay for her to be herself around men—lively, passionate, caring. She could be all those things and still be a nun. However the accusation, once made, did not go away. The hours Cathy was allowed to be at the seminary were reduced by Sister Elizabeth. Cathy feels that Sister Elizabeth was trying to protect both Cathy herself and the rest of their congregation (all those of that religious order) from what she saw as a possible scandal.

'So I didn't stay the whole day any longer. I said to the guys I knew, "I can't come for a whole day because someone here has told them I'm a flirt," and they just thought it was ridiculous.'

Despite the limited time she was allowed at the seminary she still needed to work closely with the other students, many of them male.

'The priest who taught one particular course said, "Well, normally we would do a section on evil here but if you young ladies are going to be in the group we might change it to Mary"—and I remember saying, "Evil is fine; we'll do evil," and the other girls saying, "Yes, just because we are women, don't change this stuff around!" In that course I had to lead a tutorial with a Marist seminarian.'

Her co-presenter for this tutorial was Chris Uhlmann (now a political commentator for the ABC), who was one of the Marist students. They became friends.

'One day Chris rang up the novitiate and Sister Elizabeth answered the phone. And then she came to me and said, "There is a phone call for you and it is a young man, apparently from the seminary."'

But Sister Elizabeth had lost any traction with Cathy, who could immediately see the funny side of this. Taking heart from Sister Joan's words, Cathy remained open to making friends with men. She had male friends among the seminarians but she liked none of them in a way that suggested to her that she needed to leave religious life. She related best to those who planned to lead active lives of service in the real world—the Columbans and Marists. She did not relate as well to the Conventual Franciscans, whose Catholicism was less about service and more about contemplation and preserving tradition.

'The Grey Franciscans were nice guys but they were conservative and I was not a conservative Catholic. They would pick me up and drop me off at the seminary so Sister Elizabeth expressed her concern ... and I said to her, "Well, you don't need to worry about them!" but Sister Elizabeth continued to monitor me closely.'

At first I am surprised by just how honestly nuns speak of this type of threat to their vocation. Cathy was taught that nuns can have infatuations: 'You have the infatuation, but then it is gone.' I am not surprised at the advice not to trust infatuation, as it can be such an unreliable indicator of the real state of your heart. But Cathy did not have any infatuations and neither was she worried about missing out on romance. She'd had boyfriends at school and afterwards. She'd liked them, but after about three months all such relationships had fizzled.

'I just thought that I wasn't very good at having boyfriends—and in the back of my mind was that maybe I'd be a nun,' she says, casually.

In 1979 she became a nun and moved from school to school and state to state at the direction of the order. For a long time she didn't admit to herself that she longed for children of her own. Instead, all the love and care that would have gone to her own children was showered on her students and on others in her community.

'Then, in the last year before I came to Western Australia, when I was working in Adelaide, we had a Mother's Day service. They were giving flowers, praying for mothers, and I started to cry. I remember friends saying to me, "Oh, you poor thing, you are missing your mother in Melbourne." And I went back to the convent and I started to wonder about just why I'd cried. I realised: "I'm not missing my mother. I'm missing being a mother." It really hit me then that I was never going to have children of my own and I loved children so much.'

In a single night Cathy acknowledged for the first time this grief for the children she would never have, and worked it through into acceptance in a cataclysmic crying jag. 'It was just as well I was by myself at the convent that night.'

It was not long after this that Cathy was offered the chance to go to Western Australia, and she leapt at it. Almost as strong as her conviction that she needed to be in religious life was her conviction that she needed to be working in Western Australia and, more particularly, in the remote mining and station country.

'My first placement was in Campbelltown in NSW after I'd done my training in Sydney. And there was an education assistant, Robyn, in Campbelltown who'd come from Western Australia. Her sister lived on a station. Robyn had spent Christmas on her sister's station. She spoke about the shearing shed and the heat, the corrugated iron. I was fascinated and I thought, "I wonder if I'll ever get to see a station?"'

But her congregation, the Good Samaritan Sisters, had no foothold in Western Australia and Cathy was very disappointed. Not long afterwards this changed. The Good Samaritans were first appointed to New Norcia, and then Perth and finally to Mt Magnet. Immediately Cathy began saying how keen she was to go to the outback. At congregational gatherings in Melbourne, Cathy prioritised attending the sessions where the four sisters from Mt Magnet presented. Cathy did not understand why she, from suburban Melbourne, felt so attracted by the red-dirt country and the frontier towns of Western Australia.

But in January 1991 a place opened up at the Mt Magnet convent and Cathy applied immediately and was successful.

Cathy was under no illusions about what she'd find in Mt Magnet. When Western Australia was first colonised Mt Magnet became a major centre, along with the rest of the Murchison, with its rich veins of gold and substantial grazing opportunities. Beginning in about 1860 all wealth was systematically sent out of the region. First, knowledge of land held by Aboriginal clans left, as whole families were moved to reserves. Then mineral wealth was dug up and sent away. Stations were unknowingly overstocked and so the nutrients in the soil were exported as wool and meal, breaking the natural cycle in which nutrients were consumed but eventually returned to the soil. Now, in many places the old iron-red soil looks thin, the bush water-starved, and the trees low and ragged. The ground itself looks iron-hard and resilient, but that is an illusion. In each decade the carrying capacity of the land (the number of stock that can be run per acre) has dropped.

Some of the money from the sale of minerals, wool and meat came back to Murchison—you can see it in the old town buildings—but most did not. As the resources left in trucks and trains, so did the jobs and the people. With loss of population came loss of political power. Loss of political power means fewer services—and with fewer jobs and services and less power comes rural malaise. To begin with this malaise only affects the most vulnerable in a community, and the strongest in the community may not even believe that those vulnerable people really need help from outside. Frequently those strong community members, the ones in positions of relative power, have turned down many offers of outside help over the years. But eventually the malaise has them too by the throat. So it was not hard for Cathy to believe that God had called her to Mt Magnet—a place where inequity was the rule rather than the exception and where people of capacity and goodwill were desperately needed—simply for the help she could give.

Cathy was tasked with writing a family faith program for Catholic families on stations. This program aimed to help parents pass their faith on to their children in the absence of Catholic schooling. The church has a three-year cycle of readings, so Cathy, together with the other nuns stationed at Mt Magnet, had to write an exhaustive, all-ages, three-year curriculum.

She arrived in January and began on the required getting-to-know-yous. Almost immediately she met the station families for whom the curriculum she was writing was intended. Of these, the Jones family at Boogardie was located closest to Mt Magnet. Josephine and Henry Jones had five children—some of them adults with children of their own, and others in their teens, away at boarding school.

'Their third son, Paul, was married to Janet. Janet and I got on well—she had three little kids: Jeremy, Simone and Nicholas, who was a baby. We became friendly, and I loved kids, so I helped her with them.'

She also met David Jones, Paul's older brother. David, like his five brothers, was well known throughout the Murchison region for his ability to find fun in unexpected ways, his enthusiastically deployed skills in working stock and machinery, and his loyalty to his family and to the land. He was very tall, lean, slouchy and easy in his movements, his demeanour calm (except when his ferocious temper was evoked), his features blunt and even under his curls and pushed-back Akubra hat. He was just thirty years old but already his eyes had the downward lean which comes from a great deal of time looking for stock in the far distance under a bright sun. Flashes of humour frequently brightened his face as he listened, and he generally listened more than he spoke. But people liked to listen to him. He was very funny and his insights were widely respected.

Cathy is unsure when she became inescapably aware of that extra quality to her friendship with David—the unmistakably emotional connection that seems to wrap itself around the two of you, tugging you tighter with every meeting.

'I knew a little bit. I think I knew unconsciously, but consciously I didn't.'

I cannot help thinking of the veil Cathy wore for so long. In our culture, it is perhaps the strongest symbol that a woman has joined a celibate religious order: a celebration of a nun's new status as being reserved for God and his work, set apart from the world. But in the months after she met David it seems to me that the veil had another function: from behind it Cathy was shielded from understanding that her interest in David was a romantic one.

She did feel a connection to David, but she didn't recognise it for what it was. Free from the consciousness that recognition would have brought, she simply enjoyed being with him and getting to know him better. Christmas Day is Cathy's birthday. At a shared Christmas dinner at Boogardie at the end of 1991 she learned from David's mother Josie that his birthday was on New Year's Day. Both had birthdays that were important for other reasons, and because she knew just what that felt like she sent him a card—carefully designed not to come from her alone but from all four nuns stationed at Mt Magnet.

David felt that same connection but he did not deceive himself about the nature of his interest in Cathy. He didn't see 'a nun'. He saw Cathy and he saw something that had escaped most people about Cathy's nature. Cathy was not in the convent to hide, but to see deeply into the sad and ugly places in communities and people and to help out wherever she could. She was not a woman who needed to be sheltered or protected but a woman to stand shoulder to shoulder with.

Finding yourself 'fathoms deep', as Shakespeare says, is different for everyone. Some people slide happily into love, and glory in the slide; for some the loss of self-containment is a violence done to their soul; and then there are the dreamy travellers who simply miss the 'no turning back' sign on the road. My friend Art who, like David, is a man not given to self-deception, wrote of falling in love with his wife Anna: 'I don't remember a borderline between not love and love. It was obvious even from the edge that the water was deep.'

For David, a man of the dry inland, I would draw another analogy. The Murchison is dry most of the time. Nonetheless, spread throughout are the oases. Out here they are called 'sweet patches' and in them grow tall trees, grasses and bushes, green even in the dry times. In the driest times animal life withdraws into these sweet patches to wait for rain. They are a refreshment to the pastoralist's spirit, with their promise that all the land will be green again when rain comes, and a place for life to hide out when it does not—and all pastoralists know each sweet patch on their land and visit them when they can. For David, Cathy stood out like a sweet patch in the dry land, and his destination was quickly set.

David was a direct person and not given to reflection. He would see what needed to be done or said, and do or say it. Added to this, from an early age he had picked and chosen from among the prevailing social norms. This is something that many School of the Air children do. The rest of us are taught in the primary-school playground that what other people think counts, but School of the Air children often play only with their siblings and the family pets. David was far more his own man in consequence and so, even though he was Catholic, he had never taken on the social norm of 'nuns belong to the Lord and aren't for marrying'.

He set about courting Cathy. But this was not a standard courtship, as Cathy herself had no idea she was participating in such a thing. David did need to reflect at length, perhaps for the first time in his life, on how to get to know Cathy without causing her to back away from the friendship. He attempted to be with her on all occasions, he went out of his way to help, and he began sharing all he could of his life with her.

Cathy doesn't remember exactly when it was borne upon her that it wasn't only David's family she liked so much—and, after all, both his family and hers were complex, passionate, fun-loving Catholic families—but David himself, in particular. The veil of not-knowing would sometimes flutter up, only to come down and blind her to the significance of their connection once more.

'One day Janet's daughter Simone rang me up. She was only two years old but she had terrific language. She said, "Could you come and stay at my house?" so I played along and said, "Oh yes, and what day would you like me to come, Simone?" In the end Janet took the phone and said she was coming into town and could pick me up. She asked if I could stay for a couple of days. And then I discovered that Josie and Henry were going to be away and David was staying with Paul and Janet ...'

A look of remembered consciousness flashes across Cathy's mobile face. She called a friend in Melbourne. Trisha had been a nun but she had left her congregation as it wasn't a good fit for her. Cathy explained the situation to her. Perhaps she shouldn't go, with a single young man being there too? Trisha laughed, and said "Go on, you'll have a great time," and so Cathy went. What a revelation this hesitation was! Cathy didn't know David well and knew too that she generally found men easy company and no threat at all to her choice to be in religious life yet, quite correctly, something about David, even on little acquaintance, was ringing her alarm bells.

'So there I was having breakfast, lunch, dinner with David, Paul and Janet ... and there were times when I just was talking to David. And I thought, "Crikey, this is a bit ... interesting." It was quite a different feeling than I'd had with anyone else I'd ever related to.'

She now saw David often. He'd not been a regular church attender, but now, with an ulterior motive firmly in place, his lanky relaxed frame was very visible most Sundays. She was pleased to see him every time, her response untrammelled by any awkward consciousness of just why he was there. Often he'd drop into the convent as well and they would talk.

'I don't know why the other nuns left me alone so often,' says Cathy comically, and I can't help laughing. 'The order didn't send any young ones after me for a long time either,' she adds in a thoughtful tone. And the other nuns do seem to have been away quite a lot.

'When the other nuns were all away travelling for the Feast of St Benedict, I thought, "Well, because it's the Feast of St Benedict, I'm going to have a party." And so I invited people, including Janet and Paul, and I said to Janet, "If David wants to come, tell him to come." He came as well, and it was a fun night. We had a shared dinner and conversation. Even then I didn't consciously think about it, but I was really happy that he'd come. I remember seeing him helping Janet with Simone and carrying her out to the car, and thinking, "Oh, he's lovely with little children."'

It wasn't long after this that she did know, finally and fully, how she felt about David. He had dropped in after a function Cathy had organised for children. It was a rainy day, and the children were excited, and she looked up to see David talking to Janet. David nodded to her, and smiled, and came over to talk ... and as Cathy thought to herself, 'How nice to see him', she suddenly knew just how attracted to him she was. It was a double awareness: she realised her own feelings and for the first time made a guess at David's own.

Finally Cathy was awake. Her first thought was that it must be infatuation on both sides and she knew that that feeling was not one to trust. But was it infatuation? In the midst of this unlooked-for confusion, this sense of David having overturned her beautifully balanced applecart on its pre-determined path, the convent was visited by the congregation leader for Western Australia, Sister Colleen. Cathy knew her well and had a great respect for her, having lived with her in Adelaide.

'And Colleen said to me: "Where to from here?" Because normally nuns will go to a place, stay there a set time and move onto something else. She said: "Maybe you'd like to do a theology degree?" And I would have! It would have been really good to go back to Melbourne to do a theology degree, I'd have enjoyed that. But when I was talking to her I did tell her that I wasn't sure what was happening, that it was probably nothing, but that there was a man around who was kind of ... something was happening ... but I was sure it was going to be nothing.'

Perhaps because for so long he had looked for a sign that Cathy was aware that he felt more for her than friendship, and finally he could read that in her face, perhaps because there was a chance she would leave Mt Magnet, or perhaps for both these reasons, David chose early July in 1992 to say exactly how he felt.

'I used to go for walks in the evening. I went for a walk one evening, and went past the corner hotel. Henry Jones (David's father) and David were in there, so I stuck my head in to say hello. They said, "Come in, come in!" so of course I went in, because I liked David, didn't I? We were talking, and I said I had to go, because I needed to be home for tea and I was already a few minutes late. David came outside with me. And then he said: "I love you, and I just wish I could tell the whole world." I knew he meant it and I thought, "Oh, no! What is going on in my life?" I knew then that I had to make a decision. Was I going to stay in religious life or was I going to leave?'

*

The Rule of St Benedict places great emphasis on willingness to listen for the voice of God and in doing so, transcend the limitations of your personal vision. Cathy's faith required that she not go against God's will. Was David, and marriage to him, simply a temptation away from the path she had rightly taken all those years before? She still wanted to be guided by God and to read, as if from a compass, the direction her life should take.

So Cathy immersed herself in the work that she had to do. In her spare time she walked, in every moment listening within for the voice of God. That year was a particularly good one for wildflowers, especially for everlastings, which are Cathy's favourites. Only in some years, when it rains for long enough and at the right time, do everlastings grace Western Australia's outback. In a good year they flow across great swathes of flat inland like the rain that calls them out of the soil. Everlastings grow best in the places where a puddle once sat. The deeper the water was, the higher the plant. So, where road edges were splashed with puddles, now they were splashed with everlastings. The channels that directed water away from the road and into the bush were occupied now by flowers, floating improbably above the softly grassed red earth. This hallucinatory effect is courtesy of their nearly invisible dark stems, and the way their papery heads respond to the softest zephyr.

In drawing comfort from the everlastings Cathy was also aware of their symbolism. One everlasting on its own does not achieve very much, but in assembly every pink, white or yellow flower works to create a glorious tapestry and Cathy prayed to be guided to the tapestry God had in mind for her. Although these flowers are called 'everlastings', like us, they do not last forever. While Cathy believed in an eternal life of the spirit, she believed too that there is just one life for us all on the planet. How best could she give of herself in this life?

She called her friend Trisha again.

'I said to Trisha: "I don't know what to do. I really like him, he really likes me, and he wants me to make a decision but I have to do God's will ..." and Trisha said, "Cathy, God wants you to be happy."'

Of course, for Christians those words are not as simple as they sound—they might sound like 'you go, girl', but that is not what Trisha meant. She was suggesting to Cathy that guidance would come in the form of being shown where to find that happiness. Benedictines believe too that guidance should be looked for within everyday life and conversation and community, and so Cathy listened to her friend.

That night Cathy lit a lamp, knelt down on her prayer stool and prayed for many hours. It was very late when the thought came to her that she should take twelve months' leave from the community—and with the thought came an incredible feeling of peace, like the softest and warmest blanket, wrapping around her indecision, her confusion, her sense of failure. Weeks of turmoil slid away as the peace sank into her bones. Cathy knew she had finally set foot on the right path in God's eyes.

In the morning she rang to ask for leave, eventually speaking to the head of the congregation. Leaving religious life is a serious decision. Just as when she entered religious life counselling was required in order to ensure she was not acting on a whim, she was now required to trial life outside the convent before making a final decision, to ensure she was not being snared by infatuation. The head of the order asked Cathy to return to Melbourne so this counselling could take place.

With her request for leave in place she went to see David at Boogardie. At this stage David and Cathy's love was not even suspected by most people. However, David's mother Josie, a most devout Catholic—for whom it was unthinkable that any man should charm a nun away from her calling and out of the convent, and horrifying that a son of hers should do so!—was unable to dismiss her suspicion that this was in fact what David was doing. Josie is famous for her good cheer, her honesty, her good business mind—but inside the family she's also known for her '40 questions' and she was beginning to ask them.

Cathy found David at Janet and Paul's house. He was sensibly, but most unromantically, dressed in a tracksuit. Mt Magnet in late July is extremely cold. It was clear that Cathy had something important to say, so David suggested they move somewhere both warm and private—difficult in Janet's busy house with three little children who knew that these two adults could be counted on for games and attention. This warm and private place was Janet's pantry.

With the pantry door shut tight Cathy brought David up to date. He was delighted. He's not a man for half-measures or nuances of feeling. All he wanted was for Cathy to marry him.

The next visit was out to Boogardie, for Cathy and David to tell his parents Henry and Josie what was happening. Cathy was nervous about this, because the Joneses are a Catholic family and there is a general disapproval about nuns or priests renouncing their vows—she was equally concerned about the reaction of her own parents. She heard later from Josie that David didn't actually say who it was who was coming for dinner—he had simply said to his mother, on the way out the door in the morning, quite casually: 'Somebody will be here for tea.' This was rather a typical statement by David (and, indeed, many station men) because, for all their isolation, stations can be very busy with people passing through—friends travelling, stock agents, agricultural department staff …

Cathy arrived, very nervous, homemade fruit cake in hand, and hoping that David would be in from work. He was, but he was in the shower, and it was Josie who came to the door. The sight of Cathy standing there must have transformed all Josie's teeming suspicions into an astonished and horrified certainty and she said, 'Oh, it's you!' in a voice that clearly revealed this.

The four of them—David, Cathy, Josie and Henry—sat down to dinner and the conversation was wide-ranging but did not touch at all on why Cathy had come to dinner. At the meal's conclusion, Henry took in the increasingly taut atmosphere with foreboding and immediately excused himself.

'He didn't muck around with things like this—he went straight to bed,' says Cathy, matter-of-factly, affectionately and comically. 'The three of us went to sit in the lounge room and Josie asked all her questions. David charming a nun was the last thing she'd have wanted—she believed a nun should stay a nun and not go off and marry somebody. And she wanted to know, "What is going to happen? Will you still be able to be in the Catholic Church? Can you and David get married in the Catholic Church?" She was really concerned about that. I said, "Yes, we can get married in the Catholic Church—if I was a priest leaving it would be much harder. Women are dispensable, but priests are not. They are pretty strict on releasing them from their ordination, but it won't be a problem for me."'

In Melbourne Cathy also spent time with her family. She had been anxious about telling her parents that she was leaving the church, and particularly anxious about telling her father. He had been so proud of having a daughter in the congregation, and he helped out the local sisters with maintenance and sports coaching. In fact, both her parents were supportive. Her siblings felt rather more strongly—they'd been having sisterly intuitions of a disruption in Cathy's world. They were utterly delighted by her romance with David and they cheered her on.

*

Cathy returned from Melbourne to Mt Magnet in late August. She'd been counselled, she'd lived once more in the convent, and now she was back to trial living out in the world. This was complicated by the fact that emerging from religious life meant Cathy had to establish herself in the way an eighteen-year-old does.

Within the order you don't need such things as a tax file number. You haven't accumulated savings. You haven't accumulated 'stuff' either, not even the basics for setting up a house. The Mother-General, the head of Cathy's order, had asked that she go to the Catholic Education Office in Geraldton and apply for work there. Geraldton is a four-hour drive from Boogardie, so in addition to somewhere to live, she would need a car and, of course, Cathy had almost no possessions and no money. She was utterly dismayed at the thought of setting up a house—before she left Melbourne her sister Bernadette's husband had, as a joke, given her a little present, a green vegetable peeler that she still treasures.

On returning to Mt Magnet she emptied out her room at the convent and, with the intention of it being just for a week, she went to stay in Josie and Henry's house at Boogardie, where David also lived.

'Josie showed me into my room. David's room, of course, was on the other side of the house!' This was the beginning of Josie's careful supervision of the rest of this courtship. She was determined that David and Cathy's behaviour should remain within the boundaries decided by the Catholic Church—and, after all, Cathy was only on leave. She was still to decide whether or not she would marry David and renounce her vows.

Cathy now says that religious life was right for her: it was just not right for her life long.

'I am sure I was meant to be in religious life for a time. I went on retreat in early 1992 and the priest presenting was saying that he felt a change was coming in the Catholic Church, where people will commit for a period of time rather than for life. And I thought that was interesting, but I didn't think it was particularly relevant to me. One of the things they asked us to do was to go off and draw ourselves in religious life—they gave us oil pastels and paper. And I divided the paper into four and what I drew was each of the seasons: summer, autumn, winter, spring. I didn't think about it at the time, but when I looked back it was almost as if I knew I'd completed the full cycle of my religious life.'

If there was a Bible text for this time of confusion in Cathy's life, it was surely 1 Corinthians 13. This contains one of the best-accepted definitions of love in human literature, not as a feeling, but as an umbrella term for principled action: it describes love as patient and kind; it does not keep a record of wrongs, rejoices in truth, protects, always trusts and hopes, and it always perseveres. A great deal of the Bible tells us that love is action—and in reading about this I came across the frequently debated question of what was more true—love as action or love as feeling?

Cathy was 'in love' with David, but she needed to know if she could translate that feeling into doing. She needed to know how well she fitted with David, with the rest of his life and with the rest of the family, because this is the way of things in station families: business, family life and recreation are tangled together. And, despite the request from the Mother-General that she should move to Geraldton, life conspired to keep her with David and his family at the station, and there she served another kind of novitiate.

She could find no work in Geraldton, but she was offered teaching work in Mt Magnet without even looking.

'I rang Mt Magnet School to enquire about teacher registration and the principal said, "Can you do relief teaching?" and I said, "Well, yes," and he had me in there immediately.'

The shops and main street of a small town like Mt Magnet act like antennae for gossip—rumour is refined in homes and on the backstreets, travels in with the daily business of shopping and posting and is exchanged in conversation in the shops, taking new forms with each speculation. All small towns are like this. Few small towns ever have a love story like the one of Cathy and David to wonder at—so on the day Cathy started at the school there was hardly a person who didn't know some of her story. This, naturally, included the students.

Cathy's first class was with three high-school boys who needed help with written language. Shocking the pants off the new teacher is the first tactic of struggling students. Of course, this new teacher would be delightfully easy to shock—only last week or the week before, she was a nun! What would she know about 'life'! At the start of the lesson, in a gleeful chorus, they began: 'You know what we did on the weekend, Miss? We got pissed, Miss! We smoked dope! And we had ... sex!'

Teachers need to direct and shape the relationship with the children—and when teachers are rattled or offended by this kind of behaviour from children it means the children become the ones in charge. Cathy knew this.

'I just said, "Well, I don't think those were good ideas, but that was the weekend. Let's do some work now." If I'd allowed them to get to me it would have been the end of my teaching there.'

In Cathy's years of teaching she had found that for a child to be prepared to learn, first they needed to know that the teacher cared for them as a person—not as an outcome to be demonstrated, but as a child living their life every day. The greater your capacity to care and to consistently show that, the deeper the wells from which you give and invest your time, the faster the children will come to care for you—and from there, to learn from and with you. Without those capacities a teacher can cope with the easy student, but has nothing to offer the student kept in the classroom only through the law and the relationship with the teacher. A teacher like Cathy is a gift in a school full of such students.

Not only was Cathy suited for a teaching life in the bush, her years of living 'in community' proved a wonderful training ground for the challenges of living in a multi-generation pastoral business.

'It was very good training. I thought at the time: "If I hadn't done that, I might not have been right for this." I had to work out if I could live with him, and also with his parents and the rest of the family, because we were obviously going to be closely connected. One of Josie's gifts is her ability to accept a person for who they are—even if she doesn't like what you are saying or doing, she'll accept you. And so, despite times of tension between David and me, and family tension, I decided that I could live with them all.'

The next step was for David to meet Cathy's family.

'He and I went over together after Christmas. He got on well with my family and they liked him. And next door were the O'Neils and David got on very well with Mr O'Neil who loved to tinker in the shed. Tinkering in the shed and talking to Mr O'Neil helped David cope with being in the suburbs. I had to take him out into the country every now and then so he could see the green, but he found it really hard. He stayed there two weeks—he came back before me—and I stayed until February. I arrived back in Mt Magnet on Valentine's Day, late at night, and I got off the bus and there he was with a rose picked from his mother's garden. That was the only flower I've had from him—he's romantic in his own way, not flowers, not presents—but it didn't bother me at all, I'd rather have him.'

Cathy and David married in August 1993 in Melbourne.

'You were the happiest bride I've ever seen,' said one of her sisters. Cathy went from happy bride to happy wife. She and David lived for a year in Mt Magnet itself, with Cathy picking up short teaching contracts at the school and David working off-property on drill rigs, driving trucks and mustering goats. Cathy knew that frequently nuns who had left the order and married had no children, or just one child. She was now thirty-six years old. She warned David that she might not be able to have children, or, if she had a child, she might only be able to have one.

'I really hoped I could have more than one child and I said to David we can't leave this—we have to get into this straight away,' she said. It was not the worst thing a man can be told. 'We got married on the first of August and I was pregnant in September, and I was so excited. We had this beautiful boy, Connor James, the following June. I was so happy, and David was over the moon.'

The long trip home from the hospital in Perth to Mt Magnet was made much longer by David's pride in his son. At every homestead where there were friends—and he had many—David called in to introduce his new son to his old friends.

Cathy had terribly missed being a mother and now she had her very own child. She loved being a mother. Like her own mother, Cathy was delighted by the company of children, and the physical work of caring for a child filled her with joy—and she was ready for another baby in short order.

It was a little harder the second time, and Cathy and David worried that Connor would not have a sibling. Eventually, when Connor was two, she gave birth to Gerard. She was thrilled with this second healthy son, but she longed for just one more child. Rhys joined the family one year later. Cathy was overjoyed to have three healthy sons. Then, to her astonishment—'old' though she was—she found that she had fallen pregnant again. Anthony was born a year after Rhys. Four healthy, lively, loving sons! Cathy, the girl who loved children so very much, the woman who had mourned her chance to be a mother all those years ago, could hardly believe her good fortune. These were the crazy, busy years of parenting little children, but such happy ones! Cathy and David shuttled back and forth between their house in Mt Magnet and living with Josie and Henry on the station—David turning his hand to all kinds of work as well as working on the station, and Cathy working on and off at the school.

'I only did relief and casual while Connor and Gerard were babies. They'd call and say they were desperate at the school, and so I'd come in. Then I had Rhys, and when he was six or seven months old Janet came and said that the school was desperate, and that she would mind the kids. I did two days a week for a while. Then I'd got pregnant without realising and I just said to the principal that I would be too tired and needed to stop. Then Anthony was born and I took four years off teaching entirely. I said to the school: "I can't keep giving my little kids to other people, I just need to be with them."'

Cathy had one particular goal in rearing her boys—she wanted them to be able to care for and relate to children. In her listening to them, her playing with them, her working alongside them, her loving touch and her clear rules for how others are to be treated, she was showing them how this is best done.

And all their sons have both Cathy's gentleness with children and David's extensive practical skills.

Once Anthony was at kindergarten, Cathy returned to teaching part-time. This, in fact, was when I met both Anthony and Cathy for the first time, as she was a teacher at my local school. All the children were 'on the mat' looking up at the teacher. Curly-headed Anthony was sitting at the back, beaming vigorously and angelically at his teacher. From my vantage point I could see Anthony had one hand not folded on his lap where all the other children had theirs. That other hand was behind his back, wagging back and forth. It was explained to me that on that day Anthony had chosen to be good, and right then he was being a good little puppy, wagging his tail and being obedient.

Later that day I met Cathy in the staff room, where she invited me to a party—and at that party on Boogardie station I met David for the first time. I still have a picture of them both in my mind from that night. David smiling gently, his long hands still as he watched Cathy. She was holding an enormous tray of food, listening to someone talk, clearly oblivious to the weight of the tray. As always Cathy was truly listening: nodding, echoing, laughing, her pale face alight with interest and reflective emotion. There was a lot going on, as there always is at those parties, with children running, fires being stoked, food, beer, teenagers attempting to just 'go off somewhere' and parents attempting to monitor them while still trying to attend to the conversation of other adults ... but I remember David's outright pride in Cathy very clearly.

Over the next few years, first Connor, then Gerard, then Rhys left to board at Mazenod, a Catholic boys' school in the Perth Hills. Only eleven-year-old Anthony was still at home. Cathy's leadership skills had been noticed at the school and she had moved into working with teachers as well as students. The church community also recognised those leadership skills and Cathy had become the go-to person when the priest was not available for such things as funeral services. David was continuing his mix of station work and off-property work, and on the community front he was a shire councillor and an unobtrusive giver of his time and practical skills.

Then, in August 2011, came David's accident. It was quarter to three in the morning. Cathy was woken by her friend Wendy and her sister-in-law Janet outside the bedroom.

'They came to the door and said, "You have to get up. We have bad news." And I thought immediately of David's father Henry. And then I thought: "Why is it my bad news, and not Janet's?" I put on David's big windcheater to keep warm. Anthony had woken up, and I pulled the doona back over him and said, "Shh, back to sleep." Paul was waiting in the living room and there were two policemen with him and I thought "This is not good—is it David or is it one of the boys?" And they told me straightaway, it was David. And then I wanted to know, was it only David? They said, "There was no-one else." And I felt some relief that he had not been responsible for another death.'

At sunset David had been driving and he had not seen cows crossing. One had collided with his ute and it had rolled several times and David had been killed. News like this makes no sense. Gaps open up between the words that you hear from other people and you utter yourself … and then the gaps close and time runs too fast … and your emotions grab for time as it flies by and try to turn it back and will for it all to have happened differently. Cathy fell back on politeness and found herself offering a cup of tea to them all: Janet, Paul and the policemen. They were all very caring, she says. She was glad that it was they who came to tell her what had happened. Having the boys told and how it could best be done was next on her mind.

'It was four o'clock in the morning and I said, "I'm not ringing the boys now, this might be the last good night's sleep they get for a while."' She wasn't worried that the boys would see it on Facebook, not at four o'clock in the morning. 'I waited, then I rang at about seven-thirty to start the ball rolling for them to find out. They found out at about nine o'clock in the morning.'

Cathy was very particular about how this would occur—who was to tell them, and who was to be with them as they heard the news.

'I wanted Father Maher to tell them. In the meantime I called friends who knew us and all our boys. Their son Liam was up with us on the station at the time. Liam had already told his parents, and when I rang Mandy she was crying, and I said "I just wanted you and Dave to be with the kids when they hear this news", and she said "of course". She also called for me my friend Kerry who had lost her husband in an accident when her children were very little. Connor thought he'd been called up to the office for doing something wrong … then he saw Rhys and Gerard … and he thought of his grandfather, as I had done. So Kerry, Mandy and David were with the boys, and Father Maher said to them: "There is no easy way to say this, boys—your dad has been killed." And then I told Anthony.'

Young Henry (David's brother) was in Perth and Cathy asked him to pick the boys up and bring them home. He just sat in the car park of the school, dreading sharing the news.

'He was relieved to find that he'd been spared the horror of having to tell the kids. And the school gave them breakfast, made packed lunches for all of them. It took them a while to get home. I was really happy when I saw the boys. To have them home was good.

'The good thing about having my family over east was that I had two hours up my sleeve. I started ringing them at five-thirty because it was seven-thirty their time and not too bad a time to ring them with news. It wasn't something any of us had experienced at such close quarters before. All of them were in shock—as much in shock as I was. David was the first one in our family who had died. We still had Mum and Dad, my brothers and sisters were all still alive, all of David's family, his parents. My sister Bernadette was inconsolable, her husband told me later. She said, "Those poor kids, those poor kids, they've lost their dad." Less than two years later she was dead herself.'

Cathy's oldest sister Marie was on long service leave, and she asked if Cathy wanted her.

'I said, "Yes, I want you to come." And she came over straight away. It has been good for us, we've been a lot closer. Everyone else, they had little kids, and jobs, and I said to them, "I want you here for the funeral, wait for that." They arranged flights, then they had to change them, because David's funeral took a long time to happen.'

Cathy had initially thought of a cremation, with David's ashes scattered on Boogardie. But Connor asked instead that his father be buried so that he was able to go and sit and talk to him. Cathy sent David's brothers John and Henry on a mission to find a plot in the Mt Magnet cemetery, but they returned to tell her that no spot looked right. Then a neighbour said it was possible for him to be buried on Boogardie.

'So we went through the local government department to have him buried on the station. We had to have maps and references ... It was supposed to take four or five days until we had an answer—but no answer came in that time. So I rang up. I said, "I need to bury my husband."'

The service was by now organised. When the undertaker had asked who would do the eulogy Cathy had found herself saying, without prior thought, 'That would be me.' Like leaving religious life, the decision rang true within Cathy. It felt like David speaking within her and to her, and that gave her comfort. But she'd already been comforted by two visits, in those long days before David could be buried.

'I dreamt that I saw him. It was a beautiful blue sky, a nice day, where he was. He was wearing a Driza-Bone and an Akubra. He just stood there and he said, "I'm sorry. I'm so, so sorry."'

Cathy related that dream to her sister Teresa, who listened in staggered silence. One of Teresa's own friends had called to say, 'Is something wrong with your husband?' 'No,' said Theresa. 'Nothing is wrong.' The friend said 'I'm hearing someone say, "I'm sorry. I'm so, so sorry" and I'm connecting it with you.'

A few days later Cathy had another dream.

'He had a big black jumper. He used to bring joeys home like that. And I said to him, "David, have you got a joey?" And he lifted back the jumper, and there was a tiny baby. We had lost one and it broke my heart. And I thought: "You're okay, and you're with the baby." It was amazingly comforting.'

Comforted by David himself, Cathy acted with clarity and purpose. She delivered the eulogy.

'I began it by saying I had the strength to stand up that day because David had never let me be a pampered princess—so now I could talk on this day to everyone here about the love of my life.'

Another friend spoke of David's life as a child, and David's four boys had all written prayers for him. On the day itself the boys faltered, but Cathy said to them with her fierce confidence in them blazing: 'You can do this. You can, because you are doing it for your dad.' Every boy stood and read his prayer clearly, undaunted by the enormous number of people who had attended the funeral.

'We put David on the back of a Toyota—and the boys sat on the back with him, and our best man Michael's son Tim sat with them. I sat in the front and John drove. John had done a beautiful job of digging the grave. And the men filled in the grave then and there—it was quite a beautiful thing, it mesmerised me, I didn't want to leave. It was good to see young men, old men, kids, all putting something in.'

She was to have the same experience of being transfixed by the sacred a few months later at another funeral: one at which she was officiating. A young boy had committed suicide, no priest was available, and Cathy was asked to help. The closeness to David's death momentarily gave her pause, but she wanted to help the family and agreed. It has turned out to be, she says, the most profoundly spiritual experience of her life so far.

'I had to take a deep breath. I said to myself, "You are here for this young boy, you are here for his family." The family was lovely. I did the service in the hall, and then we went out to the cemetery. I did a prayer, and then the family took over. They lowered the coffin, they played a song. The men started to shovel in the dirt and made a mound over it. The men all went round the mound, leaning on it, patting it. Then the women. They leaned on the mound and they cried. Then they put flowers on it. There was so much love.

'I thought: "I can't move. I can't take my eyes off this." I also felt that perhaps I shouldn't be here. I was the only person who wasn't Aboriginal, the only person who wasn't family ... I felt out of place but I couldn't move. I'll never forget it.'

Like the musician held suspended by music of extraordinary beauty, or the artist who cannot pull his eyes from a sunset,

Cathy, a student of the human spirit and of God, was taken out of herself by this scene of perfect love and grief.

'David started the run of deaths in August 2011, then it was Bernadette, then Mum, then Dad and Grandfather Henry too,' says Cathy.

Cathy talks a lot about the big transitions of life: who was present for each baby and how they were born—the death of each loved family member, who was there, how it all happened, how they were buried. She's a moment-by-moment thinker, not caught back in the past, but with the habit of dwelling so deeply in the moment that she can bring those moments back to mind. That ability to inhabit and expand the passing moment for those sharing it with her is one of her gifts. When Bernadette died, then her mother and then her father, Cathy found herself offered the chance to use that gift to help celebrate the lives of her own family members.

'With Bernadette it wasn't a choice. The priest said that he couldn't do the Rosary Service for her, and that needs to take place the night before the funeral. He asked if someone in the family could do it, and so I said that I would. I came early with my sisters, and I asked if they could leave me by myself for a little to "get with God". At the end I felt this sense—almost out of body—of God at work and reaching the people. Then my mum died, and the priest again said, "I can't do the Rosary on this particular night" ... and I realised that it would be better if I did it, rather than a stranger. So again, I thought about what scripture is good for Mum, what aspects of the Rosary, what fits for her life. And again God was with me, touching the people who were there.

'As we were burying Mum—putting flowers and dirt into the grave, and Dad threw some coins in—Dad said, "Don't worry Mary, I won't be long." It was like *voom*—like a heavy blow on my chest: I remember it as clear as day. That night he said, “I don’t feel very well, you’d better take me home.” And then he got worse. At midnight he was admitted to hospital with pneumonia. Then my brother rang me at four o’clock in the morning and said the hospital rang to ask if we wanted Dad given antibiotics. And I said, “Yes, of course we want him to have antibiotics. He’s our dad, we’re not just going to let him go!”

‘The doctor came in at about nine in the morning and felt Dad’s stomach and he said, “He has gut rot so we’ll just put him on morphine.”’

Cathy and her siblings explained that their father had just lost his wife, their mother. The doctor responded merely by saying, ‘This often happens.’ Cathy was incredulous at his dismissiveness. ‘Not to us, it doesn’t,’ she said, trying to help him see that everyone has a finite number of parents and they can die but once in your life. Saying ‘this often happens’ to a grieving family is akin to saying to them ‘everyone has to die sometime’. Such phrases carry a subtext of ‘so what’s the big deal?’ or ‘surely you were expecting this!’ or ‘you shouldn’t be so surprised and upset’.

‘Mum was his life, when she died he must have felt that his work was done—Bernadette had been gone nine months exactly then. Her death really rocked my dad. His baby gone, he couldn’t believe it. He must have thought, “Well, Mary’s gone, Bernadette’s gone and the rest of them are big enough to look after themselves.”

‘This time the priest asked me, even though he was present, to lead the Rosary for Dad. And the priest said afterwards he was touched by the service and that was good for me to hear. I still love that work, sharing my faith as part of leading a service.’

I had wondered, initially, if this series of losses might have weakened Cathy's faith, but clearly it has not. As well as saying that faith is a gift, Cathy says also that it is 'action'—in her own keeping-on without collapsing in a heap after David's accident, in the way people have helped her, in the kindness and care shown to her boys by their school, in the way her boys have found mentors and employers who do some of what David did in their lives, and the way her boys help each other. In all this she doesn't just find evidence of God, but of David, still caring for and helping them all.

It can be very tough financially when two income earners are reduced to one. But Mazenod, the boarding school the boys attended, reduced their fees and then found insurance money to subsidise the fees in the year following. Mt Magnet School principal, Richard Cook, suggested that she apply for a literacy consultant position and helped check through her application before it went in. In 2012 Anthony had left for boarding school.

At the end of 2014 it was suggested Cathy apply for the principal's position at the little town of Cue, an hour's drive north of Mt Magnet. Again, with some assistance in selling herself, which is not Cathy's thing, she applied and was successful. It was time, she said, for a change. She was getting too comfortable at Mt Magnet. Cathy has no interest in being kept in—or keeping herself in—cotton wool. This is something all her boys have learned from her. They do not shy away from challenges. When one of Cathy and David's sons is faced with a challenge they research the possibilities and take thoughtful action.

'They didn't collapse in a heap, they kept going,' Cathy says with pride, knowing that David is proud too.

'On Sundays, Josie always asks God to look after Henry and David. I say to her, "You don't need to ask God to look after them. They're okay, God has to look after the rest of us." It's a bit of banter between us. She always says it and I always tell her, "No, they're alright, you don't have to worry about them!"'

Cathy talks to David every day. She says such things as: 'I love you David, but I'm not ready to come up there yet.' She tells him what is happening with his sons. From time to time she can feel his physical presence, and a comforting weight pressing on her arm or her hand.

'Anthony had to write an essay in exam conditions. Last time he was asked to do this he baulked totally and just wouldn't. So I was speaking to David about it the other night, and I felt like he was with me. And so I thought, it will be alright with Anthony, he'll be okay.'

As I'm listening to Cathy share this story I'm taken back to the night when I met David all those years ago, and his very evident pride in Cathy. Suddenly I have the sensation that if I look up I'll see him standing behind her, watching her with that gentle, proud, loving smile. I don't look: I will not be able to see him. But before me I can see Cathy, at peace and comforted, strong and persevering, supported still by David's faith in her and their love for each other. And looking at her I realise that I have answered to my own satisfaction the question of whether love is primarily an action or a feeling.

The argument that love should not be considered an emotion but a set of actions is one made most often by psychologists. Love, they say, is something that you do, not something that you feel. Psychologists say this particularly to married people who are finding it hard to love. They encourage them to act lovingly and see what happens. Often it seems to work! It seems that in acting with love we can find it again. But I suspect that there is another explanation here too. Having another person act with love towards you perhaps creates that feeling in you—just as you are creating it in them.

Philosophers rebut this by saying: 'If love is simply a set of actions, then how can it continue after one person has died? If the person we direct our loving actions towards is gone, how then do we love?' And yet we clearly do keep on loving them, wanting the best for them, relating to them even when they are gone and there is little more 'action' we can take. And Cathy still loves David, and still feels that he loves her, and I can see the impact this has had on her life. So I have come to side with the philosophers on this.

On the other hand, the story of Cathy and David might also be evidence of something else entirely: that death can't end love because our spirit continues on after death. Perhaps it shows instead that even when we are dead, we continue to act with love and to feel love. This is what Cathy believes, as she believes that she came to Mt Magnet both to be with David and to serve the community. And if she had not married David we would never have kept her here in the Murchison, where she is so very valued and where she makes such a difference. This is love working at its ineffable, mysterious, bewildering best.

Lovely Boy, Beautiful Girl

John and Mary te Kloot, Marmboo Station, Longreach, Queensland

For Mary Curran and John te Kloot to have met at all required not just every star in alignment but twinkling in synchrony—she is Irish, he is Australian. Their story illuminates how each successive generation grows out of the choices offered to and made by the preceding generation. We know this applies to all kinds of things, but it's perhaps most apt when it comes to how we rear our children, and also, to how we love. So for these reasons the story of John and Mary's wonderful closeness begins with the story of both of their parents' marriages. Their parents' generations had gone through depressions and wars, and so survival was key, and their parents' endeavours had ensured that the next generation had it easier. John and Mary (and many others of their generation) could focus on more than just surviving. They could aim to have a close marriage above all else.

Mary's mother, Vera, had been a nun with the Medical Missionaries of Mary in Ireland and had trained and worked as a nurse. After two years she had found that religious life was too restrictive for her and she left the convent and continued her nursing in Dublin, though she retained her strong religious sensibilities. In her thirties she married John Joseph Curran and in 1953 the couple moved to Southern Ireland to the little village of Cappoquin, in the County of Waterford. This is where Mary and her sister, Veronica, were born.

Being married to John Curran, the eldest of six children, was not as free an existence as Vera might have expected. John's mother controlled the family, and she kept the books. Although Vera and her husband were running the family farm, they had little cash to spend. The meat supply was controlled by Granny Curran, and it was doled out grudgingly and sparingly every time.

Even the house Vera lived in did not feel like her own. This house, three storeys, beautifully symmetrical, with many paned windows, some arched, some rectangular, had thick walls, and the trees under which it sheltered were grander than the house itself.

'Once servants lived in it and were brought by carriage to a bigger house about five miles away, where they actually worked,' explains Mary. 'There were fireplaces in all thirty-two rooms. On the ceiling in the kitchen, which was very high, there were hooks for smoking hams. It was so big it needed a lot of maintenance and Mum was a very houseproud woman. When we lived there many of the rooms were closed off.

'It was owned by my father's family, and my father's sisters often came to visit, bringing their friends and showing them around as if the place was theirs. I remember the Irish winters in this house. There was no heating, Veronica and I took hot water bottles to bed and we very often ended up with chilblains. Mum and Dad sold the house (although they kept the farm) about the time I went away to boarding school at thirteen in 1967.'

Vera wanted to give her own daughters wings. She wanted them to have the freedom to choose lives outside the village. It was unusual (and disapproved of) to send children away to boarding school, but that is what Vera did. She believed in the power of education. Even on holidays Mary and Veronica could never just do nothing—if they were not helping in the house or on the farm, they were away at 'Irish schools' to improve their Gaelic. The two compulsory subjects in Ireland at that time were English and Gaelic, and Vera was trying to help her girls get ahead.

'Not that it did much good,' says Mary, for whom languages remained a challenge throughout her education.

Mary remembers her father as a gentle giant, saying little, but not averse to putting his foot down. She loved to help him on the farm, particularly with animals, and gloried in meeting his high expectations of her. That shared love of farming and practical skills built a close bond between father and daughter.

But her parents' relationship was sometimes strained. Mary remembers hearing fiery arguments over simple things. Like so many children, she worried that her parents might go their separate ways—and the anguish of that thought has stayed with her, even though such a separation never happened. Very young though she was, she decided then that such arguments were not something she wanted in her own marriage. And in Australia, out in Queensland's station country, in his very different sphere, a young John was also thinking about the kind of marriage he wanted and reaching much the same conclusions as Mary.

John, with his usual precision and empathy for his parents, shares the story of his father and mother with me. John's father, Jack te Kloot, was a grazier's son from Cunnamulla in south-west Queensland.

'For three months in 1944 he was commander of RAF Squadron 249, which at the end of the war was reputedly the highest-scoring RAF squadron, that is, had accounted for the most enemy planes shot down during the duration of World War II.' Jack was awarded the Distinguished Service Order (DSO) medal in recognition of his leadership, superior strategic skills and his flying, and returned to Australia ready to resume his life on the land.

On returning, Jack put his name into the War Service Land Settlement ballot. This was a lottery whereby returned soldiers were randomly allocated land. It had operated in World War I also, but had been revamped recently. Previously, this scheme had simply included any man who wanted to go onto the land in reward for war service. After World War II this changed and now only returning soldiers who could stock and develop the land were permitted to enter their names in the ballot. It was in one of these ballots that Jack drew Marmboo Station. This was the equivalent of winning the lottery as far as he was concerned.

Jack had made many friends during the war, and friendships that survived it were special. He had become friendly with Joan Armstrong, an Englishwoman who had been a member of the Women's Royal Naval Service for six years, mostly as a petty officer. (It still puzzles John that his father didn't have a girl waiting for his return in Australia. Jack was, after all, a rather dashing figure.) While they didn't have a great deal of time together during the war, Joan and Jack had found enough in common to make a correspondence worthwhile. This had continued throughout the war and afterwards. When Jack won Marmboo, Joan was one of the people with whom he shared his good news.

It was a great bonus to Jack that he won the property free and clear of debt. Debt had nearly crippled his father's grazing enterprise during the Depression. Jack had learned to detest and fear debt, and from a very early age he had begun to put money aside. Jack also encouraged Joan to come out to Australia to visit, and she did. After all, England had been shattered by the war effort, life there was austere and bleak, food was rationed and queued for and prospects for improvement seemed far too distant. Jack met Joan in Sydney in his US Army jeep and took her on the long journey back to Cunnamulla to visit the family property.

Jack and Joan married in 1947 and they became a highly effective team. This was just as well, for Marmboo was no sinecure. The Depression and the war had given birth to a generation of people with the kind of self-discipline we find hard to imagine today. They did whatever had to be done well ahead of time. Jack had repeatedly put his life on the line in the war and he continued to live in a decisive and forthright way; he held back nothing of himself from doing all that was needed to make Marmboo thrive.

With his aversion to debt, Jack found it hard to borrow money, but often there was no choice. He traded in stock, built fences, and added water and stock-handling facilities. He was a progressive and thoughtful farmer. Joan told her children that, 'What was good enough for his father is not good enough for yours.'

And Joan's staunch English spirit that had taken her through the war was now required for a different kind of battle. For a homestead to run smoothly, it requires systems in place, forward planning and hard work every day, even in the twenty-first century. In the 1950s, on what was effectively a new property, all of that had to be created from the ground up and with almost none of the household equipment that exists now. This is Joan's description of her early life on Marmboo from when she arrived in 1947, which she wrote at the request of a local historian.

'The country was drought-stricken and eaten out and there was very little water at the house. I described this house as a "biscuit box on stumps". It had never been painted, lined or ceiled and, although families had lived here, water had never been laid on, nor was there power of any sort. The windows were merely sections of the corrugated-iron walls cut out and hinged, then propped open with iron bars. The bathroom was a separate building with a camp shower which was filled by a bucket, hot water coming from the copper attached to the wood stove. The "private sitting room" was a hundred yards down the paddock.

'Shortage of water was a problem for some years and at one stage we used to cart a hundred gallons [378 litres] from a neighbour's dam each Sunday when we went out to the road to collect our mail (which included a regular order of bread, a dozen eggs and a pound of tomatoes).'

Even for a woman who had managed staff and accounts in a war zone, a woman of that era who was used to hard physical work, it was tough.

'On Mondays the copper was lit bright and early—outside—and the laundry fed in according to cleanliness. Eventually the hot water was used to scrub the kitchen floor (which was so splintery my first child never crawled), the bathroom floor, and finally there was a trek down the paddock with a bucket and scrubbing brush. I remember getting a large pair of wooden tongs which were a big improvement on the usual stick for the copper, and a deck scrubber which was a wonder, too.'

Though this was less than a hundred years ago, Joan's brand-new household tools were tongs and a deck scrubber! Such a contrast to the wonders in today's households. They will cut up and cook the food. Wash your clothes. There are even little robots that vacuum floors ...

'Good rain came in 1949 and the fifties were bountiful years. The first big rain found the leaks in the old roof on the house, which had been erected about the turn of the century. We had to drape a tarpaulin over the baby's cot, when before that he'd slept for many hours with a wet sheet over the cot to keep him cool.

'Over the years we enlarged the house at each end of the old nucleus, making it L-shaped and reasonably cool even before air conditioning. When the second baby came, a new bathroom and a bigger bedroom, lined and ceiled, were added. An early-model Holden replaced the old army surplus jeep, although this vehicle continued in service until the two boys grew tall enough to drive it—when they were about seven.

'Number two son was a year old when we installed a lighting plant, followed later by a wind-driven battery charger, which was very effective. What joy to have an electric iron and a mixer. The third baby, a girl, merited a washing machine (the cement-mixer type) and the second girl was born into an entirely different establishment a few years later. A 240-volt generating plant was bought in the mid-1960s and then, in 1980, came that greatest of all modern conveniences—rural power.'

Joan had help from time to time with cooking, and she had a nanny or governess for the children. The home she ran singlehandedly and to very high standards. One of John and

Mary's youngest daughter's black-and-white photographs shows Grandmother Joan on washing day. She is smiling and very slender. There are two drums through which the washing must pass. One drum is steaming. Joan, her curls ruffled by the wind, is bending over the other, rubbing out stains. Beyond that is a smaller rinsing tub, and then a final container with laundry ready to be hung.

'Of the three generations, my parents genuinely knew through the Depression and the war what it was to go without. We, as kids, had everything we needed, and,' John adds ruefully, 'our kids have everything they want.'

Most vegetables were grown on the property in line with the seasons, which meant there were only a few weeks in which you could have, for example, cauliflower or green beans. Preserves were made year round to capture those seasonal abundances. Milk and meat would both have come from the property. Bread, biscuits and cakes were all made at home. In the early days Joan made nearly all her own clothes as well as her children's.

'Mum was very good to us kids. She went without so we could have things,' says John.

Joan's children gave her great joy. The goals of parents then were not the same as parents now—with their own experience of life being so hard, many postwar parents simply aimed to make their children tough enough to survive. But the love with which Joan and Jack raised their four children was evident. John's warm, stable childhood became the foundation for his life. However, there were many distractions in Jack and Joan's married life and John feels now that worked against their being able to achieve real closeness in their marriage.

'Right from day one, there were staff around and that would have played a part in their relationship,' says John. 'There was always someone there.'

It was, he says, a very orderly upbringing for that reason. It wasn't until John was away at boarding school that he remembers the six of them—Jack, Joan and their four children—having a meal as a family.

'I always worried that my father hardly knew my mother, and that then their lives would have taken them further apart. And Dad was a very dominating character,' says John. 'There was never any doubt that he was the boss. It was good in some ways—he trusted his own judgment, he could be kind and generous—but not in all ways.' John knew he didn't want to have a marriage exactly like the one he perceived his parents shared.

Granny Curran, who had unceasingly attempted to control all around her, did not change as Mary grew up. Her sights were now set on controlling her grandchildren's adult lives. She believed she had found the ideal husband for Mary and promoted the match whenever and however she could. She could not understand that Mary's goal in marriage was intimacy. The marriage Granny proposed was one of financial security and improved family networks—Tom was thirty years older than 21-year-old Mary, and a respected local farmer.

'My grandmother thought that I should marry him, because she herself had married a much older man—and she'd been a widow for a long time because of it. She would say: "Oh, Mary, how's Tom going? Lovely boy, now lovely man, lovely man."'

Under considerable pressure from her grandmother to become friends with Tom, Mary accepted his invitations to spend time with him, and she grew to value him as a mentor and friend.

'Tom taught me a different side to farming as he specialised in beef cattle, which resulted in him going around to shows and judging cattle. He taught me how to play golf, he took me out to dinner and in general was a very interesting man with years of experience behind him. He was known far and wide throughout Ireland, which meant that whenever we went out we would be asked, "Now what will you have to drink, Tom, and what would your daughter like?" He was nice company, but as for marrying him—no! But it was amazing how Granny kept pushing it.'

Rebellion had always been difficult for Mary. It was not that she had trouble knowing or saying how she felt—it was getting people to believe she meant what she said. Her manner and voice are gentle and courteous. To be heard and believed she inevitably found herself resorting to dramatic tactics, as in the event that saw her thrown out of finishing school.

Mary had left school wanting to study home economics in Dublin, but her marks in both compulsory languages were not sufficient for her to gain entry. There was another way in. She could attend a finishing school (very different to the famous and non-academic 'private Swiss Finishing Schools' with their focus on etiquette and deportment), where she could continue to study languages and hopefully from there gain entry to the home-economics course in Dublin.

'But the finishing school nearly finished me off,' she says. 'To begin with they made me head girl, which didn't please me one bit because I knew I would have to behave accordingly—I'd been head girl at my boarding school—and I didn't want that, I wanted to have a good time.

'Towards the middle of the year, the head nun, Sister Mary Mercy, had the idea that I should do a first-aid course. I said, politely and reasonably, that this wasn't my cup of tea. Sister Mary Mercy became more authoritative and insisted that I do the course, to which I replied that I wasn't going to.' The nun was clearly convinced that polite, obliging Mary would fall into line with a bit more pressure. 'Then she told me I had no choice. So I said, "Well, you can stick it up your arse, I'm not going to." She was horrified. She told me to pack my bags and go, to which I replied, "I would be only too delighted."' She felt rather less delighted when she found herself with bags in hand and out on the street a short time later.

The only benefit of her time at the finishing school was that it was there that Mary heard about another home-economics school, this one in Belfast. Even with Vera's steadfast upholding of the value of education, Mary is still surprised that her mother supported her in choosing to attend a college in Belfast in Northern Ireland. It was 1973 and at the height of the civil war known euphemistically as 'the Troubles'.

Despite a name suggesting nothing more alarming than digestive difficulties, the dangers of living in Belfast during the Troubles were very real. It was a war zone: soldiers, guns, searches, traumatised children, limited public gatherings, bombings, attacks, bricked-up uninhabitable houses, unexplained ambushes and killings, political negotiations failing, outstripped daily by the ugly and more final diplomacy of war. Vera had grown up in the North, in a town called Newry, and she had lived within that religious tension all her life. She understood the North and had acclimatised to it as just another random element—living was a dangerous business after all! For Mary, however, who had grown up in the warmer, safer Southern Ireland, Belfast came as a shock.

'My friend Sister Lorena (who was a nun in the Mercy Order) and I had both applied to attend the Home Economics College so we took the train to Dublin and from there to Belfast. As the train was about to enter Belfast city we passed a big sign—"You Are About to Meet Your End". It was quite frightening.

'We made our way to the college for our interviews and on completion the head lady of the college offered to take us back to the train station and in doing so showed us the sights of Belfast. There was security everywhere, army men with guns stood on corner blocks and on the entrance to main streets there were big iron gates covered in wire which were guarded by soldiers. But I still wanted to go to Belfast, and Lorena and I didn't hesitate to accept our offers to attend the college. Nor did my parents stop me. My mother could have, but she didn't.'

Mary is touched and surprised and grateful to this day that her parents let her make her own decision on this. She had seen mothers who had prevented their children from doing what they really wanted with their lives. Her parents respected her wishes, even the ones they didn't totally agree with. They never stood in her way. Mary was to spend four years in Belfast, three of them as a student and one as a teacher, and never regretted a minute of her choice.

'It was a whole new world for me. The meeting of people, the talking about religion, the acceptance of you for who you were.'

She went to cafes, pubs and parties. One evening she went to see a fortune teller who told her, 'You'll marry a man with curly hair who comes from somewhere over the water, and you will have three children.' She thought it was a lovely prediction, but not for a moment did she believe it.

After Mary's parents had sold the big house Mary grew up in, it had become a bed-and-breakfast place as well as having some permanent boarders. The landlady's name was Jean Deevy. On Mary's college vacations Jean often employed Mary to assist her with serving the breakfast and evening meals.

In 1975, while Mary was home on vacation, John te Kloot came to stay in the bed and breakfast.

'How did I come to be there? My godfather was a permanent boarder in that house,' he says. 'And how did I come to have a godfather in Ireland? In the war my father was operating in the Mediterranean, and this fellow, Charles Gray, was the Wing Intelligence Officer (several squadrons make up a "wing"). They had quite a bit to do with each other. At the end of the war, when they were all going back to their own countries, my father said to Charles, "And what can I do for you?" and he said, "You can keep me a godson." That's how it happened.'

The friendship between Jack te Kloot and Charles remained strong. The te Kloots had visited him in the 1950s, and Charles had come to visit at Marmboo in 1964.

In 1975, after studying and working elsewhere, John had decided that he wanted to return to live and work on Marmboo alongside his parents. Long holidays and being a pastoralist do not mix, so before starting his new life, John was determined he'd do all the travelling that would be impossible afterwards. Europe, with all its family connections, beckoned. Staying with his godfather was naturally part of his to-do list.

'When I was staying with him he was tracing back the line of Grays to the bastard son of William the Conqueror. He'd done some interesting things. He'd been at the Lausanne Conference at the end of World War I, he was tied up with MI5, and between the wars he'd done an elephant trip surveying Burma—he used to drop names ferociously.'

John would listen to his godfather's reminiscences, help care for his elderly Pekingese dog, have cups of tea, and drive his godfather to his neglected property for another cup of tea. Not unnaturally, after a few days of this he was longing for some company of his own age.

'There were two girls who worked in the kitchen of the guest house—Mary's old home—so I asked them out for a drink. One bolted, and the other explained she was engaged.'

Jean Deevy overheard this conversation and her heart went out to John. She rang Mary to say that there was a nice Australian boy who needed a bit of young company, and to ask whether Mary had any young friends who might like to meet him. Mary decided she would come and meet him herself. If nothing else, going out with a man would make it plain to her domineering Granny Curran that Mary was not meekly going to marry the man her grandmother had selected for her.

John was disconsolately facing the prospect of another evening of reminiscing in the company of the Pekingese when Mary arrived.

'Mary walks in,' says John. 'I didn't know who Mary was or where she had come from, and she says, "Well, are you coming out for a drink?" I knew nothing about it but I thought—"Righto!"' As he tells me this he glances at Mary, his eyes full of warmth.

Mary did not fully reciprocate this profound physical attraction straightaway. Like so many of the young men backpacking at that time, John was wearing chain-metal necklaces. Mary found all those chains deeply off-putting, but John was a warm, friendly, kind, well-mannered and softly spoken young man—a lovely boy, as the Irish would say.

John, as he says himself, was 'marriageable'. He was looking for the right girl. He didn't want to find himself on Marmboo alone. And he was looking for someone with whom he could develop a rich intimacy.

'I'd had girlfriends, but none of them fitted the bill.' And right from that first night he found he and Mary could talk easily. 'And so we went out. Then we went out the next night, the next night, the next. I left after about four days to go backpacking again. Then I came back to visit Mary in Belfast while she was at college, and that was unusual for a tourist because it wasn't safe. Generally, tourists didn't come to Belfast as a bomb could go off in any public area. I was struck by the way places like the ferry terminal cleared the moment people were off the ferry,' he says.

'When you went out to the pubs you had to be searched going in, everybody was on edge, because you didn't know if a bomb was going to go off either in the area or in the pub itself where you were having a drink,' says Mary.

'Being an outsider I was just so interested,' says John. 'I went to a gathering of Mary's contemporaries—where she studied there were both Protestants and Catholics, all studying, all getting on. Everyone I met was affected somehow by the Troubles. To begin with some pretended they weren't, but they all had been—hate mail, a cousin killed, killings, bombings. It had been going on for so long and people were really oppressed by it, just putting on a brave face to try to ignore it. They wanted to get on with life and then you'd think, why don't you leave?'

'You asked them why they stay and their reply was: "This is our home. This is where we were brought up. We know nothing else,"' says Mary.

John left Belfast for more touring, but he continued to stay in touch with Mary.

'My brother and sister-in-law had come to Lancaster as they were both studying there for a year and I made my way to them for a visit. During this time Mary came across to Liverpool by ferry. We had a really wonderful weekend. We went to Hadrian's Wall, to the Lake District. It was very romantic, it really all started there.'

'Around this time John said to me: "You really need to come and see where I live." I was just in awe of him by then. He was talking about this massive farm where everything was so big. Everything was in thousands, and I had grown up on a dairy farm, just fifty acres. We could count our cattle and see our boundary fence from the house. He was speaking a foreign language: jackeroos, kangaroos, were they the same thing? I didn't know. You can only relate to what you know, so I had no idea.'

In the absence of knowing, Mary imagined Marmboo instead. She imagined the many stock horses as being equivalent to Irish race horses, worth thousands. She imagined the family plane (a Cessna 172) as something like a Learjet. The mention of staff—governesses, cook and overseer—had her picturing a castle surrounded by acres of high green grass, heavily stocked.

'I had the idea that this place was something like you would see in the film *Gone with the Wind*: a massive house with lots of servants, green rolling fields and hills surrounding the house, and on the hills, fat animals grazing happily. I thought it would be hard to see much of the sky past the hills and the big old trees dotted everywhere. Of course, this same sky would seldom be blue as it rains so much.' The foundations of these pictures were, of course, the green and grey of her own land.

John returned to Australia to take up a new life on the family station. In these first years on Marmboo, John was not yet seeing what would become painfully apparent in time—that his father was not going to be able to willingly share the business decision-making. John was focused instead on developing the physical skill set that pastoralism requires, and on enjoying the experience of getting to know the property as an adult. Children, even teenagers, see loved land differently to adults. Returning to a property means that you have to grow new knowledge around old perceptions: in childhood a fence extends forever, but working on it is easier as the responsibility doesn't rest with you. As an adult, the fence is simultaneously shorter and more work.

He wrote to Mary, and she wrote back. They also corresponded by tape for the pleasure of hearing each other's voices.

'John would send these long tapes about the workings of the property, cattle and sheep, and then right at the end, talk about how he missed me. I didn't care much about the cattle and sheep, I'd just fast-forward the tape and listen over and over to what he said at the end,' says Mary.

'One of our sons once complained about a few hours of driving to get to see the girl he was interested in,' John says. 'I said to him, "Son, I courted your mother from halfway round the world, do not give me that rubbish about 120 kilometres if you're really keen!"'

In Belfast Mary was in her final year of study and thoroughly enjoying the opportunity that being a trainee teacher of home economics provided to really get to know the students.

'With teaching cooking or sewing you are moving around the classroom, you are chatting to these young people, and so you hear about their lives and what they have been up to,' she says.

Mary was fascinated by these teenagers whose lives were so different from her own safe and tidy growing-up years. On one occasion she was teaching a class of fifteen- and sixteen-year-old girls. 'Two of them will be late,' she was told by the head of home economics. 'You are not to ask them about where they have been, just accept that they will be late.' But Mary, in her chatting with the two girls after they turned up, did find out why they were always late to her class. They had been servicing the British soldiers stationed up the road from the school.

'They said, "We go up every day. We go from eight to ten." I was horrified. I couldn't believe that this was going on, part of their everyday life,' says Mary, still unable to fathom that this prostitution by schoolgirls had been accepted, even by the school. She wonders now if the school was actually threatened or even if the school was getting a reward for their silence.

'Every one of these children would have a story to tell. And some of them had such hatred. I couldn't believe that such hatred existed in such young people. I was teaching thirteen-, fourteen-, fifteen-year-olds in the poorer areas of Belfast. I didn't come across this hatred so much in the more affluent areas. I wonder if it is like this all over the world: that a lot of the fighting, a lot of the antipathy, happens in the poorer areas. People are out of work, they sit around, they tell stories, urge each other on and probably find themselves doing things they had never envisaged—being part of an army, servicing an army ...'

Mary was also exploring the cultural differences between North and South. The North, under British rule, was very 'English'. The South, having gained its independence from England in 1916, was very Irish.

'The English are very matter-of-fact, and everything has its place and goes back in its place. The Irish have a casualness—if the thing is not back in its place, it doesn't matter. It'll be fine, don't worry about it. You do enjoy that. But I was feeling that living in Southern Ireland wasn't what I wanted. I'd enjoyed being in Belfast and since leaving for boarding school at thirteen I had spent my time coming and going from my home town so I didn't feel I really fitted in there either. I wanted to somehow keep the freedom I experienced in Belfast, even though I did have to be careful where I went.'

Mary declined the opportunity to spend her next summer holidays on a kibbutz (a communal farm or settlement in Israel and the 'in thing' for vacations at that time), and instead decided she would visit Australia, and John. The summer holidays came, and Mary had made herself ready to go to Australia—the visitor's visa was stamped on her passport and she was immunised—while somehow knowing very little about where she was actually going.

'It was amazing how I took off to a country I knew nothing about. I didn't look to see where Longreach was on a map—and my mother and father didn't say to me, "Do you know where you are going? Have you checked on a map?" All I knew about Australia was something an aunt of mine had told me—that there were a lot of sheep in that country.

'The actual flight over took thirty-two hours. I met with friends of John's in Sydney and had a day there, and then I flew up to Brisbane. In those days the people meeting you were allowed to come onto the tarmac. It was a long time since I'd seen John and I had no photograph of him, so I had no real idea what he looked like. I knew he had curly hair. I knew he had glasses.'

Nothing teaches you about the fragility and inadequacy of human memory like a long separation. You reach into your mind for the other person, but over time their face, hands and smell fade away. In just a few short months their image won't flash up on the screen of your mind. You are left with what feels like an empty description—you might sometimes dream of them, but that can distort memory rather than repair it. And after all, Mary and John had not had a great deal of time together: four evenings, two days and then a long weekend. Mary hoped that her image of a gently spoken man, in whose company she felt an unaccountable ease and joy, was a true one. She was also hoping that he was actually going to turn up.

'I had a lovely little white suitcase, my hair was done and I felt drop-dead gorgeous! I walked down the stairs of the aircraft with a big smile on my face, but I was absolutely petrified—was he going to be there? I had no phone number for him. I had no idea where Longreach was. There was no such thing as ringing him up or sending him a text. I was just hoping that this guy who had said, "Yes, come to Australia," was actually going to be there to meet me in Brisbane as he had promised.

'Then there was this young man coming from the arrivals area onto the tarmac—he had on a long coat, he was running, he was on a mission. And I was thinking to myself, "Is that John? What should I do? Should I put my suitcase down, should I put out my arms?" Fortunately I didn't do anything, this fellow just shot past.

'I walked into the arrivals area and I didn't see anybody. And my heart dropped. I was thinking to myself, "What'll I do?" I had hardly any money in my purse because I virtually had no money. There was a good friend of my aunt living in Brisbane—the aunt who had told me that Australia was a country with many sheep—and I knew I could go to her. But I was thinking, "I'll have to take the plane out of Brisbane to go back," and then I saw a hand waving.'

It had been such a gamble, Mary's trip to Australia to spend more time with a young man she had only met a few times. Would whatever it was that had drawn her to John still exist? Would they still be easy in each other's company? In those first few moments of seeing each other after eight months, each felt a deep relief: they did tremendously like this other person after all.

John was as she'd remembered and imagined him—except better. There were no metal chains around his neck and he was dressed, not as a tourist, but for the life he was leading on the station.

After the commercial flight from Brisbane to Longreach, John's father met them at the airport in the four-seater Cessna. As the smallest of the three of them, Mary was squeezed in behind the two front seats. Her first sight of Marmboo was from the air. Nothing less like the emerald land and gunmetal sky of Ireland could be imagined.

Below her were warm ochre plains and around her the bright-blue vault of the Australian sky. Even after quite a lot of rain and plants green and growing, Australia's rangelands look as if they are mostly bare earth from the air. The spaces between plants, which are easy to miss when you are down in the landscape, become painfully apparent when you are gazing down from above. Mary had quite confidently expected to see, if nothing else, thousands upon thousands of sheep, white and fluffy and busy in green paddocks. In pastoral country unshorn sheep are nearly invisible from the air, their fleeces greyed and browned with dust and twigs. Mary could not help wondering where all the sheep were.

But she was excited and fascinated by everything she saw. The incomprehensible thousands of acres, the paddocks at least twenty times the size of whole farms in Ireland, semi-wild cattle handled just once a year, the stock horses, the stables, the corrugated-iron sheds barking in the wind, the thickening of the grasses closer to the big creeks, the smell of the big gum trees after rain, the long days of mustering for shearing, the camaraderie of the shearing sheds.

'Fortunately, it had rained,' says John.

There was no Learjet. No castle. Mary was immediately pressed into riding a horse and taking part in the sheep work in the lead-up to shearing. All this meant she was quick to discard any of her prior ideas about a highfalutin lifestyle. John's mother, Joan, was away seeing her family in England, but there was evidence of her cleanliness, organisation, self-discipline and hard work everywhere. In the next six weeks Mary saw clearly both how much work life on Marmboo would be for a woman, and how very high Joan's standards were—and she fell irretrievably in love with John.

His physical presence, sleeves rolled up and actively engaged with the land, did all kinds of things for her that it hadn't in Ireland when he had been on holiday. And working alongside him during the day, talking to him at night: she was finally seeing the whole man in his context, and she loved all of him.

Having Mary with him on Marmboo was heaven for John, but he said nothing to her about marriage and forever. If one person is not happy in a marriage, that marriage isn't successful. It was going to be for Mary to decide if she could be happy on Marmboo. After all, this was the 1970s and it was a given that it was a man's work that decided the family's location. In addition, and this was as much the case in Ireland as it was in Australia, women who married a man with a farming property then afterwards said it must be sold were greatly criticised. The commitment a farmer or pastoralist's wife made was to a great deal more than the man himself, and it was not just to him and the land, but to the invested work of earlier generations. For a man to sell his inherited property due to his wife's unhappiness was seen as a forced betrayal of his heritage. Mary, having grown up on a farm, having slowly become aware that her mother felt to some degree stifled in the setting she'd married into but had also felt she must stay there, was only too aware of this.

Mary knew how happy John was in his life on Marmboo, and so, loving him, she wanted him to stay in the life he adored. But was it the life for her? It wasn't a decision she could make in Australia. She had to go back to Ireland to think it through. And besides all that, Mary had accepted a teaching job in Belfast.

'I did wonder if I could take that life on. I could see the standards that had been set both inside the house and outside on the station, and I thought, "You'd be so isolated." I had to come back, I had to look at it from afar, to see whether or not I could take it on,' says Mary.

Back in Ireland Mary had a few days with her mum and dad in the South before leaving for Belfast. In Ireland were her parents and sister, her friends and all the trappings of civilisation. It is not so much the coffee shops and the clubs that make life easier, but the sharing of the load of all the small jobs that make up our lives. In the Irish towns and cities there was a person for every different job: plumbers, electricians, butchers, nurses, teachers, cooks, gardeners and carpenters ... but there was no John.

The weekly correspondence between them continued. They chatted to each other on tape, sharing their lives and how very much they missed the other person. It took just two months for Mary to realise that home for her was now 'with John'. She recorded a message to John which ended in saying that she thought a shared life would be worth a try.

John received this most welcome message with delight. 'I had the cue I needed,' he says, and promptly responded with a formal proposal of marriage before Christmas in 1976.

'When I look back,' says Mary, 'I took on marriage as an adventure. I didn't take it on as the total commitment that goes with marriage. I thought, "Well, if I don't make a go of it I'll pack my bags and come home. But if I don't try I could regret it." Fortunately I have no regrets, fortunately it has worked out. But if my children said the same thing to me I would be horrified and probably have given them a lecture on what marriage is about!'

John immediately began planning another trip back to Ireland to see Mary.

'Of course, as for a lot of people on the land, the animals become number one in your life, and it was after Christmas. This was the time of year when storms are expected so the sheep had to be sprayed against flystrike. All the sheep had to be mustered into the various yards scattered around the property where an insecticide was applied to protect them—and that had to be done before John could leave the place. At the end of March in 1977 he arrived in Belfast. Because it wasn't his first time he was a little more relaxed. He came for just two weeks. It was unheard of then for people to go overseas for only two weeks.'

They borrowed a friend's car—Mary had only a motorbike—and travelled down through Dublin (stopping off to buy an engagement ring) so that John could meet Mary's father. He had already met Mary's mother.

'My mother hadn't thought—I mean, who'd have thought—that John and I would marry. When I phoned my parents to tell them of my intention to marry this Australian fellow I felt my mother wasn't sharing in my joy. There was something there, but she wasn't dampening the joy either. I didn't have the nerve to ask her what it was, maybe because deep down I didn't want to know. It wasn't until years later, on one of her many visits out to Australia, that she told me what it had meant to her when I got engaged. I never knew until years afterwards that to her, my engagement meant losing her eldest daughter and it had broken her heart.'

Twenty-two, madly in love, flying high on adventure and with no children of her own, Mary simply couldn't guess how her parents felt. But Vera knew what it was to say goodbye to loved ones and not see them again. Her brothers had left for England and America and effectively vanished out of her life.

On 26 August 1977 John and Mary were married in the little parish of Affane, close to Cappoquin. Marrying an Australian briefly made Mary a celebrity. Australia was regarded as the other end of the world. She might as well have been marrying the man who lived on the moon. There were lines of people outside the church to see the beautiful girl who was marrying a lovely Australian boy and going to live in that faraway country. John's mother and one of his sisters came, and in all there were thirteen guests who had at some time visited Marmboo.

'Nowadays weddings are these great big fanfare events, but I made my own dress. I also made my sister's dress and the flower girl's dress. There was none of this getting makeup and nails done that you have now. On the day, John drove me to Cork city, where I just went into a salon and said I was getting married that afternoon, and they just washed and blow-dried my hair. That was all. John dropped me home, went on to get changed and said, "See you at the church."'

On the day they left Ireland, Mary's mother, Vera, was to drive them to catch the plane, and Mary said goodbye to her father at the farm, adding, 'You will come and visit me in Australia, won't you, Dad?' Mary felt very much as if her apprenticeship in farming had been served with her father. He had offered her excellent advice on her new life: 'Be happy. Get to know the workings of the place so when your husband comes home you will be able to share in his day's activities, and don't take on a job that you don't want to continue as it will be your job for life.' She was naturally confident that he would be keen to visit her. But John Curran was a simple man, and he had never been on an aeroplane.

'Dad said, "Don't expect me to hop on an aeroplane to come to Australia, because I won't." It was just awful. I don't have to add, this didn't make for an easy parting.'

By mid-September Mary was meeting for the first time many of John's friends and family. Through it all John was by her side, quick to understand that she felt alien, that he was not just her lover and her husband but her sole support in a new land.

The trip from Brisbane to Marmboo in late spring was Mary's first intimation of just how hot it would be in summer. The temperature was then in the mid-twenties.

'I was asking, "John, does it get any hotter than this?" and he would say, "Oh, it does a bit, it does a bit."'

The actual length and the degree of heat in Mary's first Australian summer was a dreadful shock.

'That first Christmas we'd been given a candelabrum with three European candles. We came back from a Christmas Eve dinner at my parents' house and found the three candles had just laid over in the heat,' says John.

'I couldn't believe it, I cried when I saw the candles,' says Mary. 'That first Christmas was awful. I wanted so much to talk to my mum and dad and wish them a happy Christmas. Our telephone system was shared by two other neighbours so it was a very faint line. To make an overseas call you had to book days in advance, nominate a day and time you wanted the call to go through and then wait. All Christmas Eve I was waiting for the operator to ring to say we could speak. Then when the call came, I couldn't hear my parents and they couldn't hear me. It was a disaster, which was followed by tears.

'I spent that first summer sitting on the toilet—I will never know why the toilet—crying. It was so hard, going into that summer. Where was the green grass? Where were all the cows? Where was the rain? It was just so, so different. But I did stick it out. Sometimes I wonder how I did it, it was so hard—no family, no friends and living in the middle of nowhere—but I did do it, and I'm probably a better person for it.'

What kept Mary at Marmboo was John and her very real enjoyment of their life together. And she isn't a person who looks back. She had left Ireland behind, this was her new life and it was that simple.

Before children arrived Mary wanted to understand the workings of the property. She had to feel confident driving the hundred kilometres into Longreach. She learned to ride a horse, to help build fences, drive the vehicle to service sub-artesian bores and to play a part in all the different activities that make up a pastoralist's year as her father had advised her.

In the late 1970s and early 1980s many of the health and safety precautions and equipment which are now standard on rural properties simply didn't exist.

'We're so conscious of these things now but, in those days, if you took a bottle of water you were a softie. We didn't wear sunscreen.'

She revelled in working alongside John despite these tough conditions, just as she revelled in the slow process of building a home.

'We had nothing in the house here—little furniture, two single beds that were tied together with rope and a wedding present from John's parents of a massive deep freeze with two loaves of bread and some butter. I suppose you could call these the essentials! Everything we bought just came gradually and we worked hard for it. And we appreciated it so much. In Ireland before I left there were some of my friends with big mortgages and they had everything in their house. We had two fold-out chairs, and they were our sitting-room chairs, but they were very versatile as they came everywhere with us for the first eighteen months.'

Mary began finding out all she could about how children in remote areas learn to read and write.

'I had heard about children doing correspondence and I had no idea as to what it entailed. So I went over to a neighbouring property one day a week to teach the boy there. I think he ended up teaching me. He was a clever boy.'

Back in Ireland her father was ill. In fact, not long after Mary had left he had been diagnosed with motor neurone disease, a particularly awful neurological condition which sees a person inexorably lose movement after movement until, finally, they can't breathe. Mary's mother had only told Mary that her father was sick. She didn't know how to share over the phone the news that such a tragic and terminal diagnosis had been given. She was further deterred by the fact that Marmboo was on a 'party line', which meant that the whole district used that telephone line and no private conversation was possible.

John and Mary had carefully saved to pay for return tickets for both her parents to visit. (The financial control of the property was in John's father's hands: if something was not able to be saved for, Mary and John would have to go 'cap in hand' to request the money. It was a situation they did not like.) The ticket being paid for ensured that Mary's father would indeed take the huge step of getting on an aeroplane for the very first time.

'That was in 1979 and John and I went to Brisbane to meet them. At the airport I couldn't figure out why my parents were not coming out in arrivals, and then out they came with Mum wheeling my dad. When I said goodbye to my father two years before, he'd been a healthy farmer. Then to see him at the airport, in a wheelchair … I'll never forget it.'

The shock of that moment has never left Mary. This was a day in which she expected only joy, but what she was seeing heralded tragedy and loss. And yet, the memory of her father's first and only visit to Marmboo is such a happy one now. That plane ticket and three months with them were the very best presents they could have given him.

'He came in a wheelchair, but he got out of the wheelchair when he was at Marmboo. He was able to get around very well. We had a little old car here that belonged to John's sister. He used to drive the car anywhere on the property and he never got lost. It was incredible that this man, who had never left Ireland, could find his way around a 95,000-acre property! And he loved it. He loved the open spaces. He loved the work the men were doing, although he couldn't participate himself. It was lovely that he was able to be here and to see where I was living as I think from my letters going back home they both thought I lived in the Simpson Desert! For a man who was never going to leave Ireland he did very well.

'They left in August and once he knew he was returning to Ireland he was back in the wheelchair. He didn't have the strength, he knew he was going back to die. For the first month after getting home he would go into the local pub and entertain the locals with his stories of his visit to the outback of Australia. My dad was a good storyteller and I would have loved to have been a fly on the wall to hear his tales.'

Mary went over in February 1980 to help her mother with nursing her father at home, and to say goodbye to him. She returned to Australia in March.

'Ten days after I left Ireland, I woke in the middle of the night. I felt a hand on my shoulder, and I woke up. I thought it was John who had touched me so I called, "John?", but John was asleep. I closed my eyes again and I was holding my father's hand in mine and we were walking along a dark driveway, with a lot of sheltering trees. He said to me, "You'd better stay now where you are, because I'm just to walk on a little bit further." And I woke up again and I knew my father had died.'

When Joan came to tell Mary the news early the next morning, Mary discovered he had died at the time of her dream.

The relationship between father and daughter was strengthened by his time at Marmboo—and her father's last visit at the moment of his death celebrated a bond Mary had always felt to be special. This was not to be the case for John and his father, Jack.

John has had to come to terms with the dominance and inflexibility on his father's part, the uncertainty and remorse on his own part and the barrier that tragically grew between them. The honesty of the exchanges between Mary and John on this subject is a testament to the ease between them, because this is not something on which they completely agree. Listening to them both talk of his father, I wonder when the dementia Jack was eventually diagnosed with began. It is an illness that changes people in small ways before it eventually strips them of the ability to find the particular memory they need to make sense of the world or to imagine themselves in someone else's shoes. The brain begins to change some twenty years before the diagnosis can be made. With hindsight, families often realise there were signs well before the decline in thinking became apparent.

Jack's was always an autocratic character. This had excellent results in some ways. John and Mary admire how fairly and cleanly he planned the succession onto the property, and how provision was also made for John's brother and sisters. There was no bitterness, no hatred, no loss of sibling relationships, no family torn asunder—something all too common in farming.

'We four children are all still talking because of how my father arranged the estate. The critical thing was that he invested off-farm,' says John. 'And there were no secrets about the will.'

John and Mary have replicated this with their own three children. Since Ashling, their youngest, was in boarding school at the age of twelve, all their children have been privy to the will, how things are going in the business, and how it will be left.

'Every time we can get them together, we all go along and we have a financial adviser to mediate. It's up to the five of us to talk it through. The financial adviser recommends that children's spouses aren't involved—it's up to that person to tell their spouse what has been agreed. The adviser has complimented John and me for doing this. It has been the salvation of the te Kloot family and John's father led the way in this,' says Mary.

In the management of his will, Jack's dominance ensured the friendship and love between his children would be lifelong, but on Marmboo that same trait drove a wedge between father and son that was not fully bridged at the time of his death in 1997.

'We just did what we were told. We just slotted into what was here, we didn't question,' says Mary.

'In hindsight it's all very clear. Dad was in his early sixties and he wanted someone to take over the physical work. The office was his comfort zone. I always remember the occasion when there were 10,000 sheep being sold up north and we heard about them early. I said to Dad, "Let's get up there. Let's buy them, tidy them up and sell them." But he wouldn't. It was a lot of work, and he wasn't a young man, but I was. If I'd pushed it enough he might have agreed, and we'd have made a few dollars. But I didn't push it. The very things he did, he never allowed me to do.'

John regrets now that he didn't insist, that he let it go. This has, in part, driven the messages given to his children: get out there, have your own adventure, make your own way in the world.

Mary has a slightly different take on their first twenty years on the property.

'If you had been the same kind of person as your father, we wouldn't have survived living there,' she says. Meaning if John had been as autocratic as his father the arrangement would have failed at the outset. 'We are who we are,' she says. 'If we had to live it over again we'd do the same things—we might wish that we wouldn't, but I feel sure we would.'

Her view is that no-one understood better than John his father's fear of debt—how entrenched it had become in his childhood, the fight to have Marmboo debt-free. John let go of the idea of purchasing these sheep, and of other ideas like it, out of this acute understanding of his father. Some of John's underlying regret, Mary feels, is not that he didn't get his own way, but that the ongoing tension destroyed much of the relationship he and his father once had.

'As he got Alzheimer's he fought every inch of the way. When I got a computer with an accounting package, that was seen as an attempt to do him out of his job—but it was only just in time,' John says. Every conflict separated father and son further. There could be no resolution, as Jack no longer had the insight into the damage he was doing, and John had no choice but to take more and more control as his father's decline accelerated. Alzheimer's robs families of the person they loved, even as the person lives on in their midst. And for the person, Alzheimer's makes them frightened. When you cannot remember, when you cannot trust your perceptions, it is a very short step towards becoming angry or withdrawn.

'I never discussed death with my father, or the many great and exciting things he'd done in his life. Excuse me if I get a bit emotional—there were things that needed to be said and I didn't say them. There was an evening when my father was in his house and I was in my house, and I'd never had him over for a meal. But there was such a barrier between us because he'd fought tooth and nail. I say to my boys, never let that happen in our family. Fortunately time heals, and I now choose to remember my father for the positive things he did for me, his family, the community and this country.'

With the word 'family' we are back to what matters most to John and Mary. They had grown closer with every passing year. After three years Mary felt ready (as ready as anyone ever does) to take on mothering on Marmboo. In March 1982 Conor was born, then two years later Cormac, and three years later, a daughter, Ashling. Mary's mother came out to stay for a while with the birth of each child—she was to come out often until her death in 1997—and was quick to see the situation in which the young couple had been placed.

'My mother could understand what life was like with John's parents being rulers of the property. She could understand that well because that's exactly what she'd had herself with the dominance of Granny Curran. She understood that it wasn't an easy life.'

Though it was sometimes difficult, Mary has no regrets.

'I had no friends in Australia. I couldn't go down the street with a friend for coffee. John was my husband and my lover, but he was also my best friend. And I treasure that.'

And John feels the same way.

Their close friendship was vital in building what they both, as a result of their own childhoods, felt was the most important thing in the world: a happy home. 'The children have lovely memories. John and I never fought. They had the freedom of the bush. They would be outside helping John. They were responsible children, like adults, helping where they could with the work, and yet they were children with their playtime.

I said goodbye to them at an early age with boarding school. The boys were ten and Ashling was nine and a half.'

Sending a child away to boarding school is an extraordinary act of sacrifice and trust.

'You're so used to having your children around. They're educated on the property, they work and play here. Then, one by one, they leave home and the nest is empty. When the first one went, it was as if we had lost the child. I remember saying to my mother how awful it was. I felt we had lost our little boy,' says Mary.

Even before Conor went away to school, Mary and John made sure that they valued the times when the whole family was together. The care they took to do this was even more pronounced once Conor had left.

'We always knew that our time together would only ever be for a few weeks, and we all made the best of it.'

Mary organised the house so that evenings were kept for talking because she says it's 'the nicest thing you can do over a meal in the evening time'. On Marmboo, even in the middle of a hard workday, if a good conversation begins over morning tea or lunch, that is honoured, too.

'Don't go back to work—keep the conversation going—work is not that important,' says John.

Despite the drought, Marmboo is not a property that carries any debt: of course, it is nearly twenty years since John's father died and this debt-free status owes much to John's organised and meticulous farming style.

Yet over Marmboo the skies remain obstinately blue. It's drier than they've ever seen it. It is baking in the worst drought anyone can remember. John is in demand to speak to journalists about the drought due to his uncomplaining attitude and ability to speak to the point. In 2015 a photograph of John standing by a wire gate—unsmiling, head slightly bent, before a broad expanse on which grew no grass, no bush, no trees—made the front page of *The Weekend Australian.*

'Sometimes I get down because it is so dry and John says, "Oh, we'll be fine, we'll get through it," and then he'll be down and I can say the same thing to him,' says Mary. John and Mary are reflective but, despite the continuing dry, they are not at all grim. With each other's help they have made peace with a great many things in their lives—the fact that you cannot make it rain on your property or stop it raining on your neighbour's property is but one of these.

'When you're in a drought you're wishing time away. You want tomorrow to come. You wish for a cloud in the sky; you want next week to come for a change in the weather; you want next month to come as you'll be one month closer to the promised wet season. One should never wish time away, especially at our age!' says John. He tells me it is an observation Mary made initially, and that he shares it whenever he can. 'Nothing else I've ever said on radio has had the reaction that had.'

Drought, like fire and flood, is a direct attack on the soul of a place. Where fire suddenly exposes and flood suddenly suffocates, drought slowly starves. To protect itself the land must seal itself over. And the people who live on the land feel it in much the same way as a family feels it when someone they love withdraws from them—there are many extra burdens that come with drought, but this one is rarely acknowledged. You have existed in a relationship with the land, given to it and received from it, and that rich and satisfying exchange has mostly disappeared. This means that during drought the quality of the other relationships we have becomes a great deal more important. John emphasises the protective effect of high-quality relationships when he talks about drought. This isn't all that he says. Putting relationships first is how he and Mary have always lived.

Mary and John will be all right. They have each other. They have never been afraid of taking on new roles, these two, and they have their sights set on the next stage of life.

'We both feel it's time to hang up our boots,' says Mary.

'With this in mind we hope to sell the property and move to our house in Maleny, Queensland. Change is not easy at the best of times, but as we get older it becomes so much harder and this is our main reason for wanting to make this big move in our lives sooner rather than later, when it could be all too late.'

Even though Mary and John are leaving the industry, their concern for it remains. In his media appearances John has been sharing an idea to help farmers survive drought. Mary and John, out of their own experience of going through drought with minimum debt, believe that if people have less to worry about financially, they will be less stressed. If people are less stressed they'll make better decisions—not just better business decisions, but interpersonal, land-care and animal-welfare decisions. The financial stress resulting from this drought is costing marriages, lives and childhoods. It is this that Mary and John, with their abiding focus on healthy family life, seek to have addressed ahead of all else. John is suggesting the creation of a 'future farming fund'. This would be partly funded by farmers themselves (at a quarter of a percent levy on farmers' pre-tax income) and enabled by legislation.

In 2015 Mary and John celebrated thirty-eight years of marriage.

'There's no recipe out there for a successful marriage,' says Mary. 'There's a lot of good luck, and it's so important to talk to each other about the big and little things that come your way in life.'

That they turned a chance meeting into an intercontinental courtship is testament to them. Mary concludes her first letter to me by saying, 'our passion of all those years ago has become true love'. For their resulting marriage to not just survive but flourish in Queensland's pastoral country shows how sometimes—not always, but sometimes—that almost painful feeling of being physically drawn to another person is no more or less than a profound intuition. They simply had to be together.

There is a photograph of a courting Mary and John. John with his curls and lion-wide face is smiling at the photographer and on his arm Mary is excited, reckless, on the adventure of her life. She's looking into the distance, the bright Australian sun shining on her wavy hair, her Irish complexion and gentle chin. They are still easily recognisable as the couple in the photograph. Mary's brown hair is creamy white now, but her face still has that pared-down elegance, her skin is clear and bright and she is smiling. John's glasses seem to have changed rather more than he has. There's a deep easiness between them which makes them great fun to be with.

Mary and John are grateful every day for their good health, and their delightful family, for their good luck in meeting at all, for the wisdom of their ardent bodies and hearts all those years ago, and for the easy, unfailing connection they still have with each other that lies at the heart of their happiness.

You Turn Me On, I'm a Radio

Kath and Steve Baird, Kiewa Valley, Tawonga, Bogong High Plains, Victoria

The Australian Alps of Victoria—the High Country—are the rarest of our rangeland environments. Unlike mountains in other parts of the world, they are ancient, pre–Ice Age, and the soil here is, correspondingly, hauntingly old. On this old soil, living almost in the sky, gathering most of their water not from rain but from snow, plants here cooperate to survive. The taller trees with their shaggy rough outlines create a downdraft, pulling down the snow and stopping it from drifting elsewhere. At the foot of every tree are the ground covers: the grasses and bushes, little plants with many small roots creating pathways into the soil for the snow as it melts. In this way water reaches the tree's own roots. In the highest places the tall trees don't grow. Here the rider on her horse is above everything else on the plains, her gaze, like the light, bouncing from mountain top to sky, with no barrier in between.

'We call the beautiful open high plains "up top". Alpine mint grows vigorously up top, and when you brush against the mint it releases the most exquisite smell in the whole world,' says Kath Baird, who with her husband, Steve, has lived at Spring Spur, high in the Bogong Ranges for thirty years now. Kath and Steve have been married for thirty-six years, having fallen in love on meeting and moved in together just three weeks later.

I had first heard of Kath and Steve from their son Lin. 'I'm looking for great love stories,' I had said. (So often the word 'love' makes young men uncomfortable, but not this one.) 'You want to talk to my folks!' Lin said without missing a beat. He could not be more comfortable with the word, or prouder of his parents and their love for each other, which began with that lightning bolt: love at first sight.

Should we trust love at first sight? It is hard to accept that in a fifth of a second (which is all it takes) you can gather enough information about another person to decide to marry them, but people do. Falling in love is a violent sensation—which explains the sayings 'struck by lightning' and 'falling off a cliff'—but it also feels timeless. The lightning was striking before you were born. You've been falling for an eternity. It's always been the two of you. It seems hardly a sensible state in which to make a life-changing decision, but for the people for whom it happens there is hardly a decision to make. Everything in you is captivated by this other person, all at once, without your volition. This was the feeling that swept over Steve and Kath.

'I'd discovered in adult life, as well as the responsibility, there was a lot of fluff and rubbish,' says Steve. 'There were things you were meant to do and say that weren't important. When I met Kath that all disappeared: here was the person with whom none of that was needed. We just fitted, without the need to explore that fit, without a great deal needing to be said. There was Kath and there was me, and together we made something bigger.'

His description brings to mind Shakespeare's phrase 'the marriage of true minds'. The people we know best and deepest, the people we most respect, all shape how we respond to the world. As we build their vocabulary into the silent language of our thoughts, as we learn to see the world the way they do, we extend, we enlarge. Even when Kath is not next to him Steve doesn't feel separated from her.

The phrase 'love at first sight' induces nearly as much cynicism in some psychologists as the related phrase 'soulmates'. Generally, the research literature agrees that this feeling is not just sexual attraction or the hormonal cocktail of limerence, or a feeling of overwhelming friendship, but all three shouting the news: I want this one! And, if we have a soul, that, too, is shouting the news.

So how can someone know so rapidly that they have met the person with whom they'll have the most fun, the easiest and deepest conversation, the best chance of helping and being helped by? The short answer to this is 'love maps'. Apparently, from our very earliest years we are building a map of the kind of person we want to love. This isn't something we are conscious of, but nonetheless—unseen, from a potpourri of family members, characters in books, people we meet, family legends, classmates, people on TV, friends and from our growing knowledge of ourselves—this map grows in our mind.

Sometimes that map is so very exact and so absolutely mutual, each person so transparent, so necessary to the other, that the map makers fall in love straightaway. Even from the outside, if an observer knows enough of each person, such instant commitment can make sense, and this is the case here.

Steve grew up in a family where none of what he calls 'fluff'—being seen doing the 'right' thing, being part of the mob, keeping up appearances—mattered. This attitude was rooted in the family's history and most particularly in the legacies left by war service, of long engagement with the land and of the family practice of art.

'My grandfather Lin and his brother fought in World War I. Both men returned damaged, physically and mentally, by their war experience. They were allocated a block in the Mallee under the Soldier Settlement scheme and confronted hard times.'

Many of these soldiers survived war but not the Mallee, as they didn't have the skills to work the land. Without a farming background, contracted to pay rent on their land to the government, living with battle nerves and the old bodies that war bequeaths young men, many suicided. Steve's grandfather and great-uncle had fought in and witnessed the carnage of the war; now they were seeing a second tragedy where people's lives were again overturned by the demands of society and dictates of government. And while the Baird brothers did have farming skills having grown up on the family farm at Ballarat, they did not do well in the Mallee.

'It was a battle with the rabbits and the markets and drought, and in the end they abandoned the farm and the debt. My grandfather started a new life with eight kids, but that battle and country remained entrenched in his psyche.' This was true not just of Steve's grandfather, but of his children, who witnessed the struggle and losses, one of whom was Steve's father, Bob.

'My dad was six years old before he saw rain. He saw it when they moved from the Mallee into the north-east High Country. And so Bob always understood and taught us about the rarity of water in the Australian landscape—he became a water-treatment engineer, ensuring safe water supplies for the little country towns,' says Steve.

Looking for water is the constant adventure offered to those exploring Australia. On weekend trips, through all kinds of landscapes, Bob laid bare for his children the working together of man, water and time. Steve was taught to see the fall of the land, to trace in his mind's eye where rain would run as it gathered momentum on slopes, to imagine water greedily lifting topsoil, leaf litter and seeds, to recognise the places stripped of their living wealth first by poor management and then by fast-moving water. He also learned how to look further down catchment to find where the water had gone, and to see the beneficiaries of all those nutrients, compost and seed bounty—lakes edged with sediment and grasses, rivers at the heart of valleys, springs, rock pools defying the fall of the land and the magic of river meeting sea. Where water hid beneath the earth fascinated his father, too—the guessed-at caverns and sandy beds, the basins and channels, the chanciness of finding a supply enough for a town, or for a bore to water stock.

Steve's mother, Pat, had been an only child at a time when this was unusual. Her family home was a quieter one than those of many of her friends. In her own family she wanted something different: more people, more passion. On meeting and loving Bob Baird she also valued the whole boisterous Baird clan. She set about creating a family life that focused on sharing, including and celebrating. In her home there would always be people to play with, to help with the load, to cook with, to talk to and to build alongside. Steve's parents also valued art. They kept materials for children's art available, and made time for the children to create. Steve still remembers his excitement at the prospect of drawing. Among the family friends were professional artists (such as Leonard French and

Fred Williams). Childhoods show children what is possible or not possible, and alongside his belief that adventures come if you set out, Steve came to see art as everyday, as valuable, as something he could do.

Art had become a habit with him before he left childhood, and on his travels he carried notebooks in which he documented particulars of what he discovered about the natural world and the history of each place.

With the advent of the Vietnam War, Steve experienced for the first time acute pressure to comply with wider society's values and to 'do as he was told'. His birthdate was one of those selected in the conscription ballot for Vietnam. But Steve believed he was a brother to all of humanity. Supported by the same tide of thought among family and friends, he successfully objected on conscientious grounds as a pacifist. To do so he had to appear in court. The entire experience left him more determined than ever to lead a life in keeping with his identity and values.

At an even younger age Kath, like Steve, had concluded that the dictates of society must be resisted and that the only discipline is to act with love. Again, like Steve, she came to understand this as a result of living under acute societal pressure. Being a child during the Vietnam War (known as the 'television war' as it was the first war to come into people's lounge rooms) was traumatising for her, as for many children. However, what happened to Kath was a result of the era she grew up in and the malignance of a particular teacher.

'When my dad came home from World War II all he wanted to do was go to university. And he put himself through, paid for his education himself. That was the Menzies era, you had to work bloody hard to get through uni. Education was so important to him,' she says.

Kath's father wanted a good education for his children, too, and felt the best security lay in high academic achievement.

Kath understands her father now, and the fact that at all times he was only trying to protect and help his children, to make them 'safe', and perhaps particularly protect Kath herself, with her sensitive and creative nature. Sadly, his determination that Kath succeed academically only served to make her more vulnerable at school, and the price she paid for that was a high one.

'Dad was very tough on us, especially when it came to learning. He had a very busy life, and a busy political life. I actually dreaded him coming home because he was just so strict. He'd come in and say, "Right, what homework have you got?"'

Kath started school very young. She was bright but she was also a child who was passionate and intense. This aspect of Kath meant she was not emotionally ready for the swamping demands of playground politics or the need to please teachers. The idea that starting formal learning earlier creates higher academic achievement in most children is a seductive one. But when a child is not ready it instead teaches them that they are 'dumb' and that school is 'too hard'. With the best motivations in the world Kath's parents put her into school when she was four and a half.

'Dad made me go for a scholarship at Mentone Girls' Grammar. I just didn't want to go for the scholarship, I knew I wasn't going to get one! He kept saying to me, "Of course you can get a scholarship." His expectations of us were just so high. And I didn't get one, I actually failed the exam and ended up being kept down a grade. I was made to repeat Year Six in the Girls' Grammar Primary. It crushed me.'

It is known now that keeping children 'down a grade' puts them on track for worse educational outcomes and mental health problems—their confidence rarely recovers from this affront and educational outcomes are poorer as a result.

Teachers are now advised never to propose it. In Kath's case it did more than disadvantage her. We speak a great deal of the power of teachers to play a big role in improving a child's mental health. Of course, the converse is also true. Teachers can also harm a child's sense of self.

'On the first day the teacher said: "I'm going to read the roll out, and anyone doing the second year of sixth grade must stand up." And I thought, "Oh" and then I thought, "There must be someone else going to stand up, because it wouldn't just be me, she wouldn't make just me stand up, surely?" My last name was Viney so there were lots of other names first. And of course no-one else stood up, no-one. Just me. So I had to stand up and say, "This is my second year of sixth grade." And then she made me move, and come and sit behind her daughter, because she had her daughter in the same class as me. So her daughter was in the front row, and I had to sit behind her, that was my place for the whole year.' Throughout the year the teacher continued to victimise Kath.

'I was a good swimmer. It was sports day, and I swam a little harder this year for my house and I was in lots of events, and Mum said, "Do you want some barley sugar?" and I said, "No, Mum, no-one is allowed to go to the kiosk." Mum said, "Oh, what a lot of rubbish" and bought some barley sugar for me. The next day was the day that man landed on the moon. I was sitting with all the other kids in the television room and I was so excited to see this happen. Well, this horrible teacher told me to come outside. She said to me that she had seen me with barley sugar and that I'd been deliberately disobedient. She said, "You must go and write out: *I must not be deliberately disobedient* a hundred times," and I missed seeing man walking on the moon. I cried all day. And that year I started what is called trichotillomania.'

Trichotillomania, or hair-pulling disorder, is one of the most common ways stress overflows into self-harm in children and young people. Like every type of self-harm, it briefly soothes but then quickly leads to a feeling of shame and alienation. While this is a very common disorder, the accompanying humiliation means that sufferers don't ask for help, and never learn how many people who feel just like them are in the world.

'The way I started pulling my hair out was by biting the ends. I had beautiful long wavy blonde hair—I was quite an attractive child—and then I couldn't reach anymore, the bits were too short to reach in my mouth. So then I started plucking it out. I ended up with these massive bald patches right through my teenage years. I struggled with that for a long time, because I thought, "I'm nutty, there's something wrong with me." I had no idea other people did this, too. Eventually, I went to see a psychologist and he was lovely. He said, "Kath, you know why she sat her daughter in front of you, and why she treated you like that?" and I said, "No." I didn't understand, I'd never understood. And he said, "It was because she was taking the attention from her daughter, she was making you the scapegoat, so that her own child wouldn't get bullied by the classroom for being the teacher's daughter." But she turned me into quite a rebel, that teacher.'

With nothing left to lose in the way of approval or appreciation, Kath became anti-authoritarian. She'd been bullied and stung into masking her sensitivity and creativity, into hardening her outside and stopping her growth on the inside. To protect herself she became another kind of person. She wore coloured underwear (which was considered terrible at the time) and started smoking. She was cheeky, rebellious and hard to reach.

One of the hardest things about being a parent is doing your very best and finding you've had the opposite result to what you intended. Kath understands how parenting her through this unhappy time would have felt for her parents. She also sees the impact of social mores on their parenting decisions, and, keeping that in mind, can find the people they really were despite the shackles of their era.

'I don't blame Mum and Dad, it was that era, that generation—they weren't good at saying "I love you". They just wanted to bring me up, give me a good education and get me qualified in something, that's what was most important. I know Dad made mistakes as a parent, but I now know what pressure he was under financially and politically. He was a really amazing person, a visionary, my dad.'

Kath's parents, Bill and Eleanor, were builders who had a dairy farm on the side, but they were also politically active. They campaigned against capital punishment and conscription. Even when they were doing it tough financially they advocated for and assisted those who were doing it tougher. Later in his political career Bill supported the development of a new educational facility and was elected to the board of directors. Wonderfully, this new facility was to make good a great deal of the damage done to Kath by other schools.

Huntingdale Technical School was a democratic or 'free' school. Even now, this type of education is considered radical. In these school communities each child's voice and vote is treated as equivalent to that of an adult. Children experiment in creating the community, negotiating, planning and doing the work. They see then what happens as a consequence of their actions for themselves. Everything is put to the children's vote: rules, consequences, innovations, contribution and staffing. And when it comes to the children themselves, each child has full control. They choose what and how many subjects they will do, or if, indeed, they will do any study at all. It can sound like a recipe for disaster, but study after study has shown the opposite: graduates of such schools go on to contribute outstandingly to society.

At Huntingdale Kath could be in charge of herself. She discovered herself anew, what healed her and began the journey of finding what she had to give to the world. To her parents' delight the hard, rebellious, cheeky mask (so painfully worn) began to lift and underneath they could see again the bright-eyed, spontaneous, lover of life they'd lost years before.

'Huntingdale saved my life,' Kath says, 'I did drama, I did pottery, I did film and television, I put on plays, I did everything I loved. I never finished at Huntingdale Tech, but I was able to tap into that creative part of myself.'

Putting on plays let Kath for the first time understand her rather peculiar creative gift of turning a group of separate people into a team focused on sharing. Her optimism, her understanding of the costs of creative endeavour, her belief that society needs to empathise more, better, deeper and her ability to help people relate to each other, became (and remains to this day) an anchor and a haven allowing others to shine, contribute and learn. Her canvas is place and time, and her media is mixed but always includes other people.

Kath left home and moved to Melbourne. She lived there for two years, working in aged care. But city life palled. At twenty she moved back to the farm and worked both for her parents and in a library. Her parents at that time were leaving the dairy industry. England, previously a big market for Australian dairy products, joined the European Economic Community in the 1970s and prices for dairy products plummeted correspondingly. Oil prices soared and drought gripped much of Victoria. Kath's parents were just one of many small dairy operators—farms with perhaps just seventy cows—who had no choice but to leave the industry.

Kath's parents now needed a new way to make money. For the Vineys, finding a new enterprise was easier than it was for many other ex-dairy farmers. Their farm was surrounded by state forest. The family had a rich heritage of horse skills. The Vineys put the two together. Soon Kath was helping her parents in their new business of taking tourists on trail rides through the forest. A few cows were kept for milking.

Kath's days were built around the work of caring for the family's horses and dogs. She regained yet more of her childhood love of life. The dogs helped return to her the excitement and the fresh, earthy, poignant perceptions of her young self. The horses, with their strength and their desire to explore (which is every bit as strong as that of a dog), reinforced her curiosity, confidence and courage. The city was never to compete for Kath's affections again: in this time her allegiance to horses, dogs and life on the land was secured.

Then, in 1978, at the house of a mutual friend, she met Steve and they fell in love.

'He smelt of wintergreen oil. He was wearing a beautiful embroidered jacket and he'd done the embroidery himself. And I thought, "Ooh, a man who can sew!"'

Each saw in the landscape of the other person the map they had been charting since childhood. Here were the strangely familiar contours, the underground rivers and upwelling springs, the dreamed-of lost continents. Astonishingly, wonderfully, here was that longed-for partner in adventure. Kath invited Steve to her family farm.

They had an astounding amount in common. They were both beginning artists and creators. They were both from families of social reformers, political activists and artists: families conscious of and active in what was happening outside the small, safe family sphere. Each family was one in which ideas and ideals were discussed, art was appreciated and created, risks were calculated and adventures taken. In each family the doors were flung open to admit people who needed extra support and nourishing.

Steve was twenty-five and looking for something, always on an adventure, learning, reflecting, noting down and moving on. He'd studied architecture, but he didn't want just to design but to build, and to build not just buildings but landscapes. Landscape artists frequently refer to the 'genius of place', an identity unique to that one part of the earth created by the combination of what is there: the ecology, the land forms, the impact of man and water and time. It was with this that Steve wished to interact, and not just on paper with his mind, but with physical materials and his hands. For that he needed other skills, so he worked in plant nurseries, learned carpentry, helped on building sites and kept moving.

Steve is handsome—a dark handsomeness of the even-featured, steady, calmly in the background type. In contrast, Kath is always somehow in the forefront. Her colouring is of the blonde-bombshell variety and her dazzling, hopeful smile adds a show-stopping glamour to the most prosaic of scenes. Their storytelling is also contrasting. Steve speaks with the purposeful phrasing of the experienced raconteur, Kath with the emotive force of an actor. To convey how she talks in text requires regular use of italics and capitals.

'He told me he was a vegetarian, and I thought, "Oh, I don't know what I've got for a vegetarian." So I made what I can only call White Rice and Tomato Stodge cooked up in a frying pan. It would probably be called *risotto* now! Steve came again the *next* weekend, and then the *next*, and then he just *stayed*.'

Kath is wonderfully entertaining to listen to, as is Steve in his entirely different way. Where Kath knew horses, Steve knew water and land.

'I always say that when I married Kath, I also married horses,' says Steve.

Kath was now, at only twenty, breeding her own horses. She was delighted to share with him all she knew. And he returned the favour, teaching her how to read the movement of water on her own family farm. Steve also brought his habit of investigating the stories that surround any artefact.

'I always had a strong sense of history, of craft and the skills around making things by hand, so when Kath introduced me to horses I was keen to explore the whole story of the horse, particularly in the Australian bush.'

Kath opened up to Steve the love of the animal, and he opened up to her the heritage and stories created from the interaction between horses, humans and land. It didn't take long for Steve to unearth the story of the Australian stock horse and the heroic effort it had taken to bring them back.

'The Australian stock horse wasn't a breed to begin with. It was the horse that evolved in Australian conditions, helped along by people who knew horses, culling and selecting and breeding for Australian conditions: not much water, hard underfoot, hot. "Jim, I like the look of your stallion, he's a good type," that kind of thing. From the 1860s until after World War I there were horse-breeding operations that produced horses for the British Army, coach horses, stock horses,' says Steve.

In *The Man from Snowy River* Paterson wrote a description of the Australian stock horse. In it he dwells on the unflinching courage, the enduring toughness, the dextrous tread and the sympathy of the horse to the rider's goals. Useful, beautiful and brave, they were nearly all gone by the 1930s.

'The Australian stock horses were sent in their thousands to the British in the Boer War and were used again in World War I.

But then the machines took over their work in agriculture, and in war: motorbikes, tractors, utes. To preserve the breed, a loose association formed, and they began by creating a list of characteristics and breeding to it. About forty years later, in 1971, they opened a stud book and decided which horses would be the foundation sires and dams for the breed,' says Steve.

And then Steve found that one piece of horse heritage was disappearing fast. 'The seventies saw a crisis in keeping the skills and tradition of the packsaddle: the old saddlers were dying, the handlers and riders were going, the knowledge was disappearing from the landscape,' he says. Packhorses were used throughout Australia for many years, most particularly in remote regions: the early mailmen used them, as did station hands on their long runs to build and maintain fences, the drovers and of course, the explorers. Steve was utterly hooked. Here was not just the right girl, but for him the right quest: a race against time to preserve a vanishing and precious heritage. Preserving that tradition, they felt, was a job that somebody needed to do. Without committing to the job of saving the packhorse tradition, they decided to learn as much as they could about it from those willing to teach them.

'As someone who was always looking for adventures and journeys into the bush, in the grander sense, travelling with packhorses into remote places was a perfect fit,' says Steve. The tradition is a mix of linked skills: saddle design, making and caring for the saddles, packing them with the right things, packing effectively, balancing loads (of up to eighty kilograms per horse), caring for the packhorses, training horses to work together, camping out with horses, planning for safety and managing emergencies.

'At this time a few of the mountain-cattle families included horse tours in their mix of business and we got involved in riding and working with a Gippsland mountain cattleman, Clive Hodge, of Valencia Creek. Clive held the Moroka Run up on the side of Mount Wellington. He was a hard man, but he was generous with his knowledge of working with horses in the bush. I was like a sponge and probably made a nuisance of myself. Kath and I had some great experiences in those days, before we had kids. We rode the High Country from Kosciuszko to Bunyip with him and learned our lessons the hard way,' says Steve.

The years flew by. Steve worked as a builder locally, and together Kath and Steve helped out her parents with their trail-riding business. They built a house in Tonimbuk. On meeting the Bairds I felt their song must be a sunlit, steady, simple piano piece in a golden major key. They are neat and elegant, as lovers and riders of horses so often are, and practical. Spilling from their smiles is their spirited warmth and hospitality, their interest in their fellow woman and man and child. But that's not all their song. These two have lived big lives. Quite early on in their relationship they found that each separate family tradition of getting caught up in larger events had been somehow multiplied in their shared lives. Their story is peppered with dramatic and tragic incidents, and naturally, this only fed Kath's pre-existing anxiety.

'Did I tell you about the time,' says Kath, 'when we were held up by three men?'

It was 1982, two o'clock in the morning and Kath was pregnant with Lin. She and Steve were driving along the Princes Highway when they saw a car crashed by the side of the road with a young girl in a chiffon dress standing beside a man, who was waving for help. They stopped to help. When they pulled up the young man was revealed as an aggressor. A gun was put to Kath's head, and, as Steve went to protect her, another gun was swung into Steve's head with force.

'It would be so easy to kill you,' the man yelled, 'BANG, BANG!'

As she cradled an unsteady and shocked Steve's bleeding head, Kath was sure they were both going to die.

In fact, the biggest manhunt in Victoria's history was underway at that moment for these men, who were wanted for rape and theft. There had been no car crash. The car had been smashed up to mimic a car crash and thus attract a Samaritan with a new car in which the criminals could escape.

Kath was forced inside the car, where she discovered three young men, all with injuries. Steve, who had a fractured skull, was thrown in on top of her.

All this violent activity caused the interior car light to come on. The young man closest stared at Kath.

'Hey,' he said, leaving Kath amazed at some people's ability to make small talk no matter the circumstance. 'Aren't you Kath Viney?'

The men took the young girl with them, and with her as a hostage, escaped in Kath and Steve's vehicle. The manhunt would go on for days, but the girl, says Steve, was brave and clever and escaped, following a spur line of trees down to a river. On the other side were the police searching for both her and her abductors. As she walked into the river, a policeman strode in to collect her, lifting her in his arms, a moment caught by the press in what became one of the best photographs of the 1980s.

Steve followed with difficulty as Kath ran from the car and found a farmhouse and help.

She had coped valiantly, but in the long moments of terror by the roadside the anxiety Kath had kept at a distance for so many years returned. There's no answer to anxiety; it keeps you on the treadmill of trying to find reassurance, and the reassurance only works for a little while, and then you need more. For people living on the land there is no need to invent terrors—such as a carjacking—our loved ones face hazards on the most ordinary of days.

For death to threaten in such a random fashion made all of Kath's other fears appear even more likely. Kath's imagination, which had woven together other people's ideas into performance, was every bit as good at presenting her with nightmare scenarios. This part of our minds—our imagination—partly exists to help us keep our loved ones safe. A wild imagination can work magic in the arts and make us the most intuitive of friends. In the everyday world a wild imagination in overdrive can flood the body with an ugly cocktail of adrenaline and cortisol and make us ill. Kath fought back against anxiety by immersing herself in motherhood, the horses, the Tonimbuk community, and, at that time, it worked for her. Lin was born, then Clay. Kath saw in each boy's birth an opportunity for the family—the whole family—to grow closer. She transformed the arrival of her babies into a whole-family show in her own home, aided and abetted by her doctor.

'I said to Mum, "I want you to be with me." She was very anxious about that, and I persuaded Dad, too. I said, "Come on, Dad, you can do it!" I had a midwife and a doctor—it was a responsible homebirth—and the doctor had been to university with my dad, which was so serendipitous. He said to Dad, "You didn't see your own children born. You'd love this." I held Dad's hand as Lin was born, my first, he turned his head and he was looking right at my dad. I remember just glancing at my dad and he was crying. He had tears streaming down his face, but he was smiling. It was pretty special.'

Kath and Steve grew shared skills in riding, packsaddling, business management and running tourism—but as Kath's skills and confidence grew, she and her father agreed less and less. In particular, they could not agree about something of great value to both of them: the management of horses.

'They were too alike,' says Steve. The prospect of losing again the warmth of the relationship she had rebuilt with her father was not something Kath could bear. 'Kath decided the best thing she could do to preserve her relationship with her dad was to move away, and make a new life elsewhere. We decided then that we would preserve the packsaddle tradition and take people into the High Country,' says Steve. In 1986 they left the forested-in farm and their home in Tonimbuk for the open high plains of the Alps.

'I did a quick road trip with my mate Andrew in an old Toyota driving right up through western Queensland calling into old saddleries and buying bush gear and saddles. We got some war surplus packsaddles that saddler Harry Downs had stored in pig fat,' says Steve.

With this recently purchased tack and gear, a truckload of horses and two little boys, Kath and Steve set off for their new life. They rented land and a small cottage and, having purchased the goodwill of the previous operator and her riding business licence, established their tour company, Bogong Horseback Adventures.

In 1987, a year after she and Steve had moved to the Kiewa Valley, Kath's dad was killed tragically and unexpectedly in a horse-riding accident.

'When Dad died so suddenly, I was just so grateful that a few weeks before I'd given him a hug and told him I loved him. It was at my sister's wedding.

'I said to him, "Thanks for holding the service up so we could be here," and he said, "That's okay, that's okay." I hugged him and I said, "I really love you, Dad." I'll never forget it. He put his arm on my back and he just patted my back and said, "Oh yes, yes, yes,"' Kath says, imitating her father's tone, of a person deeply touched but determined to contain their emotions.

'He always treated me like I was the emotional one, the one who was too sensitive, the one who didn't finish school. After he died, I remember thinking, "I'm going to say that more." I promised myself I would say "I love you" to my boys every day.' And she does. 'Mum always said to me: "You were the one in this family, Kathleen, who built on family, on your own need for strength in family—not many daughters would let their father be there for the birth of their children."

'She said: "I'll forever be grateful to you for letting me be so close to your children." And it was very important for her to have her grandchildren in her life after Dad died. Lin was six and Clay was four. Her involvement with them kept her going.'

After her father died Kath's anxiety became more aggressive.

'Of course, Kath's dad died unexpectedly just as we were starting our business and I was away for days and weeks in the mountains, riding horses in the same kind of environment,' says Steve.

Kath began to have frequent panic attacks. This neat phrase belies the ugliness of being so anxiety-racked that your body systems react as if your world is ending in anguish and torment. When the attack subsides you are left feeling unfit for the business of living. But Kath refused to surrender to fear, and continued on the path she and Steve had planned—preserving the packsaddle tradition, opening up their lives to enrich other people's, helping other people find a connection to horses and to land.

'Connecting with the High Country is something that just happens,' says Kath. 'It doesn't grow on you, it hits you in the face. People fall totally in love with this landscape: it speaks to something really deep in us. The Indigenous people felt this, too, and to connect with land is something not only Indigenous people do. That connection is something that happens to any human being.'

So despite the agony of her anxiety and despite the difficulties of a pioneering lifestyle in their tiny, freezing house, Kath believed that the right thing to do was to keep going as they were.

Kath had finally brought her trichotillomania under control. 'I hid the affliction for years from Steve,' she says, 'and one day when I was quite bad I blurted it out in an ashamed emotional way, Steve hugged me and said, "I don't care, Kath, I will love you if you have no hair at all!" and from that day on I started to heal.' But she was determined nothing like that would occur in her sons' lives. When Lin and Clay went to school, they were creative, artistic, sensitive and adventurous. 'I could see when they were starting to have the same kinds of difficulties I did, and I was down there, talking to the school.' Finally Kath's own trials at school were something she could really value. With understanding for how her parents had been fettered by the time period, Kath did her best to set aside her own generation's prejudices in child rearing. Painful experiences as a child often create a very good parent. Such parents remember how very lonely children can feel, how ashamed, how powerless—how very hard childhood and adolescence can be.

In 1988 Kath and Steve pulled together the wherewithal to begin paying for the little property adjacent to where they were living: Spring Spur. Together they embarked on breeding their own horses, horses that would thrive in high altitudes, had the temperament for packsaddle work and for people, for working as a team. In other words, a special brand of Australian stock horse. Kath and Steve shared all roles in a balanced partnership: making up provisions, caring for Lin and Clay, maintaining the homestead, teaching and caring for trainees, managing their stables and conducting the tours. In the spring, summer and autumn Steve took horses and people into the Alps and was away with them for days at a time. In the winter months, when 'up top' is covered in snow, Steve was away for even longer stretches, conducting tours for the Diamantina Touring Company in Central Australia and the Western Desert, making the extra cash the family needed. To his notebooks he added sketches of clay pans, salt lakes, abandoned objects and desert plants that cunningly gather and fiercely protect their water.

His feeling of being with Kath endured on those long journeys, and it continues to do so.

'You can be with someone who is not there. In the afternoon, even though I'm with a group of riders, I might just drift away with my horse and be alone for two or three hours, but I'm not really alone. Solitude is something I enjoy—long drives on my own, or astride my horse rhythmically travelling across country. In fact, I need and value that solitude—but I'm not really ever alone.'

He is referring again to his extended sense of self of which Kath is part. For Kath, solitude is not so enjoyable. Thinking of another person in their absence quickly leads the person with anxiety to worry for their welfare. A person's physical presence is what reassures Kath: seeing, touching, talking to, learning about, feeding, telling that person she loves them.

She is very much the same with her horses and dogs. Watching horses nose-to-tail, both surrendered to sleep, hearing the beat of her dog's happy tail upon the floor, enjoying the mad playful early-morning gallop to the water trough, the way an animal leans into her scratching hand or gazes at her: all of this is deeply reassuring for Kath. So in addition to her interest in finding better ways to care for people, she is also always looking for new ways to care for these other companions, too. She found both in a revolutionary, innovative method of handling horses.

'In 1990 we saw an advertisement in the paper that read, "Do you have a problem horse?" Below the question was advertised a clinic with one of Australia's best-known teachers of Natural Horsemanship, Wayne Banney. I said to Steve: "Do we have a problem horse? We will need a truck!"' Kath and Steve were captivated by what Wayne said, becoming early adopters (and sharers) of thinking and handling techniques which respect horse psychology. 'It's taken off like mad now, of course. The only part of the horse industry holding out against it is the racing industry,' says Kath.

Understanding animal psychology better is one of the most powerful and little-known new 'technologies' in Australian agriculture. Its power was first demonstrated with horses, but the same way of thinking applies to many different species. To begin with, Kath says, horses are herd animals, and they are also prey animals.

'People are the horses' predators. Their eyes are at the side of their heads; ours are in front.' She is making the point that humans immediately convey their predator status to horses—and that we have to work hard to convey that we don't wish to eat the horse but instead are worthy of being trusted. The ability to empathise with the horse is key. From Wayne Banney, Kath and Steve discovered that what frequently creates 'problem horses' is miscommunication between human and horse.

'We as humans need to understand their language, not vice versa,' says Kath. When you understand what they are feeling, when you can respond in that same language, when you are utterly consistent, then, and only then, can a horse trust you and relax into doing as you direct.'

Even before instituting training techniques based on horse psychology, Kath and Steve were proud of their horses. Each horse is part of the intergenerational pageant of the re-created Australian stock horse. Their foundation sire, Inca Gold, was leased from a friend. In his veins ran the blood of four of the fourteen foundation sires listed in the stud book created in the 1970s—including the renowned blood lines of Radium and Bobbie Bruce, all exemplars of the breed.

There is another heritage that the Bairds have also bred into their horses.

'The brumbies are part of the Australian stock horse story anyway. Some graziers used up top for grazing—which doesn't occur now—but back then they always kept an eye on these herds. They'd turn out one of their own stallions to run in with them over summer and improve the breeding. They would muster them and run them through the yards, cull anything that looked inbred. They might capture and break in a particularly good-looking filly,' says Steve. 'During World War I, breaking in and selling these horses was a profitable second income.

'Recently, through the noughties drought, the government used salt baits to trap the brumbies. Horses will go a long way for salt and there's not much in these mountains. The trap yards were cleared daily, then the horses were kept in our yards down in the valley until they were collected by the Brumby Association for training and sale. Among those horses there was one beautiful mare ...' So some of the horses working in Bogong Horseback Adventures are cousins to the wild brumbies on the mountains.

Part of what the Bairds now offer (sometimes in partnership with Bianca Gillanders) is natural horse-person training.

'When we're teaching horse psychology, words can only do so much. In just an hour of observing the behaviour of horses in the wild, people can learn far more. For themselves they learn to identify the leader—and that's usually an alpha mare—from how she directs the group, how they are looking to her all the time,' says Steve. From the backs of their domesticated kin is the best way to observe the brumbies, say the Bairds.

In this way you can discover for yourself the language of horses. Tail swishes, ear flicking, nuzzling, the cautious turning and looking in a new direction—this communication is all directed at helping group dynamics and ensuring the herd is safe. You watch the leader and see how she corrects the other horses only until the lesson is learned and then stops immediately, and you begin to empathise with the weight of responsibility upon her. For your own horses to be happy, and for you to be safe, you need to become as much like her as a human can.

If you had asked Kath and Steve many years ago why their business was successful they would have given you the wrong answer: their intelligent, educated horses, insights into horse psychology, the revival of the packhorse tradition, teamwork, adventure, their unique access to remote parts of the High Country, Kath's terrific provisioning. They weren't to realise for many years that the one aspect of the business which they hadn't carefully planned was the essential one.

'When we looked back through our Visitors Book we saw the comments were things like, "A wonderful week with the Bairds",' says Steve. 'We realised then that it was time with us that people valued most. It was the family tradition that my mother, Pat, began in our family and that had been part of

Kath's family, of having an open door, of letting people into the heart of the family, of the kinds of conversations that happen around our table.'

In 2003 the Bogong High Plains were struck by lightning and caught fire: two-and-a-half-million hectares burned and smouldered for weeks. What remained was snow-gum skeletons and burned ground, a far cry from the bushy, grassy heathland. The bookings for that season had to be cancelled. Steve's work away became more important in terms of financial survival. This situation was repeated after another serious fire in 2006.

In the absence of the men she loved Kath worked her way through a new level of anxiety. By now her sons were overseas in dangerous environments on horseback. Spring, summer and autumn she busied herself still more with her horses, the many trainees that came to learn horses and hospitality, her visitors and her welcoming: using her skills drawn from the theatre to turn the passing moment into a celebration for her guests. She and Steve took increasing pride in their ability to strengthen and create bonds among their guests: re-teaching the art of conversation, the love of shared adventure and the practice of empathy (not just with horses but with people, too) that lies at the heart of their own lives.

Every year she and Steve together would contribute their expertise in the packhorse tradition (which they had done so much to restore) at festivals like The Man from Snowy River Bush Festival. Winters were always without Steve. Outside her window the snow would be falling and Kath would quell her anxiety and send loving thoughts to him in the desert and to her boys in the mountains far away in South America.

On his travels across country on his horse or as he drives, far away from the distractions of small talk and 'fluff', Steve is always busy with the mental discipline of puzzling out the story behind the landscapes he sees, of building lasting impressions in his mind, and thinking about the words and the lines that will best hold it on the page. These are times of intense concentration.

'When I see a landscape I want to know the geological narrative—how the place was formed—as well as the human narrative. What happened here?' he says.

Steve found time to open his old notebooks and to be surprised by how much they conveyed of how land is marked and changed, of the story of what happened. He began to elaborate on his sketches. The resulting pieces of art quickly found a market. In his art, as in his storytelling, Steve aims to teach people how to read the Australian landscape and recognise in that landscape both our history and our future.

'The nomadic movements, which are still celebrated and still partly there, were movements in response to where the water was in the landscape. The conflicts of first contact between Indigenous and European Australians were about water,' he says.

He tells this not just as an interesting historical fact but as something for us to think about, as less and less rain falls on the land. There are many puzzles in the Australian landscape. Yes, less rain is falling, but that does not entirely explain the increasing ferocity of our bush fires or the speed at which farmed land degrades.

'I'm a follower of what Bill Gammage outlines in his book *The Biggest Estate on Earth*,' he says. 'We're going to see more fire because the modern practice of suppressing and minimising fire creates a very different and volatile environment.'

I also admire this author's work. Early Australian landscape artists recorded vast open grassy plains and, like many

Australian schoolchildren, I was taught that these paintings revealed only the limitation of the painters. Their European childhood meant that they could not see what was really in front of them. I was encouraged to pity these first visitors, who were not 'real Australians' and had painted idealised portraits of parkland instead of the rough Australian bush. It was children like me, who had been born here and knew the land in a way those artists couldn't, who were the real Australians, and who saw the bush as it truly was. This was a lesson taught not just by teachers but by some of my favourite writers, such as Ethel Turner. Our generation would certainly not suffer from the Eurocentrism that had so clouded the visions of those first landscape artists, and we could be proud of that. I swallowed all this hook, line and sinker.

This story undoubtedly fed our nationalism. After all, there is an added sense of possession and belonging when you feel part of a group who has knowledge denied to others. But the story wasn't true. Those painters had simply documented what they saw, and since that time the land had changed. It seems that in our wish to forget that Australia was inhabited before those portrait painters stepped ashore, we didn't consider another and more obvious explanation for the scenes shown in those paintings. Hundreds of years had passed, the land was no longer cared for in the way it had been and the Australian landscape had altered.

In *The Biggest Estate on Earth* historian Bill Gammage adds to these paintings the extensive written work of the early explorers and farmers and proceeds to destroy the false story we were told. His work reveals that Australia was a vast estate, managed cooperatively: the enormous plains on the best soil had been brought into existence by fire-stick farming. Those open, grassed landscapes that greeted the admiring gaze of

European artists were created by Aboriginal people's purposeful, planned, strategic use of fire.

That is not all historians can tell us. The puzzle of just why land degraded so rapidly is being answered, too. How could the early settlers possibly have put such high stock numbers on properties that within fifty years couldn't carry half or a quarter of that number? The conventional wisdom is that they, too, were 'too European' to assess correctly the carrying capacity of Australian land. (Those of us who have farmed Australia in recent years said to ourselves that we'd never have made that mistake.)

The modern agriculturalist had fallen for the myth that, if not uninhabited, this had not been cared-for land at the time of colonisation. That no-one had worked it. We didn't believe the stories of early generations that the soil had been friable, deep and fertile, that grass had grown in thick mats upon it. Previous farmers hadn't known vulnerability when they saw it, and had simply, blindly overstocked the country.

In his book *Dark Emu*, historian Bruce Pascoe outlines the agricultural practices of Aboriginal people. In just one example, grain was harvested, planted, irrigated and the seeds from the best plants were traded. There existed a 'grain belt' stretching across Australia. So, in fact, there had been plenty of feed for sheep and cattle: the stocking rate set by early farmers was a response to that cultivated abundance. When the cultivation practices stopped, that supply rapidly declined. In short, the reason that agricultural land degraded so fast is that Aboriginal people were no longer able to continue the practices that had supported its abundant fertility and our grazing practices didn't change to match.

Voices like those of these two historians, voices like Steve's, of people who are concerned with the puzzles of the Australian landscape that 'hide in plain sight', who can interpret it for us, are increasingly important. The tasks of reversing erosion, producing safe food, storing more carbon and simultaneously preventing fire, all require Australians to understand our continent better.

What has prevented us from seeing the careful cultivation of land by Australian Aboriginal people in the thousands of years before colonisation? This is a question that Kath, particularly, has asked herself. She has also asked herself: 'How do I act with love to change this?' On arriving in the Bogongs she was horrified to find a group of rocky peaks with the official name of Mt Niggerhead and known locally as the 'Niggerheads'. She wrote in protest to councils, to newspapers, to government departments. A storm of controversy broke out in response to her request that the name should be changed. Should the name 'Niggerhead' instead stand as a testament to racism endured? If it was changed, which of the Alpine traditional owners should have naming rights? Was a name change a contribution towards reconciliation, or was it simply 'political correctness gone mad'?

It is in discussions like these that Australia is slowly finding its soul, but if soul-searching is painful individually, it is far worse collectively. There are so many more competing versions of the past and investment in each of these is deep. After all, as George Orwell wrote: 'He who controls the past controls the future. He who controls the present controls the past.'

In the end Kath, like most people, heard about the name change some time after it had occurred. The Victorian Government consulted with local Indigenous groups and the peaks are now known as the Jaithmathangs, and the central peak as Mt Jaithmathang. More powerful than the name change is the story of that change: Indigenous people in the present were allowed to shape the story of the past and with that given ownership of the future.

In 2007, as the naming controversy Kath had unleashed raged on, Kath's mother fell ill.

'I nursed her here. We had the most amazing special time, I'll never regret one minute of it. Mum said to me, the day before she died: "You are just both the most incredible people." She was holding our hands and we said, "We love you, too, Mum." Her death was so peaceful, I can't think of it without feeling love.'

But after her mother died Kath's anxiety went up another gear, and this time, for the first time, she couldn't bring it back under control by staying busy and loving harder.

'I ended up with horrendous psoriasis. I could not squeeze a lemon as my hands were so badly affected. There was now all this fear overtaking me. I'd be out on a pack trip and my hands would be slippery with sweat. I could not walk out the door without feeling like an actor, like I was in a play, everything felt surreal. I had tried a lot of medication before, but it had taken away my passion. I'd rather have passion than not have anxiety, so I'd stopped them.

'People said, "You must be stressed. Your liver must be stressed, try a liver tonic." I tried a liver tonic, acupuncture, everything. Then one day I went to the hairdresser's. I thought, "I'm even anxious about coming into the hairdresser's, what sort of idiot am I?" My hairdresser, Kate, just hugged me and said, "Kath, by this stage your brain would have changed with all these years of stress, your brain is a mess. If your doctor doesn't give you this drug you can come and see my doctor."

'Well, I went to see my doctor and I told him what Kate had said and he said, "Well, that's funny, because that was the drug I was thinking of for you." For the first three weeks I felt a bit drugged, then I had another anxiety attack and they upped my dose and I haven't had a panic attack since. I feel this enormous weight has been lifted.' She still feels anxiety, but she is, she says now, liberated, almost a different person. This is just as well, because they have all, Lin and Clay, too, continued to lead exciting lives.

Adventure, freedom, art, observing, fixing, making do, packing, designing, cooking, compassion, cleaning, listening, storytelling, being part of a team even when you were only little—learning all that, helping their parents the whole way, the Baird boys, both with Steve's dark hair and Kath's dazzling, life-affirming grin, completed school and went to university. Lin studied multimedia, Clay filmmaking, and then, at the start of the 2000s, they left Australia. They set off, in true Baird fashion, to have adventures (and to take notes as they went). They worked in horse outfits from California to the United Kingdom as cooks and expedition leaders. Not until the late 2000s did they come home to become formally part of the thirty-year-old and multiple-award-winning family business.

There's none of the women's-work-versus-men's-work divide here, and that is just as well. It is now clear to the whole Baird family that it is around their family tradition of open doors, hearts and conversation that their business will grow. This means cooking more meals, growing more food, building more places to accommodate the growing number of trainees and paying guests, breeding more horses, and everyone is involved with everything. Their little property, Spring Spur, from which Bogong Horseback Adventures departs and to which they return, is being developed to reflect this. In 2003 Steve's mother, Pat, wrote a verse which captured that dream, and those words inspired the design of five-star accommodation for their adventurous guests.

First the stable for the beasts, second the house for shelter, then the garden for sustenance
Each growing strength and form, beauty of structure, together they make a place in the mountain arms
People are like the things they build, be it bricks or breakfast, food is cooked together, enjoyed together by love and laughter
Keep building this rambling, unruly and embracing thing called family.

The resulting new building was created to reflect the genius of this place: horses, theatre and tradition, the Alps and adventure beyond, the family with their door wide open, and at Kath's long family table, good conversation and nourishing food. Every single Baird helped in the design and Steve's architectural mind and experienced hand drafted the plans. They describe the resulting structure as 'Showground Pavilion' style: and it is a big, peaceful building that sits gently on the land.

On the walls hangs Steve's art. He is making more time for it now.

'Artists develop their own vocabulary. I don't have patience for details, I'm not drawing the landscape but the story within the landscape,' he says. Many of Steve's trees and plants have a wistful curl and humanlike quality that remind me of Leunig, but Steve also compartmentalises land types or parts of a story as many Indigenous artists do. Most recently he has been painting two series which feature the companion horses of the explorers.

'Billy was Burke's famous dapple-grey horse. You see him in the early newspaper illustrations enjoying the departure party they threw for Burke and Wills. He's high-spirited and bold. Then you see him labouring, becoming a good little workhorse. He reaches Cooper Creek with them, and then the Gulf of Carpentaria, but then on the way back, they eat him.'

Each of these paintings is a story fragment that forces us to think again about how we treat the animals in our lives, about what is humane and what is not, to empathise with the horses, the explorers, the Aboriginal people and the water-starved, sunburned, story-laden land itself.

'People say to me, "You are living the dream." But you don't plan these things. Life unfolds,' says Kath.

Often though, life unfolds in response to how we live it. Kath and Steve's story began with love at first sight and has grown into a shared life's work. I thought at the outset that their life's work was the building of a family business in the Australian High Country around the restoration of the packhorse tradition. But their life's work is living the most radical of ideals. All their actions—to empathise, to rehabilitate, to preserve, to give, to take turns, to strengthen, to allow, to set free and to make safe—spring from their dedication to that revolutionary ideal. Their shared life's work is love itself.

Like a River

Rebel Black and Michael Matson,
Lightning Ridge, New South Wales

To reach Lightning Ridge you have to drive through the NSW plains country. It is blue-chip farming land, but fences aren't well maintained, there are towns of empty shops and paddocks with good feed but no stock, which is often a sign that the farmer cannot afford to restock. The east coast of Australia is so much richer than the west, despite the mining boom, so I had not expected to see rural areas with such a denuded look.

Lightning Ridge is home to Rebel Black and Michael Matson. They have a story to tell of a life and love that runs deep, one that is tied to the land where they live. Rebel directs me by mobile to their house in the opal fields—there is no standard signage here. Rebel grew up on a property east of Coonabarabran, a property similar to those that we are driving through, but her family's interests and reach went well beyond the gates of the family farm. Her paternal grandfather, Roderick Black, a giant in rural politics, believed that rural media was vital to rural voices being heard, and that in turn was vital to creating and keeping prosperity in the bush. He had no faith in the market to deliver these things—he believed in market controls to ensure prices that would allow people to keep growing their products. As Australians currently mourn the sale of farm land to overseas buyers, it is clear how very prescient he was: without reliable prices that include a margin for profit, farmers have steadily slipped further into debt, making selling the farm inevitable. This desire to keep what is earned in the bush working for the people who live there has become Rebel and Michael's passion, too.

Lightning Ridge is famous throughout the world for two things—opals and fossils—and to showcase them properly the town is building a new Australian Opal Centre. 'It's a centre of excellence in all things opal: science, education, research, value-adding and telling the stories of the people of the opal fields in all of Australia,' Rebel explains. 'There's a collection that's been accrued—still is accruing. This collection is worth about three million dollars. Opalised fossils, opal and heritage items from the opal fields have been donated by people from across the world: miners, collectors, buyers and retailers. Opals are Australia's version of the crown jewels and they're also natural treasures.'

'Who wants the crown jewels when you've got opal,' says Michael, who has just emerged from the shower and caught the tail end of what Rebel is saying. He is completely serious.

So is the opal community of Australia and Lightning Ridge. They need thirty million dollars to complete the construction of the Australian Opal Centre. They want this place not just as a focus for the town's endeavours, but as a catalyst for regeneration across the region. Rebel is the chairperson for the project.

'We have partnerships with universities, people that are studying our collection. The dinosaurs in Australia—particularly the dinosaurs here—are turning our understanding of dinosaur evolution on its head. Opal miners are finding new species here often. The centre we have already fills a vast number of functions, but the new building will also have space for conferences, a theatre, discovery rooms, labs and gallery space for exhibitions. It's thirty metres by a hundred metres, two storeys, built underground, fully off the grid—it's a Glen Murcutt building, designed for this landscape. There are people all over the world waiting for this building. I'll take you and show you the big hole in the ground we've dug already. We're very proud of our hole!

'And it won't be just for the visitors or the people of the opal fields, it's going to be a beacon for the kids who live out here, the ones who never leave their town,' Rebel says. 'I want them to know they can dream big and make it happen; that they can be scientists or palaeontologists or opal miners or jewellers or engineers or architects. This building and the project will inspire all of these things and some we haven't even thought about!'

'Have you seen much opal?' Michael asks.

The only opal I've handled was sent to me as a gift by a reader of another of my books: it's a tiny black opal. The giver had been told it came from Cue, my closest town, but research suggests that this isn't possible, although black opal was once mined in Coolgardie, and so perhaps it came from there. However, even this little piece of black opal seems to hold a world, if I just look close enough. Carl Jung wrote that the very best symbol for the human soul was stone. Surely then, the very best stone to symbolise the soul is the precious opal, with its play of colour, its fluid nature and the way each opal feels like some miniscule, exotic planet.

'No two are the same,' says Michael, liking the idea of opal as the soul stone. 'Every single one is its own creation by Mother Nature.'

Michael also brings out some fossils to show me. Here are yabby buttons, minute pine cones, a lungfish jawbone, a shark's tooth, twigs, the bones of some dainty marsupial, a plesiosaur tooth, mussels, bird bones, land snails, dinosaur bones—all from ancient times long before ours.

'A lot of people who dig opal throw this away, it's not worth a dollar to them,' says Michael.

He reverently tips the fossils out onto a white dinner plate and hands me a jeweller's loupe for better viewing. They are so prettily delicate. I pick up the fossil of a land snail, an elegant spiralling twist no longer than the nail of my little finger. I can just see the facets on the shell, the careful turnings where this tiny builder ensured her house met the peculiar mathematical criteria of her species so very long ago. A fish vertebra, over one hundred million years old, gleams as freshly as if it had just been filleted. When I fit the loupe to my eye, lean closer, I can see a roseate glow, a run of violet colour. If only it were brighter! 'I want to lick it—is that okay?' I say.

'Just do it. We're all rock lickers here,' says Rebel.

So I lick it, and it comes to brighter life. I'm looking past the glistening fresh surface now, I'm looking in. The veins and nerve supplies of the bone are picked out in shifting three-dimensional colour: a palaeontologist's dream.

In the late Cretaceous period, Lightning Ridge was a freshwater billabong, fringed in Wollemi pine—type ferns, on the edge of the inland sea. It was a bright, watery place that maintained not only all the animals we no longer see, but those we still find today. There are the glittery-winged dragonflies, so beautiful and yet so insatiable and voracious, both in larval and adult form. The water beetles, the scarlet fairy shrimps and the shovel-headed shrimps—hunting and hiding, multiplying after rain, dying in the dry times—would have been food for the yabbies, and the yabbies the food for the monotremes (like platypus and echidna) of the Australian Cretaceous period.

'At Coober Pedy they find lots of fossilised plesiosaur bones, but here we find fossilised plesiosaur teeth. Like modern-day sharks they swam up to the fresh water to mate, to drop lice, and then swam back to the sea. The behaviour was the same. That's what the palaeontologists think anyway,' says Rebel.

All opal is old, old, old. It was formed as water dripped down from massive inland seas through the bed into the earth, and on the way collected silica. This silica-laden gel eventually would reach a cavity or creep out along a hard bed or infiltrate and ultimately replace another mineral. Some of that water remains in the stone: three to ten percent of their content is water.

I say that I've heard there are three different theories on finding opal, and am about to start talking about box trees, which are considered to be one of the main markers of opal below.

'Probably all three theories are wrong,' says Michael. 'You're far better off reading what you can see in the land. It's all to do with what was.' He has a geologist's eye for deep time and he reads the land not from above, but from within it, interpreting the red-and-purple shadings of iron, the fall of the different soil types, imagining the sliding and settling of the silica gel under the pull of gravity. Michael puts away the fossils and brings out a cracked sandstone rock. He lets it fall open in his hand: two halves of a holographic crystal in blue and green, radiant and flaming. This is an opal nobby, and Michael cracked it in half with his pick. The opals are packed up: it is time for dinner.

We are sitting around the table eating Rebel's extraordinarily good cooking. Food can be all kinds of things, but this food is the cleanest, most delicious fuel for the human body. The savoury sprinkles, the homegrown vegetables, the Murray River cod caught by Michael and Rebel's handmade chocolates are all restaurant quality, which is not surprising as the couple used to own a restaurant.

'When Rebel's cooking,' says Michael with deep satisfaction, directing his sweet smile at Rebel, 'the food's always good.' Rebel smiles back at him with pure delight. Her competence on a range of fronts does not mean that she has no need of appreciation—a mistake people can often make when meeting someone like Rebel. It is too easy to forget that people try hardest when they care most—and caring most means you are also at your most vulnerable. Rebel cares a great deal, does many different kinds of work, and appears intimidatingly competent no matter how much she tries to show her journey with all her failures. But she is sustained in her work by Michael, who sees what it all costs, how hard she tries, how bravely she risks and how deeply she feels. Michael's loving praise is vital to her.

Their restaurant, Dig In, won state awards for innovation in tourism and it won regional awards for the excellence of the food. When they tell me they gave the restaurant away, it is clear to me that I have only scratched the surface in my understanding of what motivates Rebel and Michael.

Rebel is clearly multi-talented. I find I can cast her like a great character actor—those women who play the unusual and eccentric characters but are almost unrecognisable from part to part. Her bone structure is of the grand-dame type, but her colouring is soft—she's not a redhead, not blonde, nor brunette, but between them all. Her eyes are a rich Mediterranean blue. I'd happily cast her as the journo with deep networks, the too-smart-for-her-own-good kid, the fired-up self-starter flying by the seat of her pants, the soft-eyed wise woman, the lonely girl, the business guru, the powerful community organiser and advocate, the wild child, the timely hostess who can add grace to any occasion, the spirited cook-gardener—and all of these things she's been and is. It is no wonder that figuring out who she was meant to be, and what she was meant to do in the world, were so very difficult for her.

I ask—and apparently everyone does—if Rebel is her birth name. It is. Her mother thought it sounded both feminine and strong. Neither she nor Rebel's dad shared the view of others that the name has connotations of 'wildness' and 'naughtiness' and were surprised by the criticism of their little girl's name that flew around their farming district and friendship circles. However, Rebel isn't rebellious in the 'naughty' sense. She's a non-conformist, a trailblazer and an innovator, far more proactive than she is reactive.

A country childhood provides a love of nature that will give lifelong comfort and balance, and it teaches children how to work hard and to keep going even when tired or sore. It also teaches children to look for those counterbalances and comforts early, because a farm upbringing means that you know about suffering, compromise, uncertainty and death almost from the beginning. When such a rich, complex life experience is made available to the kind of person Rebel is—perceptive, empathic, passionate, sensitive, motivated—the end result is a child who has seen more, thought more, cared more, felt more and hurt more than other children their age. Such children move into the halfway house between adulthood and childhood much earlier, and are out of synch with their peers. It is therefore no shock to learn that at eight years old Rebel was raising money for charity.

She had a happy childhood on the family farm—and the farm became even more important to her as a teenager. Her parents put their children on the payroll very early and this decision helped meet Rebel's need to be valued for what she could give. The unconditional love of family members and the real physical effort in the natural world gave her a break from the restless emotional long days of unhooking and reweaving her thoughts to see if she could discern who she was. It was not something she seemed able to discover at school. Having friends accept you for who you are is vital for a young person's mental health. When you are innately different—and a child who initiates raising money at the age of eight may be admirable but is certainly unusual—those differences typically are most painful in the teenage years. Finding a 'tribe' or subculture is the most common way of coping, but sometimes there just isn't a tribe into which you fit, even if you try very hard. Loneliness is something that you accept even as you find ways to blend in, to be silent and to sell an acceptable version of yourself, sometimes, even to yourself.

Occasionally this process of self-discovery is short-circuited by a focus on 'what you are good at'. Our society so often confuses identity with work role, so this is not surprising. Rebel was good at articulating ideas, at writing, at advocating: surely then, she should be a lawyer. Work role and identity and future all secured in one word! Law also seemed to fit with the conviction others had that Rebel should put her communication and advocacy gifts to work in improving the lives of people who live in rural and remote communities.

Rebel left school in 1996 and then studied law, only to leave university after two years. She didn't know exactly the work she wanted to do, but she did know that law wasn't going to take her there. That was followed by one year of working, partying and generally not living up to her own expectations. 'Self-destruction was a pathway I was well and truly on, but always with the sense that I was better than that—that it wasn't going to be the rest of my life, but maybe a blip on the road.'

In a resurgence of her farming family values—so rich in adult role and responsibility—she set her sights on rejoining the world of the grown-ups and making her mark there.

She applied for two jobs: one in Lightning Ridge, which had already impressed her as the 'arse-end of Australia' and where she didn't want to go, and the other in the Kimberley, where she desperately did want to go. To win *The Ridge News*'s editorial position required her to perform in spelling and grammar, which she did.

'On top of this, the boss thought I might stay a bit longer than most and it turned out he was right.'

The job was offered to her and she held off a little while on accepting, in the hope of the Kimberley job. She heard nothing from them. Then, when she'd been at Lightning Ridge a week, living in her uncomfortable flat without air conditioning, the call came that the Kimberley job was hers. She didn't take it: when Rebel takes on a job her commitment to it is real.

'When I moved here to Lightning Ridge I didn't know anyone, and I'm an introvert—running a newspaper, meeting people I'd never met before, dealing with them all day, it was pretty intense for me. For the first two months, after work, I just sat in my one-bedroom flat and smoked and drank and thought, "What the hell have I done," and also, "I'm not going to quit."'

At the age of twenty-one and three months into her first adult job, Rebel met Michael at the pub. Michael was twenty-seven and grieving the loss of his marriage and in particular regretting the implications of that for his two young children, Tori and Kyle. His children, and his ex-wife, too, were still in Lightning Ridge and he saw them often, but it wasn't as it had been.

Neither Michael nor Rebel was ready for the other person to appear in their life. Sometimes, falling in love happens anyway.

'For me it was instant connection—I knew, and I knew that he knew,' says Rebel. They became friends in one long night of easy chatting, learning the bare bones of the other person's life. For Rebel it was simple: 'I just knew I wanted to be around him, even though we were both struggling.'

Although she was younger and hadn't known Michael's kind of grief herself, Rebel's empathy was instant. And she had wounds, too: some people seem to be born feeling an existential grief at the pain and suffering in the world with the accompanying urge to heal as much of it as they can, and Rebel is one such person.

'I lived next door to Michael's children. He helped me move from my flat, where I couldn't open the window, into the house next door so the kids and I became great friends over the back fence, even without him. They used to sing out to me at six o'clock in the morning, "Come play with us." Michael and I were friends quite some time before anything else happened. Then the kids moved to the coast and that was pretty sad. I just think there was a lot of pain and unresolved stuff for him—and for me. I was working through who I was meant to be and what was the right thing to do. I was paving my pathway. We were never not going to be together, it just took some figuring out.'

Very gently and with some stopping and starting, they became romantically involved. Michael's sadness eased. In committing to Michael, Rebel stepped away from her self-destructive pathway.

At work Rebel's energy and imagination and networking skills were increasing the size, spread and sales of *The Ridge News*. Networking on behalf of the paper helped her engage deeply with the community of Lightning Ridge.

'This place is incredibly giving,' she says. 'Forgiving as well—I think I was quite arrogant and fairly bombastic and I came in a bit like a bulldozer and was on every committee.'

Being acknowledged for the irrepressible bubbling of new ideas that comes with her energy, skills and drive was important to Rebel, but sometimes she found that though her work ethic and skills were welcome, her ideas were not. Being appreciated for your work ethic and your skills but being disqualified from offering new ways to do things can feel as though you are being used. When only some aspects of your character are considered to be 'socially acceptable' it hurts. Rebel continued to share her skills, but found that she was sharing her ideas less, as if the spring from which they bubbled had been capped by the disapproval of others. Rather than becoming closer to who she wanted to be, only fragments of that whole person were being let through—the closest to being all of herself was achieved when she was with Michael and the children.

'Michael has never not believed in me and rarely said no to crazy, outlandish ideas,' she says. 'I'd done a leadership program and I said to the others doing the course, we'll have the reunion in Lightning Ridge and we'll cook the meal for you in our new outdoor restaurant.'

There was at this stage no restaurant. Michael was mining and Rebel was working full-time as an Arts Development Officer. (In fact, all through the years the restaurant was open both were working full-time: Michael mined and Rebel worked in community development.)

'So we built it. We built the kitchen out of shipping containers and five tables out of concrete. We decided it would be a camp-oven restaurant, and the night before we opened I thought I'd better have a crack at using a camp oven. It was slightly nerve-racking, but no-one got food poisoning.'

Dig In opened in 2004, three years into their relationship. They launched with capital borrowed from their parents and ran on Rebel's experience in restaurants from several years before, but the whole thing was new to Michael.

'The restaurant was my dream—I came back from a night at the foothills of the MacDonnell Ranges listening to the didgeridoo playing under the stars. I said to Michael, "We have to do this—it's a gaping great hole in the whole of New South Wales," and he said, "Oh, okay." He wasn't convinced, but he built it, and he cooked every night, not enjoying most moments I'm sure. He did a great job. The old ducks loved him, the old guys loved him. It just wasn't his passion, but he did it.'

The restaurant, even though it only opened by prior arrangement, was made more complex by the limitations under which they operated.

'We did the first three years without a stove. I prepped everything on butane burners. We did a wedding for a hundred and twenty on butane burners. Michael's mother was amazing, she knew people, food, production lines, fast prep. Whenever we had a group bigger than ten she was there helping us—my mum helped, too, and Michael's dad was the builder. We couldn't have done it without the support of our family.

'We ended up with a set menu—always golden syrup dumplings for dessert. They're good, bloody easy and cheap. There's such a small margin in food so you have to be smart.'

Rebel and Michael's restaurant was about much more than food. They employed elders to tell Dreamtime stories, local singers to perform and their staff were eclectic and interesting.

Listening to Rebel talk about business models is illuminating. She loves the constraints of business as a spur to creativity the way a poet loves the limitations of a ballad or a haiku. I'd understood that running a business meant that you catered to the consumer, but Rebel doesn't think so. She believes instead in finding a way to locate the consumer who is interested in what it is you can do.

In terms of business she is bold. She simply commits.

In 2008, and using all the skills developed at the restaurant, Michael and Rebel carefully designed an enchanting, never-to-be-repeated evening for their loved ones. They married at Never Never Creek in the Promised Land. (So magical are these names I had to look them up: it really is a place.) Rebel was to receive the most meaningful of wedding presents on her return from their honeymoon—what she describes as a 'deep learning'.

'We decided to surprise the children, and they were so excited to see us and Tori said to me, "I really missed you," and I just broke down inside. It had never occurred to me that I was much more than someone who cooked food and cleaned up for them. I loved them, but I hadn't realised that they loved me.'

Rebel and Michael closed the restaurant just as it was starting to really hit its stride. This was mostly because there were other things they both wanted to do more, but Rebel feels there was another element to her decision as well. She has thought deeply about this as interrupting a pathway to success is not something Rebel wants to ever do again. She talks often about mindsets: that a belief or a story can underpin a set of behaviours that can prevent you gaining something you want. In this case, she suspects she partly closed the restaurant because her mindset was that life was too hard to allow quick success. Their restaurant had been such a swift hit and if she had recognised that at the time, she says, she'd have had to change much of what she believed, to find new stories to tell herself about how life works. (Of course, she's gone to find and tell those new stories anyway.)

'The restaurant had been closed for a couple of years when we worked out that having it closed broke our hearts. It had a good energy there, everyone had a great time, it was a good little business, it just was that Michael and I had other things to do. And so there was the plan to give someone else a crack.'

It was a wild plan, giving the restaurant away. It didn't work out as they had hoped, as a cost-neutral win-win. They lost money. Rebel and Michael say they've taken from this an enduring lesson: people are less likely to value something given for free.

Getting to know Lightning Ridge and Michael went hand in hand for Rebel. 'Opal is Michael's passion, his addiction,' she says. 'It's the love story, really: he's here for the opals and I'm here because he's here.

'People used to say to me, "What do you live in Lightning Ridge for?"' She mimics the dismissive, critical tone in which this kind of rhetorical question was asked.

The risk for people like Rebel, who have stayed in a place or moved because of a loved one, is becoming a martyr to the situation: choosing not to find a solution, and instead taking advantage of the compassion their circumstance can create.

'Lightning Ridge always felt like my home, and I adore Michael and I wouldn't want to be anywhere else, but there was still a feeling that I should be somewhere else, that I couldn't just be here and love it. I wasn't consciously doing it, but I had bought into that "life is hard" mindset—I'd bought into the story the landscape tells. Once I let go of that people stopped asking me why I live here.'

So many people in rural and remote communities feel like Rebel once did, but not all of them manage to cross over into having meaningful lives in the place life (and love) has planted them. The idea that the worthwhile, important lives can only happen in the big cities—in Sydney, Melbourne, London, New York—so often underlies this. This is counterbalanced by the idea that Australian identity is formed by our wide brown land, with its opal skies. Bush dwellers might not lead the important lives, but it is living in hardship and isolation that creates the culture of place so important to other Australians.

Rebel once bought into these concepts, but no longer. She says instead that rural and remote people can live deeply connected lives, where things work out well, where it doesn't have to be hard, and also that those lives can be every bit as important as a life of making it big in a city. In support of this belief, Rebel co-developed an online community called THE (Thriving Healing Evolving) Rural Woman, in which rural women from around Australia find friendship, inspiring conversations and life and business coaching; it's a place to grow, to thrive—to 'bloom where you are planted'.

'My involvement with the Australian Opal Centre is a big way of blooming where I'm planted, and it is also about creating a catalyst for change out here. Through the work I do with rural women I see two very strong beliefs embedded in rural people: "life is hard" and "there's not enough". And that belief in scarcity means people feel like they're in competition. So the Australian Opal Centre is also about calling out that scarcity culture in a very big way. We can cooperate rather than compete (and there are genuine win-wins) and we are worthy of this investment.'

Rebel is trying to secure the government funding and private sponsorship required for the Australian Opal Centre.

'From just about every level of government what I hear is, "Your biggest problem is that all the players in your industry don't work together." And when I workshop that afterwards

I think: "What does working together look like? It's showing up, it's investing time and money, having everyone in the room, everyone standing certain in what we're trying to do and contributing. That's exactly what we're doing! What the heck more do they want?" And I realised I'd been telling all levels of government they need to sit around that table with us, yet they tell us that is not how it works. They say that each department works on its own. So while they say, "You must work together," and we are doing that, they don't know how to work together themselves. So they can't recognise it when we are!'

While Rebel and the rest of the committee are trying to find a new way of communicating 'working together' with government, they are not stopping there.

'The community raised the funds to dig the hole for the building. If we could get two or three wealthy individuals to fund the centre, to take the gamble with us, to share the excitement of that part of the opal story ...'

Michael also grew up in a culture of giving when you had something to give, helping out when you had time and supporting other people's dreams. Indeed, it is hard to imagine many other places where a character like his could have been formed.

Michael's parents, Lindsay and Heather, moved to Lightning Ridge after Lindsay, then a builder, asked his boss for a pay rise. The answer was no—someone else would take his job for that same wage, so there was no need to pay Lindsay more. This answer struck Lindsay as deeply wrong, so revealing of a society that had stopped valuing the individual that he quit in disgust. This revulsion propelled him to leave not just his job, but Melbourne. He and Heather hit the wide, open road hoping to find black opal and make their fortune, or if not that, then to live life on their terms.

Putting down a mine is hard work now, but it was even harder work then. With Lindsay on the crowbar and Heather on the shovel, they were hand-sinking shafts, down through the soil and shincracker rock laid down in the last few million years on their way to the much older opal dirt, six to eighteen metres below the surface. These days, miners use an auger for this work.

'There's such hardship that sits around that story at that time in history, but also incredible mateship and camaraderie,' says Rebel.

This was balanced by the darker side of Lightning Ridge: rumours rushing like wildfire from claim to claim, the thieving 'opal ratters' and the need to protect your find and equipment against their depredations.

That's the thing about Lightning Ridge. It's a place where people have made fortunes and will continue to do so.

'Anyone can come put a hole down and maybe become a millionaire. People do it, they do the mining course and register a claim and sometimes they're rich and sometimes they're not. It's the last frontier for entrepreneurs,' says Rebel.

Opal mining does make some people rich, but it makes others patient, persistent and philosophical. It makes you these things, or it does your head in or breaks your heart. It is purely the province of the small miner: large industrial methods don't work in opal mining. Added to that, the rules stop empire building, because no-one can hold more than two mineral claims in their name.

Michael has always wanted to prospect and mine for opal. In the long hours underground, alone in his head, he appears to have developed the ability to care only about the essentials of life: other people to love and help and team up with, places to mine opal, time to sort opal, time to plan and build things for mining more opal, good food on the table, time to garden, places to fish, places to explore. He's a sage, a philosopher, with a dearly bought wisdom, but I'm not sure all of it has been dearly bought. I suspect that early in life he hit upon his recipe for happiness and has returned to it time and again.

Looking out of the window of Rebel's four-wheel drive as we travel through Lightning Ridge, I decide that Michael was remarkably lucky to grow up in such a fairytale place. Not fairytale as in pretty, because it is not, instead it is fantastical: when the rest of Australia legislated out eccentricity, marching to your own crazy beat and the matchless ingenuity of making do, it all moved here. Mullock piles left from opal mining interrupt every streetscape and house yard. Some houses are barely recognisable as houses. Homemade mining machines rust into the rust-coloured land and every day this landscape shifts and morphs to the whims and needs of the people who live here.

There are no street signs and numbered car doors ease you through the labyrinth of the opal fields, where houses appear to have randomly and unsteadily unloaded themselves from trucks and hunkered down next to a dig. Other houses have latched themselves onto something else—a caravan, a tram, a shed. Roofs are of mismatched heights or they are crazily high-domed or flow unsteadily down.

I am particularly struck with the 'Universe Observatory' or 'Astronomer's Monument' built by Polish man Alex Szperlak. He changed his name to Robinson Crusoe, and using concrete formed up in twenty- and sixty-litre drums, built this loco rococo structure, which calls to my mind a nest of towering, angular cactus plants. Over every surface he has scribbled arcane symbols that refer to the works of Copernicus, Galileo, Newton and Hoyle, in homage to them, but also to tell those of us with mundane minds that he, Robinson Crusoe, was as visionary and just as misunderstood.

We've left Lightning Ridge behind and are approaching Michael's mine. We must spend some time down there, says Rebel, because underground is the place Michael is most himself. A collar of corrugated iron sits around the top of the mine, a long piece of drill steel is suspended across it, and from that a long ladder descends some eighteen metres. Michael comes up to greet us and to guide us down the ladder, and Rebel gives me a quick smile as I begin to descend—and waves her phone at me to tell me that she's going to be productively occupied above ground while I am below.

In the opal mine the walls and floor are mostly of a whitish-dun clay—stiff, soft, nearly waterless. The occasional red-and-purple shadings are put there by iron. The mine is spacious and balmy: fresh air is pumped in. Michael, from under the cloud of soft light cast by his miner's hat, warmly encourages me to keep digging. I have the awful feeling that if we do find good opal in his mine he would want us to keep it: the expression 'generous to a fault' springs to mind. Even though Michael has told us a number of million-dollar-day stories of people finding a king's ransom of opals in just a king-size mattress of dirt or happening upon a thick vein of opal or even a large thigh-bone of opalised fossil, he hasn't yet found a fortune in opal. Despite this, his generosity to other miners and in the community is well known, and he ceaselessly presses pieces of opal he insists 'I'd not get much for' on me.

'Follow the colour,' he says in his warm, easy drawl, an addict sharing his addiction. 'Keep on going, you never know.' I want to find opal, and with my screwdriver I keep digging because the opal obsession has me already, and also because, there, in the torchlight, in speckles and trailing dashes, like a guppy flashing past in its tank, I see opal travelling deeper into the clay. This is black opal, and the only place in the world it is being found in volume right now is here.

I keep digging, circling around and behind the sliver of opal before me. Every now and then I slam my hand into the wall—it is painful, but I don't care. And then, it's gone. The play of colour that was living on the wall is no more. Despite all my care it has flaked off and dispersed on the dun-coloured floor. I thought I'd found a nobby—an opal rock—but instead it was a nano-thin layer of opal painted over clay.

Michael is quick to commiserate. I know already that his particular dream is to find the mind-blowingly rare red opal and he tells us of the time he'd found a seam of red opal. It was the size of a dinner plate, the pure red of a robin redbreast and it lit their mine like light behind stained glass. He and his father dug around it with excruciating care. Finally it was time to lift it and, just as happened to me, the opal crumbled into tiny pieces like icing sugar and poured away before their horrified eyes.

Michael has been looking for opal nearly all his life. Added to a childhood made extraordinary by his good parents, a fantastical morphing landscape holding good, bad and crazy guys, the myth and legend of the opal fields, he only needed a quest to complete the recipe for a storybook childhood, and he had that, too.

'I went to the original open cut, where the old timers had been—they'd write on the roof with their candles. A lot of the drives are only a foot wide. You crawl in on your belly. Kids now wouldn't be allowed—bad air and cave-ins,' says Michael.

It is easy to miss opal when you dig. Along with opal dirt, opals are vacuumed up and out of the mine. The day's diggings are then taken to be agitated in cement mixers in a process called 'winding it down'. The cement mixers are all located together along the banks of a dam (which supplies the water) and reclamation or settlement pond (where the non-toxic opal clay drains to): a shared facility run by the Opal Miners Association.

When he finds opal Michael rubs it down to gauge its quality, and then he sorts it into parcels containing opal of similar quality. The next step is selling.

Many houses in Lightning Ridge have a 'buying now' shingle out the front, but the local buyers aren't the only people shopping for opal. Opal dealers charter planes to fly in to Lightning Ridge—or they may come in posing as tourists or even students in order to gather information anonymously, and then purchase large quantities of opal.

Opal jewellery has featured high-domed, oval stones, but this is a tradition that the industry is beginning to move away from. I'm yet to see any of the new opal jewellery, but Rebel assures me it is very different to what I might have grown up seeing.

'About ten years ago they started a design award for free-form opal, to encourage carving and cutting the opal to keep a more natural shape and retain more opal. It was a real catalyst for the industry to change and for the market to adapt,' says Rebel.

At a local shop, I meet Vicki, a friend of Rebel's. Vicki has the opal bug, too: she's a designer and retailer. It is here that I grasp just why high-grade opal is valued as much as diamond and gold. The first tray I see shows carefully matched small stones glowing in a rainbow array. I hadn't realised before that opal can do it all: sapphire, amethyst, aquamarine, emerald, ruby, amber and onyx. It's a chameleon stone, but this copycatting is a piece of dazzling illusion. Opal is not at all like any other gem.

'Opal doesn't have a crystalline structure like other gemstones. So, for example, under high magnification you'll see that a diamond might have a quadron or a trigon crystal structure,' says Vicki. 'We call those inclusions—the natural fracture or fissure of that crystal. But opal is amorphous. When you look at an opal under the microscope it has inclusions as well, but they're not fractures or fissures, they're patterns.'

'It's like the patterns exist in the "headspace" of the opal,' adds Rebel, and I understand. It is almost as if the opal has imagined the colour into being.

And there are other opals which look like no other gemstone: there's the matrix opal, where opal colour flickers in and out of the rock hosting it, and the honey potch, which reminds me of sap bubbling from a tree and glowing in the sun. Potch is opal without a play of colour. It lies discarded on the mullock piles along with the occasional piece of missed opal. It took a while for the jewellers to see the potential of the honey-coloured potch, but they are using it now.

Some of it looks edible, like a candied jelly.

'It just plops out from the sandstone,' says Rebel.

Some of the most extraordinary pieces look as if they have just been found and lovingly rubbed and then left strictly alone—this is the free-form jewellery which seems to be saved for the biggest of the black opals. Per carat, some are worth more than diamonds. Their colours sparkle out against the natural backing of black-and-grey potch. Had I dollars enough I could purchase an opal holding a night of fireworks, or one containing my very own piece of tropical reef, or a Bollywood-set piece of silk-clad dancers, or a flight of glittering budgerigars, or even an ever-living enchantment of wildflowers shifting on the wind.

Behind me Vicki and Rebel have started talking marketing, and this is clearly a conversation that has been going for years.

Without a big player (such as De Beers) and big dollars, marketing opal requires an ingenious approach. Once Vicki contributed black opal to adorn a tall and beautiful hat that was on display at all the big fashion shows around the world. Opal mining and selling is a cottage industry in some ways, albeit the most glamorous cottage industry I have ever heard of.

None of the challenges deter Michael—not the mines barren of opal, the opal ratters, poor opal prices nor the built-in barriers to its marketing. To him all opals have an intrinsic value, but for Rebel they are opportunities waiting to be taken in rural repair and regeneration. She's another kind of true believer altogether: she believes in the power of the human spirit and is always looking for ways to give it wings.

In addition to her involvement with opal and her online community, Rebel has two new enterprises underway. As I write she has just featured on national television in a piece looking at food security in the Australian outback. This passion for production methods that heal the land is another heritage from her farming childhood—and she's expressed it by establishing a hub for social entrepreneurs in Lightning Ridge.

On the two-hectare site that once housed their restaurant, Rebel is inviting entrepreneurs to establish a business connected to food or land or community. In this venue she is holding permaculture, sustainability and food-security workshops.

'Three years ago people said to me you should bring people to Lightning Ridge to learn gardening and traditional wisdom. I was saying, "Who would drive that far?" I couldn't see it then, but now I see that anyone who sees the value in those things for their own lives will drive. And they are. The marketplace hasn't changed, I have.'

She's increasingly feeling that the word 'sustainability' is the wrong one—her permaculture teacher suggested an alternative.

'If we just sustain, we run the risk of staying the same,' she says. 'We need to regenerate and evolve. Regeneration implies improvement and revitalisation and evolution is moving—that's what we need, not more of the same.'

The other enterprise Rebel is adding to her stable is a healing practice. This was born of her own experience of ill-health. For many years Rebel's health had been in decline.

'I thought, what is wrong with me? That had been the quest from when I'd been about twenty-one or twenty-two, to find out what was wrong with me. And I'd gone to everyone, I'd seen gastroenterologists and had allergy tests. And I started using food as a way of trying to fix it, and I did that for about a decade. I was gluten-free, sugar-free, lactose-free. I didn't eat red meat, watermelon ... there was a long list.' By the time she had been on this quest for a decade she was sick and depressed.

'Finally I found a GP who actually listened. She said, "I think there's something psychosocial going on—have you ever looked at emotional freedom technique or NLP?"' These words unlocked in Rebel a life-changing insight.

'I realised I'd been searching for what was wrong with me. I'd seen myself as a problem to be fixed. It was a light-bulb moment, and I thought: "Start looking for what is right with you!" I'd spent years thinking that food would fix the problem and it didn't. I had to be open to the emotional and the spiritual—to living and healing the whole. This was really the gateway to self-love.'

As Rebel began answering this question for herself she noticed a new beauty and depth in the love between her and Michael.

'When you love yourself you can allow others to love you. Any sort of resistance that Michael's and my relationship had over the years was not in the context of the relationship we had, but in the context of the relationship I had with myself. So while I could not like myself, or love myself, for many days, how the heck could he? How could I even see that he loved me like that? Whereas now I can see how much he loves me, and he hasn't changed: I look back over the years and his expression of love to me has not changed—my willingness and ability to receive it has.'

Rebel's new quest has transformed her life. She reminds me of a choose-your-own-adventure character, writing her own book, and finding herself at a dead end. Perhaps in the back of a cave or deep in a forest, with the way she has come closed behind her and all alone. And then comes that light-bulb moment where she 'flips' the problem and looks not for what is wrong, but what is right. And now there are pathways everywhere and companions beside her.

'We're not taught this in school. No-one teaches you how to feel love or be loved. And if you don't have people in your life who will sit you down and say, "Here's what love is—this is how you receive it and give it," then you'll just go on to model what's around you. People pattern their own relationships on what they've seen and witnessed. You have your parents' marriage essentially: good, bad or indifferent. It's monkey see, monkey do, unless you decide your own pathway.'

The evidence for Rebel's metamorphosis is everywhere. She is now well. She can eat everything. The love between her and Michael is rock-steady and joyful. Most noticeable of all is that Rebel is beginning to make the contributions and have the influence on the world she's dreamed of for so long. She conceives of this as part of her coaching as she sees a negative mindset as something that can be healed. Often, she says, people don't need to be educated in a business skill set such as 'time management' but rather, helped to develop a mindset that empowers them really to use those innate skills.

'When I work with the mindset first, a woman's business and life just flows. It just unlocks the person's innate ability so they get out of their own way. Last year I invested thousands of dollars in business coaching and it was great, but I got to the end of the course and I thought, "I know this stuff. I don't need someone teaching me how to market my business; I know how to market my business. I'm not marketing my business and that's the problem!" Many women are the same. They know what they should be doing—so what's holding them back? That will be their mindset, the limiting belief, the fear. So it's not about working on strategy or skills, it's about peeling back the layers to work on the stories behind the negative mindset. With a healing I can do in an hour what might take months of coaching: a negative belief system, life pattern and mindset can be identified and healed easily.'

Rebel's desire to make the most difference in the least time is very clear. Three years ago she was stampeded by the feeling that there wasn't enough time, but now she knows it is not necessary to 'do everything today'. These qualities of waiting, trusting and persisting, when there's nothing except gut instinct telling you to keep on, are ones that she has long admired in Michael.

We talk of love being a glue, but in the presence of lovers like Michael and Rebel, you realise that 'glue' doesn't quite capture it. You have two individual hearts and minds. Then along comes love and years of living alongside each other and that separation no longer exists. With two people with such separate skill sets and focus, it is in this area of dreams that the overlap has occurred. Rebel never wants Michael to have to stop exploring and mining opal; Michael never wants Rebel to stop exploring and mining for knowledge of the human spirit. They each work towards the other's dreams—Rebel wants to see the opal industry grow, Michael wants to see Rebel's plan for more people to build meaningful lives in remote places blossom. Of course, this is how things are now in their lives—to begin with, their surface differences meant they had to consciously steer a course between their unrelated dreams.

And I can see now that as well as being dreamers, Rebel and Michael are both explorers. Michael is drawn by the contagious excitement and sparkle that spills out of Rebel as she sets her course for the unexplored and untried, and Rebel draws from Michael's steadfastness and unwavering focus on what actually does matter most. With the deep ground of their love as a scaffold, Rebel's and Michael's vibrant achievements and Australia-wide influence remind us that important lives are being lived out here in the outback. To explore and innovate at the cutting edge you have to live on the frontier: that's what they do and that's where they are.

Holdin' a Good Hand

Cissy and Bill Bright, the Top End, Northern Territory and Queensland

Every weekend, all across Australia, there are race meets and rodeos, campdrafts and gymkhanas in which you can compete. So while the Northern Territory is huge, there are regular gatherings of horse people and you tend to bump into the same folks over and over. These are the sports of the outback. Isolation is no barrier to success, as long as you have a horse, some makeshift obstacles and some cattle.

Each rodeo or race day lifts our many-hued soils up into the air. Red from the centre, blue-grey from Queensland's Darling Downs, chocolate from the plains of New South Wales and a soft grey from the powdered limestone of the Nullarbor. People, horses and cattle kick soil particles into the air and in the early morning they spin gold in the light. All through the day and into the evening the dust rises, and as the angle of the sun changes so does the colour of the dust.

Bill Bright first saw Cissy Priest riding through just such a shifting, spinning dusty cloud in a campdraft competition at Borroloola in 1977. 'Wow! Who is that?' he said.

There is a difference between the rodeo and campdrafting cultures. Bill was a rodeo man. In rodeo the boots are decorated, the shirts emblazoned and sometimes bedazzled. Presenting well is part of campdrafting, but this is less important than in rodeo, and your campdrafter is a more tightly tailored item. Plain, bright shirt, snug jeans, riding boots: it's a polished, body-conscious look.

Added to this fine tailoring was the impact of Cissy herself: her questing, elegant profile, the determination and sizzling energy radiating from her slender, strong body, and her sheer good looks. Bill had never seen anyone like her before.

'She was like something out of a glossy magazine,' he says. 'I was very impressed.'

But Bill didn't get to meet Cissy that day. In fact, they did not meet until 1978 at one of the biggest events in the Northern Territory, the annual Brunette Downs Races.

'Cissy was there for the campdrafting and at that point I was doing rodeo. I was there for the bull riding and bronc riding,' says Bill. This was Bill's recreation, but his paid work was not so very different. At only twenty and seventeen, Bill and his brother, Ken, were working together as mustering and bull-catching contractors.

'People come from far and wide to the Brunette Downs Races. I was there with my friend Jan Darcy, and Bill and his younger brother, Ken, came to where we were sitting in our tent,' says Cissy. 'He knew Jan, and she said to him, "Have you met Cissy Priest?"

'Bill said, "No."'

Cissy draws out the 'no' as Bill must have done all those years ago, conveying his interest in this particular introduction.

'Jan said, "This is Ciss."'

Cissy saw a tall, spare-framed, good-looking kid with a remarkably attractive smile, years her junior.

'And I said, "What are you doing?"

'And he said, "I'm just here for the rodeo."

'And I said, "Well, could you hold this mirror for me, please, I want to put my makeup on. Just sit there and hold it for me, because we're going to the ball."

'He said, "Okay."

'I sat there and did my face, making myself rather glamorous. Jan and I put on our long dresses in our tent in the middle of nowhere. And then I said to him, "What are you doing now?" He said, "Going to the ball."

'And I said, "Well, good, you can take us there, please!" He took us up to the dance and I danced with him and talked to him all night. I said to Jan afterwards, "What a nice bloke, what a shame he's so young. We'll have to find a nice woman for him to meet. We can't have him wasted."'

It was the start of their friendship.

'It was funny. I met him at the next rodeo and the next campdraft I went to. I thought, "He's such a nice young fella," and I just used to sit and talk and go out with him and we'd have fun.'

In this way the difficult discussions which some couples postpone until much later were where Bill and Cissy started. Cissy was married, Bill was much younger, and they simply canvassed each other's opinions on delicate issues right from the beginning with no thought to impressing or pleasing the other. They were friends and it was a decidedly intellectual friendship. The things they talked about were of interest to them both—such things as how to be successful and what success really was. 'I liked how he thought about friendship and marriage and relationships, but not for one minute did I think I was ever going to marry him. His mum and dad were a really good example for him. They got along, they worked together. It was all very interesting because he wanted to be like his mum and dad and the last thing I wanted was to be like mine.'

'Ciss is very warm and nurturing,' says Bill, 'and that was why she was attracted to my family and my ideas.'

The Bright family culture of 'one for all, all for one' and their tight focus on putting relationships ahead of everything else, made great sense to Cissy.

'If you have to neglect your most important commitments—your personal relationships—then whatever you're doing is demanding too much of you. I subscribe to my brother Ken's point of view that "there's not enough of me to worry about everyone else". There's plenty to take up my mental and physical energy just looking after the people I really care about,' says Bill. Like Cissy, Bill has little interest in succeeding in the eyes of wider society. He cares only for the good opinion and confidence of the people he loves.

The closeness of Bill to his siblings and to his parents, their team approach to life and their habitual sharing of their deepest thoughts with each other was something new to Cissy. For the first time she was hearing and seeing how a happy family worked as she slowly got to know Bill in their long conversations at gymkhanas over eighteen months. Her family had operated very differently.

Both Bill and Cissy grew up with little money but, whereas Bill's parents had created a family team who all pulled together, Cissy's parents did not. In addition, the feeling of being needed and wanted that is crucial to a child's happiness was missing from Cissy's childhood. Cissy experienced it as sterile. It is often said that children can't miss what they never had, but of course they can. As soon as Cissy saw affection, she instantly realised it was lacking in her own life. She was the youngest of seven children and didn't have a particularly close relationship with either of her parents. 'My parents didn't show any emotion, any affection to each other. They never argued or raised their voices either. That's what I thought all parents were like. But I remember one couple who used to come to church holding hands. They used to smile and do everything together. I remember thinking, that's what I want to be like when I grow up. I want to marry my best friend.'

Cissy did not only feel 'on the outer' within her family—not drawn in, not special, not necessary—but also within wider society due to her family's poverty. While Australia aspired to being a classless society, it was not. A young girl with Cissy's background would be expected to work in a shop. Desiring to own the shop and employ other people would be 'getting above herself' or 'not knowing her place'. In little country communities like the one Cissy grew up in on the far north coast of New South Wales these social divisions were perhaps more marked than in the cities. If children did not work out what 'poor' meant, they would be told.

Having the deficiencies in her grooming ruthlessly pointed out by other children was one way in which Cissy learned how her family was perceived by society. 'We didn't have many clothes: just one hat for wearing to Sunday school and church, and at Sunday school and church they used to pick on us for our clothes. They weren't very nice,' she says.

This 'picking on' was the beginning of Cissy's discipline in ensuring that her personal appearance conveyed the message that she wasn't to be ignored. And, just as she had found a marriage to admire other than that of her parents, she found a significant role model in terms of presentation outside her family to copy. In this she was beginning to develop what has become one of her lifelong habits: seeing what works for other people and making that trait her own.

'I remember another lady from church. She was Dutch and she had five children. And she could have been a model. She was always so neat and well turned out.'

It takes a very strong character to transcend family norms and society's expectations. But Cissy belonged to that rare breed of child who refuses to allow other people's expectations to shape their lives.

'My sister and I used to tell each other we weren't going to be poor all our lives. We were going to get somewhere,' she says.

As impoverished children looking for a way out of poverty do, Cissy painstakingly added up her assets. She could present herself well, she had the energy to work hard and she could ride. It is unusual for poor children to have access to horses, but Cissy was already working in her elderly neighbours' dairy at six, helping with the milking. This elderly couple had a horse.

'He was an old grey, flea-bitten quarter draughthorse with one eye, the ugliest horse you'd ever see. I thought he was beautiful, I thought he was glorious, he was everything to me. And they gave that horse to me.

'I used to go and catch him, and ride him back down the hill. I didn't have money for boots or a hat. I used to ride him bareback in shorts. And then one day my mother came home with this beautiful little English saddle and a bridle—she had a little school-bus run she did and she'd bought the set from the tyre man who put the tyres on the bus. On a Saturday I'd ride across three or four miles of paddocks to the pony club in town.'

In addition to knowing her strengths, Cissy also knew from early on in her life where she wanted to go.

'My aunt and uncle ran a movie theatre in Southport. Back in those days, when it was hot, they used to open the doors on the big movie theatre—there wasn't air conditioning in those days. And us kids would sneak in the side door. One day there was a cowboy picture on.'

The cowboy films of the 1960s showed people seeking their fortunes in a society where you created your own identity afresh, a place where hard work was rewarded and where being considered a 'good rider' really meant something.

'I was watching this picture thinking, "Wow, when I grow up I'm going to the Wild West of Australia and I'm going to find a rich station owner!"' she says.

It was not wealth for its own sake that Cissy desired. Nor did she desire status. What she wanted was a particular kind of life, a life with good horses and time to care for them properly, a life where you rode in company with the people you loved, and a nice house, welcoming to all, well kept.

Australia's Wild West, as far as Cissy was concerned, was the Northern Territory. It was frontier country, cattle country, a place where horses were ridden every day. In 1966, when Cissy was fifteen, it had been featured (again) in the form of an article in the *Australian Women's Weekly* on the station Brunette Downs.

'Flat and empty is the landscape, all 4750 square miles, but in some lights movingly beautiful.' A caption read: 'The station keeps 1400 work horses.'

Only two properties in Australia were bigger, and they, too, were in the Northern Territory. However, it was Brunette

Downs that had received the most media attention due to a recent change of hands and half a million pounds of improvements. How Cissy wanted to see it for herself! There were just a couple of hitches in her plan.

'I had no idea how you got there, and women couldn't go to work on Brunette Downs if they weren't married.'

In 1968, when Cissy was seventeen, she met Max Priest, who came from the Northern Territory.

'He was head stockman, a top rodeo rider. He was an impressive fella, older than she was, and he wanted to marry her,' says Bill.

'I thought about it and I said to Max, "Yes, I'll marry you." I decided to get married and sort it out later. I got married to Max and went to the Northern Territory.'

It became a steadily more unhappy marriage, even though Cissy's dream of living on Brunette Downs had come true.

'When I left my ex-husband I said, "It was all his fault." A few years later I stopped and looked back into the circle and said to myself, "It was half my fault." And it was: I was young, I was naïve and all those little things add up to half the problem! It does take two people to get it right or two people to get it wrong. When you let someone do something, and let them do it over and over, you're teaching them that's okay. If then all of a sudden you've had enough, but you've told them for the last ten years it was okay ... well, marriage doesn't work that way.'

What Cissy says now is, 'If I think no, I will say no.' She is rigorously, ruthlessly honest with everyone, but most particularly with herself.

'I found myself pregnant at nineteen and I thought, "Oh my goodness, what am I going to do?"' she says. Somehow she had not even considered this possibility.

'I thought, "It might go away." I thought, "I'll just ignore it." I kept riding, I did everything I wanted to do.

'But I really did have a baby. Vickie is the loveliest girl you would ever meet, but back then I didn't know anything about children. I don't know if Vickie would have survived if there hadn't been the nice ladies at Brunette Downs—there were these old ladies there and I used to give her to them to look after.'

Baby Vickie was beautiful and her parents loved her, but a failing marriage is rarely helped by the arrival of a baby. Cissy and Max's union became increasingly miserable. Despite the difficulties, Cissy still values those years.

'If it doesn't kill you it makes you stronger. You have to make use of your experiences. You don't make the same mistake twice that way.'

Cissy met Bill while still married to Max and friends is all they were for a very long time. Bill, too, was in a serious relationship.

At this stage Cissy was employed at the homestead at Brunette Downs. She was overseeing the Aboriginal cleaning staff and her supervisor was the manager's wife, Mrs Green, who was to become a major influence upon Cissy.

'Mrs Green gave her an idea of what sort of a life she wanted,' says Bill. 'Cissy was very attracted to Mrs Green's cultural standards—far more attracted to that than to the prevailing cultural standard of the husband going down to the pub and drinking with the boys.'

Brunette Downs lived up to Cissy's hopeful expectations. And it was not, of course, the 'empty landscape' promised by the *Australian Women's Weekly*. Cissy found herself in a world of ceaseless, complex activity with a tiny metropolis at its heart. Looking up, she could see the birds on their journeys between water, food and nest—flocks of budgerigars twisting and glittering like living tinsel hung across the sky, ducks in laboured flight and the graceful predatory arcs of the nomadic kites. At first light, out across the savannah, Cissy could see the cattle moving out to pasture and at dusk she admired their stately return. In her own realm there was the industrious community of men and women travelling in and out from the homestead, some of whom were becoming the kind of friends she hoped to keep for the rest of her life. Most interesting to Cissy was the homestead itself, welcoming and grand, clad in green lawns and tall trees, a city in miniature, with a movie theatre, swimming pool and laboratory, all on the banks of Brunette Creek.

The creation of a homestead like this is the product of many generations, and Mrs Green had all the qualities needed for her turn as custodian. She was a generous and gracious woman. This was revealed in her determination to take every imaginable step to ensure the comfort of all who lived and stayed in her house, and also in the way she gathered Cissy into the heart of Brunette's social life.

'It was quite a social centre, Brunette, in those days,' says Bill. 'The Duke and Duchess of Kent went to stay there. The winners of Miss Australia used to go there. And Ciss used to be invited to be part of any celebration that was on in the big house. Max, her husband, was always out in the stock camp.

'Mrs Green took Ciss under her wing. She told her that the way you present yourself tells people a lot about your standards and Ciss aspired to the high standard that Mrs Green set, from how to dress and present yourself to running a house. That's part of where Ciss's high standards of tidiness and cleanliness come from. When you were cleaning the bathrooms at Brunette, if you found an open cake of soap it had to be replaced. The beds had to be made to a certain standard. If the boots were put out they had to be polished properly. It was very Victorian.'

The old-fashioned and formal way in which the homestead was run owed as much to the manager of Brunette Downs as it did to his wife.

'Rumour has it that her husband was an ex-prisoner of war who'd vowed to himself that if he ever got back to Australia he would maintain a very high standard. And he did. He put a tie on for dinner every night.'

Then Bill draws out for me the parallel between the station manager and his wife. Just as Mr Green was determined to leave behind him those grim years in a prison camp, Cissy was determined to leave behind her very ordinary beginnings.

So often I am finding it is Bill who helps me understand Cissy, and Cissy who helps me understand Bill. Each enjoys the chance to talk about the circumstances that created this other person that they admire so very much. And I need the help. It is easier for me to understand people of my own generation or younger because I know the Australia into which they were born. Bill and Cissy's early lives were in an Australia more formal on the surface but less rule-bound beneath. In comparison, lives now are cushioned, and there's some barrier or another (from electronic screens to air conditioning to legislation) that takes away some of life's immediacy and its pain.

Nothing makes this clearer to me than Cissy's account of Bill's early years.

'He was mature far in excess of his years. Bill had buried his father—literally buried him—and then his little sister. He had to dig the holes and bury them both,' says Cissy. 'It wasn't a nice thing to have to do. He wasn't the usual young fella. He is an exceptionally caring man.'

Remarkable lives (where people's fortunes change substantially and they change them back through their own efforts) seem from the outside to be lived in episodes. Bill's life is one of these.

The first episode was a childhood that was in many ways made golden by the tenderness and warmth of his home life. The Brights were cattle people. His family left Charters Towers for the Territory in 1969, drawn by the opportunity and the freedom. His father had built fences for other people, then became a station manager and had finally been able to purchase Robinson River Station.

His parents' marriage was a good one. They loved each other, they loved to be with their children and to do things as a family. The bonds among them all were very close, as they are when you do everything together: the school, the playtime, the chores, the adventuring. These bonds are still there. Nothing, not time, not adversity, nor the entry of new people on the scene, has ever shaken Bill's family out of their caring for each other.

'Mum made a special effort to show that there were no favourites. Nobody was more special than the others. We all felt part of the one team. Even us kids would do what we could to save money for Mum and Dad. We were proud to go without if it made things better for them.'

As well as her duties on the station, in the homestead and teaching three children, Bill's mother was also tenderly caring for his youngest sister.

'The youngest sister got a raging temperature in Hughenden. They took her to the hospital and they didn't know whether she would live or die. It was meningitis and then she developed encephalitis. His mother prayed all night to keep her alive,' says Cissy. 'She ended up with brain damage and even lost the ability to walk. Before she had been completely normal. It was a terrible, terrible thing to happen. They took her home and they cared for her.'

Despite this tragedy the family remained a happy one. They had not lost heart, and it was in 1974 that Bill's parents purchased Robinson River Station. It had been a whole-family decision to buy. Perhaps if it had been left just to Bill's parents they might have chosen differently—because his father had a debilitating kidney condition. There wasn't a great deal known about it and there was no internet on which to research these things.

'It wasn't a situation where Dad went around looking for a place and had to have a place at any price. He was managing properties and doing quite okay without owning land himself. This was an opportunity that just came along and smacked him in the face. We talked about it as a family. It was the fact that all of us kids badly wanted to go there. Ours is a family that just likes doing things together—we just couldn't miss it. And any objective assessment of the economic circumstances would have told you you'd have rocks in your head not to do it. But there are many, many things that are well outside our consideration when we're making economic decisions that can affect the outcome.'

Buying a pastoral station is approximately equal parts purchase of land and risk. So much can go wrong, or right. It can rain and you can feed thousands of cattle day after day. Calves are born. It keeps raining. The cattle price can rise and rise, and your cattle can be worth far more at the end of the month than they were at the beginning. Equally, it might not rain. Fewer calves are born. The cattle price might plummet. Hedging against failure is difficult and sometimes, with the best will in the world, the cards are stacked against you.

Yet the gamble is always being taken. It is often said 'to make a small fortune in the pastoral industry you need to start with a large one'. Even knowing that, people buy. Yearning for such large tracts of land is a very human instinct and a hard one to resist. Here before you is your own giant garden to improve: your dirt, your trees, your fences and feed, places where you need to add water or handling yards or more fences, as well as the dangers, places and mysteries you plan to explore.

With no school nearby the Bright children were placed on a kind of distance education known as 'correspondence'. Workbooks were posted out, and the children had to work through them. Ensuring the children did so was the role of their mother, made all the harder by the appeal of a new property to investigate.

'My mother taught the three of us on correspondence in between the many, many other duties she had on the station. Our schooling was not ideal, not because of any lack of trying by Mum, but because we weren't particularly good pupils. We thought we'd be far better off learning the things Dad was doing, out on the run,' says Bill.

Children often do learn more in a good conversation with an adult than in formal study. If, as well as talking, the adult is teaching them a skill that can be used instantly in the real world, no class on the planet can hold their attention better. In these years Bill was able to contribute to building fences, mustering stock and the occasional observation of animal or land health that his parents had missed. Nothing could have been more meaningful to Bill than helping his family and developing his skills, and I am sure his parents loved these times, too.

Having your children working alongside you is another of the great appeals of station life. That close engagement with your children is deeply satisfying. To know also that they have the skills to grow their own food, work a good day and be part of a team is wonderful for a parent. In this, at least, things worked out for the Brights, but in financial terms they lost a lot.

'The cattle prices at the time were good. Dad knew the property, he'd mustered it and he knew that the cattle were on there. At the prices prevailing when we purchased the place we could have paid for it in twelve months. Dad had borrowed $174,000 to buy the station; 2006 square miles of country, with 12,000 to 14,000 head of cattle on it. It was like winning the lotto. But that was 1974, and the big cattle crash came weeks after we signed the contract. Within six weeks of having the place we had 3000 steers, bullocks and bulls mustered, ready to go, but nobody would come and look at them. They weren't worth the freight. It was a wonderful opportunity but at the worst possible time.'

A new episode had begun in Bill's life. When Bill was eighteen, his 39-year-old father died. His poor health had been caused by a highly heritable condition called polycystic kidney disease.

'It was in a big rain, the police flew out with a body bag, and said, "Yeah you can bury him," and they flew back to town,' says Cissy.

Then his little sister died within two years of her father.

After his father died all three children were tested for the kidney disease that had killed him.

'How lucky are we,' says Bill. 'Fifty percent of a person's offspring are meant to get it, but only I did of the three of us, and I have only one child, and she doesn't have it.'

The Bright family's strength comes from their shared resilience: in all predicaments they stand together and, as a group, they advance. They kept on living.

'After my father died my mother married another fella, who was a family friend of them both, and she had three more daughters.'

The family sold Robinson River. The three remaining Bright siblings, Bill, Ken and sister, Patricia, known as 'Patch', took away from those years a reverence for their mother, extraordinary skills in land and stock management, a close bond with each other and one lesson bitten deep into their souls: it is not enough just to watch the cattle and the land and keep your costs low. The external circumstances that affect the cattle market can never be ignored.

'It's a lesson firmly ingrained in my brain: however good it looks, it can go wrong. It can *always* go wrong,' says Bill. 'You think about it, the fundamentals of the cattle market when they closed the live export in 2011 looked as good as they could possibly look. But that *Four Corners* footage of the terrible stuff they were doing with cattle when they got over to Indonesia, it shut the market down.'

Bill is referring to the ABC documentary broadcast in May 2011 of an act of extraordinary cruelty towards an Australian animal. This created public outrage over animal welfare and, in the wake of that outrage, live export of cattle was banned. With their market suddenly gone, many pastoralists lost their business, much as Bill's father had done all those years before.

'So even though the market fundamentals were strong—anybody trying to make an economic judgment about the way forward with the cattle market would have said it was strong—there are always intervening factors. It might not rain, you could have some political argument with the people you are doing business with—predicting the market is like predicting the weather. There are too many moving parts to be absolutely confident about anything. It is too complicated and large for the word "rational" to have any meaning. Always have an exit strategy.'

These were the kind of thoughts that Bill would share with Cissy whenever they met throughout 1978 and into 1979, at gymkhanas and rodeos. The long, intimate conversations between these two young people, superficially so different, in essentials so alike, were resulting in a friendship stronger than either had expected at the outset. For nearly two years they didn't realise where those philosophical conversations were inexorably leading. 'Then it was eighteen months later, and I thought, "This fella really is nice, he really is serious, but he's so young!" But Bill didn't care about the age difference. He was much older than his years. He thought much older.'

He was, says Cissy, older than she was in all the ways that counted. Many twenty-year-old men would have been intimidated by her, but Bill was not.

'People say to Bill, "Have I met Ciss?" And he always says, "If you have to ask, you haven't met her,"' says Cissy.

It is true. You could never forget Cissy. You just have to listen to her strong voice, to feel the blast of that warm, courageous personality, to begin to appreciate that a life where you don't give way to fear often is a better life. Being around Cissy makes me feel more courageous, after I've first been astonished at what she thinks everyone could do, if they really tried, if they brought every resource to bear on the task.

Bill puts it this way: 'There's not much of a backward step in her.'

In 1979 Bill suggested they should leave their respective partners and join forces—and Cissy realised that Bill was now her best friend, and her childhood dream was within her reach. However, they both emphasise that they had not 'fallen in love'. It was more a realisation that they were a natural team—Cissy's drive, energy and gut instinct and Bill's ability to synthesise and apply his family's legacy of wisdom and knowledge, both of them with extraordinary self-discipline—and knowing that they were in total agreement about what was important in life.

It was at this time that Vickie was ending her primary years and approaching high school. This usually requires children to leave the bush and attend boarding school.

'Some very good friends of ours, Ken and Sally Warriner, offered to take Vickie for a while. And Vickie liked them, they liked Vickie, and we respected them. Then, when Ken Warriner was working for Kerry Packer, Kerry offered to pay for Vickie to go to Ascham Girls School, with his daughter,' says Bill.

Cissy left behind the formality and civilisation of Brunette Downs and joined Bill and Ken in catching bulls. The catching of bulls for export is highly profitable but dangerous. In the vast expanse of the Northern Territory cattle breed up and with just once-yearly handling—sometimes not even that—can only be considered wild animals.

'We'd catch bulls all day and then in the afternoon we'd load them on a truck, and Ken or I (we took it in turns) would drive them to the meatworks at McArthur River. That was a six-hour round trip. And then we'd be back catching again at daylight in the morning.'

With handling, these feral bulls do become steadier, in a way that the real wild cattle do not, but on first encountering humans they are explosively impulsive. The four-wheel-drive vehicles in which the bulls are caught are customised for the job with bars, and are simply called 'bullcatchers'.

'Every morning we'd hop in those bullcatchers and I'd close my eyes because I was so frightened,' says Cissy. But the lonely little girl who had grown up feeling herself to be on the edge of her own family had found a new one—a family in which everyone was valued equally—and she was determined not to let them down.

'I was sure I was going to get myself killed on a tree, every morning. Then I'd say to myself, "If I'm going to die, I might as well die with my eyes open." And I'd open my eyes.'

Cissy is exhilarated by the unpredictability of cattle in campdraft and so I know that it takes far more to scare her than to scare me. That bull-catching terrifies her tells me all I need to know about how dangerous it must be. Every day is a journey from trepidation to outright terror and then relief, but a short-lived relief. You will be doing it all again tomorrow. Every musterer would feel the wild tang of adrenaline, the chill of danger and have eyes and ears wide, ready to act—and every bull pinned and yarded and trucked out would grow the team closer. (I suspect that daily exposure to this life-threatening situation also enhanced the romantic attraction between Cissy and Bill: it is something danger is known to do.) Ultimately, bull-catching, like so much of what Cissy and Bill have done and still enjoy doing, is a confidence game.

You have to be confident that there is a way to avoid getting hurt. You have to believe that even if you do get hurt, it won't be too bad and you'll survive even if it is painful for a while. Campdrafting is like that. Riding in rodeos is like that. Buying pastoral properties is also like that. No-one could have understood the risks of pastoral enterprise better than Cissy and Bill, but they had faith in themselves. One day they would buy a station and create a highly profitable cattle business on it. They would work hard, live lean and wait for the chance to come.

And those waiting years were good ones. They worked side by side out in the bush: bull-catching, contract mustering and saving hard.

In 1982 Bill and Cissy's daughter Jackie was born. In 1983 they came in from the bush to celebrate and formalise their commitment to each other in marriage. The wedding was held at the house of friend Jan Darcy, and both Vickie and Jackie attended. And then it was back out to camp and work.

Instead of a stove with a rangehood the family had a campfire and camp oven and the Territory's open sky. Baby Jackie grew up with leaves and stars dangling overhead. She grew up without radio or television: at night she heard the voices of the men who worked for her parents and the deep, plaintive calls of cattle settling for the night.

All through this time Cissy's standards for presenting herself and her home never slipped.

'You need to try to look nice for the person you're with. Some people dress up and look magnificent to go into town. Then they come home and put on their old clothes. Their husband never sees them looking stunning. What's the point of that!' she says.

Very early in her competitive riding career Cissy had decided that if she couldn't win the riding competition she and her horse could at least look the best.

'She always reckons it's true that you can't judge a book by its cover, but that the nicer a book looks the more chance there is someone will look inside,' says Bill.

Yes, they were living under the stars and out of swags much of the time. There was no running water or electricity. No telephones. But it was still a home.

'When we were first together we spent a lot of time in a swag, or under a tarp in a stock camp, but I guarantee it was the best, tidiest stock camp in the country, because Cissy did the best with whatever she had,' says Bill.

They raise each other's game, these two, both doing their utmost and inspiring the other to further accomplishment.

'Some of my best performances have been achieved trying to live up to Cissy's high expectations. Sometimes I've thought they were unreasonably, even foolishly high.' But Cissy's ideas proved not to be unreasonable or foolish at all. In these years Bill learned to trust Cissy's gut instincts and her wisdom, to evaluate critically every pathway and find the one that would bring Cissy's expectations to fruition.

The combination of Bill's caution and Cissy's ability to see an opportunity flashing past got them ready in just five years to take the biggest gamble of all: the purchase of their own property. In 1985 they purchased Kiana with the intention of turning it around.

Operating a cattle station is a tremendous amount of work. Building one from scratch, which is effectively what 'turning around' requires you to do, is even more work. This is what Cissy and Bill set out to do on 3313 square kilometres.

The best cattle country in the Northern Territory is the open black-soil plains of the tablelands. Brunette Downs, where Cissy and Bill met, is located here, on this rich black dirt. Further north there is the Gulf Country and that carries the least cattle per hectare and so is the least valuable. The land between the Gulf and the tablelands is called the 'transition country' and this is where Kiana is located. Not great cattle country, but good.

'If you got a map out and drew a line between Mount Isa and Katherine, Kiana is about halfway along that line,' Bill says. 'We were lucky. We worked very hard for a long time. The property was available when we had the circumstance to purchase it. We had the skills and ability to catch the wild cattle, to build the fences and do all the things we needed to do to be successful.'

Bill doesn't define the word 'luck' in the way most people do. He does not mean 'good fortune' but rather 'opportunity'—in this case, an opportunity to work very hard indeed. Both Bill and Cissy have a genius for understatement, so what was actually done on Kiana in the years after purchase must be deduced.

From the air many homesteads look higgledy-piggledy: buildings belonging to different time periods compete for proximity to the big house and the main sheds. Not on Kiana. Overhead photographs show the manager's house with new outbuildings radiating out obediently. There is even a full campdrafting arena with commentator's box. None of it looks more than thirty years old, and it's all Cissy and Bill's work. But fixing up the homestead area is the very smallest part of turning around a station.

Attention to detail throughout the operation is required. Something like 'fixing fences', which sounds straightforward, is not. Poorly thought-out fencing impacts animal health and welfare, mustering ease and, therefore, profits.

To 'fix fencing' Bill and Cissy had to consider the best combinations of land and vegetation types, a reliable set of water sources, ensure that each paddock shape would muster well and include handling yards at a good muster point where required. Then the fence had to be built, when it was actually needed, when putting it in was going to contribute to profits, and not before.

One fence in a pastoral station paddock may require a hundred kilometres of fencing. This is work done partly on foot. The terrain is rough. There are now thirty paddocks on Kiana. And upgrading the fencing was just one job among many.

Wrapped around all the different jobs that had to be done was the development of the business itself.

'The business has to be good enough to withstand a downturn. You've got to be able to hold on through the hard times while you're waiting for the good times. That's key to it.'

As Bill speaks I am irresistibly reminded of the different strategies plants and animals use to survive the boom or bust climate of Northern Australia. There is lower rainfall in the transition country (where Kiana is) than there is in the rest of the Top End, but the pattern of a wet summer and a long dry still holds. In the short summer season it rains until the land floods and grass and animal life explode from the hot wet earth. The billabongs first fill and then flood, and out of them peer not just the wrinkled faces of turtles and water monitors, but the goannas, who are generally considered land animals. In the heat everything that possibly can becomes a water dweller.

In the other months there is little rain. The grasses wither, grey and blow. The once widespread animal life begins to contract into the waterholes. There was abundance, but now it is gone. How to survive this time of little-to-no food and rain?

This is the same challenge that Bill and Cissy were presented with—staying alive financially in times of no income.

The animals and plants of the Top End are resourceful. Some make it through the long dry by living off extra fat stored in their tails. Others are only alive in the wet and leave eggs and spores to wait for the next big rain, a strategy known as 'shut down and wait'. There are yet others known as generalists. These animals haven't invested in adapting to a niche in which they flourish but instead adapt to a range of foods and habitats. And all of these strategies, translated into human terms, were found and put into practice by Bill—after Cissy had made clear to Bill that she expected him to find a way.

To begin with, Bill and Cissy are generalists. When one income stream dries, they move their business swiftly to where another is flowing and grow the skills to match. Even after they had purchased Kiana they continued for ten years to contract muster on other properties to earn money. But then the contract work began to dry up. At that time Kiana, although much improved in fences and water, could not support enough cattle to be really profitable. Bill and Cissy needed to get another business or do something profoundly different on Kiana.

The decision to invest further in a marginal business was a risk, and it took five years of trial and error for Bill to succeed, and succeed beyond his own expectations.

'It lessens your fear of failure,' says Bill, 'if you know your partner is totally committed and wants you to try it. If you fail it is a team effort. With many of the things we've achieved, if Ciss hadn't been fully on board and encouraging, I wouldn't have taken the risk. Winston Churchill said, "The pessimist sees difficulty in every opportunity; the optimist sees the opportunity in every difficulty." When I shared that with my daughter Jackie she said, "Well, Dad, you're an optimist only when you've exhausted every other possibility."'

Bill eventually increased the production off Kiana by more than one hundred percent, and he did this by adding a supplement of extra protein, minerals and energy to what his cattle ate. This meant the cattle did well all year round, even in the dry. He had given them a buffer against decreasing food quality to equal the 'fat tail' with which native animals survive the hard times.

In one recent article on the vagaries of the cattle trade, Bill is referred to as the 'magician of the Gulf savannah' not for his swag of stockman's skills, but for his ability to handle and seek out multiple incoming streams of data and put into practice good business decisions with time to spare.

'Many people get themselves into the situation where they invest in infrastructure, for instance, or even genetics in their cattle for the long-term gain. That's all well and good, but it doesn't matter how good the long-term gain is, you've got to be able to pay for it in the short term.' This ability to stop and wait, to resist the impulse to spend, is another key to Cissy and Bill's success.

While Bill and Cissy worked towards their goal of becoming rich, they were also determined to enjoy the journey. The campdraft facility north of the homestead was built to this end.

'Campdrafting developed in the early days when there were no yards. If you wanted to draft certain animals out you had to do it on horseback. The competition developed because there was a fair bit of different opinion as to who had the best horse. It was designed to see who really did have the best horse,' says Bill.

'It consists of cutting a single animal out of a mob of eight to fifteen cattle. You show the judge how well you can cut it out. Then you call for the gate, and there are two pegs and a gate that you go around in, in a clover-leaf pattern. The judge assigns a score out of one hundred: a very good score is ninety.'

By 'cut' Bill means separating out that one animal from the rest. This is challenging because cattle are herd animals and resist being separated initially. With handling, though, they quickly learn to comply. Both rider and horse show off their teamwork, athleticism and cattle-handling skills in this sport. Together rider and horse turn, block, move in parallel, chase and precisely direct the animal.

It was a bush competition that turned into a popular social and recreational activity, not just for people on isolated properties and in rural communities, but for anyone with an interest in horses. Cissy had introduced Bill to it soon after they met and shortly afterwards he was winning competitions.

'I'd broken my leg and I gave him my horses. He won the first campdraft he ever went in, and then he won the first three, which is almost impossible. But you see, Bill is a cattleman and, if you've got a horse you can put anywhere, a cattleman will get your cow around.'

In a few years campdraft was to become the Bright family's sport of choice.

'My first daughter, Vickie, when she was about seven, used to ride all the time. Then my other daughter, Jackie, wanted to ride. And I wanted her to have something to do when she grew up so she wouldn't be watching television as people do or be at the pub drinking. Out in the middle of nowhere you can't do ballet, play football or cricket, there are no social activities, so we taught her to ride,' says Cissy.

'There wasn't much of a social life for our daughter: campdrafting was a way for us all to connect on the same level. It's difficult for parents and children to connect. It gave her an interest too—feeding the horses, training them. If you did everything right at home there was the possibility you could win on the weekend,' says Bill. And attending such an event was reward enough by itself for an isolated child.

'We would camp out on the flat. We'd be in swags, sit around the fire, cook a steak, tell jokes, sing ... it was a very village-like atmosphere.'

Gradually they realised just how good Jackie might be.

'Jackie's always had a keen interest in horses and Ciss cultivated that interest and gave her every opportunity. There was a lady on the station next door who was on the shortlist to go to the Olympics, a very good rider. She decided to get married, have children and go to the station instead. Ciss used to get her to come over for a few days at a time to teach Jackie to ride.'

Many of these years were lived without television or radio.

'We've always made a conscious effort not to measure our progress against other people's. Don't worry about what everybody else is doing, just do the best you can with what you've got. Focus your attention on what you're doing,' says Bill.

This is one of the things made easier by isolation. There are not just fewer distractions but less opportunity for comparisons. But there are disadvantages to missing important information and in 1986 Bill decided he wanted a television.

'You'd spend the whole year in the bush and the news was something you heard through anecdotal reports from people you met. I remember hearing you could get TV in the bush through satellites. I said to Ciss (this was when we didn't have any spare money): "There are a dozen bulls up in the big swamp on the boundary—we might go and catch them and take them to Mount Isa and buy a satellite TV with the proceeds."

'One of the first events I clearly remember was the space shuttle *Challenger* exploding. I'd never really seen the news. Then to see that in real time felt like an earth-shattering event. It felt like the world had changed. I had that same feeling when the aeroplanes smashed into the World Trade Center,' he said.

All those years of living remotely heightened the power of this event in Bill's consciousness. Once Bill would have only heard about such events at the Borroloola Races. Now he was watching, connected to everyone else, as the world abandoned one era and embarked on the next—he was part of the whole world taking the corner and rushing onward, leaving behind the never-again attainable past.

Bill's diagnosis was never forgotten by Cissy: she knew it was likely that at some point he would become very ill.

'I probably wouldn't have managed it as carefully if it wasn't for Ciss: not drinking or smoking or eating the wrong things, or gaining weight,' says Bill.

Despite these careful measures it became clear Bill was going to need a kidney transplant. His life was changing again, he could do less with his body and he began to focus more on exercising his mind: reflecting, writing and cataloguing his thoughts.

The years when Bill became sicker were hard ones for Cissy. For the first time she had stopped enjoying life.

'When Bill was ill I forgot to find the good in life. I was too busy trying to make money because I knew the time would come when I couldn't. I forgot all the important things,' says Cissy of these years.

They had purchased fifty-two acres in Warwick, Queensland, close to both medical facilities for Cissy and Bill, and campdraft facilities for Jackie. On this acreage stood a grand old lady of a house, fading and dilapidated in her tatty dress in the sun. With care Cissy stripped back all that was decrepit and peeling, added rooms, polished and painted. She built into the running of the home the high standards and welcome to all that she had learned at Brunette Downs.

The old lady is glorious again. In 2005 Bill and Cissy sold Kiana, staying on as managers until 2007. When they had purchased the property it had been destocked, disorganised and degraded. Now fully restocked, with all plant and management systems in place, it was worth a great deal more. And so the little girl who'd felt so deeply the discrimination against her family's poverty, and the young man whose dad had been so unlucky in the pastoral business, the best friends who'd met in the Territory, both dreaming of making millions in the cattle business, had done it together. They had gone from poor to rich in twenty-eight years.

In 2008 Bill and his sister, Patch, were both operated on: a kidney from her to him. Since then Bill and Cissy have done all kinds of things with that gift from his sister—'My wonderful sister,' says Bill—but particularly they have focused on enjoying the journey.

The bonds between Bill and his siblings, always close, have tightened and deepened through the years. 'Ken and Patch were both willing to be donors—and here's another twist for you,' Bill says cheerfully. 'Cissy's daughter from her first marriage, Vickie, married my brother, Ken.'

This is in the very best traditions of romance. When Vickie left Ascham School, she moved to Darwin to work in hospitality.

'She worked at the Beaufort: a big hotel in Darwin, a big international complex. She had that job through her contacts and she really excelled at that work. And Ken was a commercial helicopter pilot at this stage. And they connected there. It was quite a surprise to Cissy and me! In no way was it a bad surprise, because I think Vickie is a wonderful person and I think Kenny is a wonderful person. They are two very good people.'

The Bright family team is made even stronger by Vickie and Ken's love story. Bill's delight in their happiness together is very apparent. Not unnaturally, this most unusual set of relationships is much discussed.

'We were all at the campdraft at Chinchilla. There was Ciss, Ken and I, all sitting on our horses at the cut-out pen. There were these two old fellas talking about our family relationships and how everything works in the grandstand. A friend of ours was sitting behind them and one old fella said, "No, no, the story is that two brothers married a mother and a daughter," and he pointed at Ciss and said, "and I think this girl here is the daughter." Ciss loves that story.

'Now Vickie and Ken live on the property we have at St George and they have their own helicopter-mustering business, and manage the property for Ciss and me as well,' says Bill.

They have their own daughter now, Abbie, who is both cousin and niece to Bill's daughter, Jackie, who is herself now married with two children, Riley and Jett. In campdrafting circles Jackie is a celebrity. Campdrafting friends to whom I read some of this story immediately asked—is this Jackie Knudsen? It is. She is as good with stock as her father, every bit as glamorous as her mother and has won the Australian Lady Rider award three times.

'She won that title right up until she started her family,' says Bill. 'And she won the Condamine Bell—one of the biggest events on the campdraft circuit—when she was six months pregnant.'

Bill and Cissy are now based permanently at Warwick. Bill has undertaken various business ventures, and Cissy has added beauty therapy to her extensive repertoire of skills. Obviously, neither of them needs to work. 'I don't think you ever really get over being poor,' says Bill. 'Unless Cissy is doing something productive she's not really happy. If we have a day off she generally feels worse at the end of the day than she did at the start.'

Cissy's interest in the art of beauty resulted from her many years of living where there was no-one with those skills and the fact that she can do it without exacerbating her bad back.

'I put my finger through a blowtorch and wrecked my fingernail,' says Cissy. 'And when my youngest daughter got married I had my nails done. Normally I just had Band-Aids on them because they looked pretty ordinary. And there was nobody where I lived who could do your nails, no-one who could make them look civilised, like a normal person's. So I thought I'd learn to do them myself.

'People would say to me: "Oh, your hands look beautiful," and so I started doing theirs. And I do a new course every year, and that way I meet a lot of nice people, and I have some lovely clients now. I can sit and do it and I'm out of the dust. I'm just about to go and do a makeup course.

'I enjoy what I do and I enjoy the fact that I see women now. You know, I've probably lived a pretty exciting life compared to most people. I don't want to do any more things that frighten the daylights out of me. Every day it was the speed and adrenaline rush from everything. I don't care if I don't get another big adrenaline rush in my whole life. I've had so many.'

In mustering, she says, they would inevitably accidentally muster in a few of the wild cattle, the water buffalo. Hairy, snorting, impossible to domesticate, all they wanted was to get out of the mob of cattle. Unerringly, they would choose Cissy and her horse as the most permeable part of the barrier created by the musterers.

'They used to pick me out because they must have smelt I was frightened of them. They used to chase me everywhere. I just got tired of all those things. I think I've broken thirteen major bones in my body. I've broken my shoulders, legs, shoulder blades. I've been kicked in the jaw ...'

Sitting in her beautiful house, bringing precision and care to the art of making a friend lovely—this is what Cissy wants to do at this time in her life. But she still loves campdrafting, as does Bill.

Just recently their campdraft training has expanded to involve two types of wild cattle: not water buffalo, but American bison and Indonesian banteng. It is with these that she and Bill practise their campdrafting. Where domesticated cattle will learn the course and therefore no longer provide any challenge to the campdrafter, these wild cattle will respond day after day in the same way. Bison and banteng don't want to separate from the herd and won't be directed or work with the horse.

'A friend of ours breeds them and he gave us some. These animals give you confidence because they do the same thing every day.'

Cissy is working to become competitive again in campdraft.

'I don't get nervous in campdraft,' she says. After all, compared to bull-catching or accidentally mustering wild buffalo along with a herd of cattle, it is a tame pursuit. 'Bill reckons he needs to make me a bit nervous so I'll concentrate more. I like to be competitive now, just so I don't look like the silly old lady who should have stopped ten years ago. It's not an easy thing to do, but I still don't get nervous.'

Partly underlying their persistence in this high-speed, unpredictable sport is the desire to stay relevant in and connected to the lives of their children and grandchildren and to the wider campdraft community.

'When we go we take all the kids with us, we all go together as a family. If I don't keep riding I'll have no horses for my grandchildren to ride and campdraft. I want to make sure my grandchildren want to come and see me and that we have something in common! We're all going away next week. My daughter is riding and both my granddaughters, too. One granddaughter is five and one is fifteen. We're all doing it together,' she says. 'While I can climb up and hop on my horse I'll be campdrafting.'

Bill is still working in the family team into which he was lucky enough to be born. 'It has just got bigger,' he says. 'And we all work very hard at maintaining a very good relationship with each other. We all value the relationship we have.'

With all of this in their lives Cissy and Bill are satisfied.

'Success is often defined in the narrowest possible terms,' says Bill. 'For some people accruing wealth is success, but I think satisfaction is a better definition. If you are genuinely satisfied with your circumstances—if you are living on a river somewhere and hunting all your food and looking after your children and you are genuinely satisfied with that, you genuinely don't want anything different—that's as good as it gets.'

In deciding to marry it appears to me that Cissy 'followed her gut' (as she always does) and Bill used something approaching a due diligence procedure (as he always does). 'It seemed to me we had the basis for a relationship, and history has subsequently vindicated that judgment. When you are young, most people wrongly believe that love is the starting point for a successful long-term relationship. Love is the end result, I believe, of a successful long-term relationship. Friendship should be the starting point. We had the same aspirations, we both wanted a long-term relationship with someone we could be best friends with, and business partners and parents,' says Bill.

Bill's parents had talked to their children about the choice of life partner and just how very significant that choice was, and what criteria to consider in making your choice. Cissy's parents hadn't.

'We don't go to school and have a subject called "life" and learn how to find the best person to marry—and we don't have experience in that either. Unless you have good parents who actually put some time into you, you don't know these things,' says Cissy.

After listening to her I wonder if we need to add a subject called (possibly) 'Life, Love and Mate Selection' to the school curriculum.

Bill and Cissy's kind of love story is told often in Regency romances. Friends decide to marry for reasons other than love. Then comes the dangerous situation where they must rely utterly on the other person. From that close camaraderie grows love. It is all rather more condensed in these books than in Cissy and Bill's case, but it is the same story. I am charmed to find that this kind of beginning to a marriage works every bit as well in real life as it does in fiction. 'Bill has the loveliest smile I've ever seen. He's a genuine, honest, good person and he brings out the better in me. A lot of people look at their partner and take them for granted. I try to find something nice to say, not every day, but often—something that is true. You can't say to someone, "Oh, I love you," every day, because you might not feel it that day or even that week,' says Cissy.

'I always reckon friendship is the most important part of it. When the emotional and physical heat lessens, as it inevitably will over a number of years, then what you are left with is friendship, so you'd better make sure you get that right. If you've been with someone for twenty years and you still like them and enjoy being with them and talking to them and doing things together, you can call that love. That's what I call love,' says Bill.

There was a pot of gold at the end of Cissy and Bill's rainbow, but despite the hard years spent growing that gold, that isn't where their attention goes. They focus instead on the wealth of good relationships they've built up. They are still each other's 'best mate'.

When I think of Bill and Cissy I imagine them when they first met, a good-looking couple in the roughest of station utes. The girl has her foot on the accelerator and her heart in the moment. The man holds a map and has his mind tracking a multitude of possibilities. The terrain is rough, the dangers real. As we watch, the ute takes off for the future—and when it arrives it is no longer a ute but a helicopter and the couple within love each other all the more for the chance to share the journey.

Never Tear Us Apart

Tania and Tim Wiley, Broome–Wiluna–Marble Bar–Port Hedland–Broome, Western Australia

Western Australia's coastline echoes the rugged outlines of a giant's ear: Perth is decorously located on the lobe, whereas Broome is studded on the tip of the upper ear in rebellious competition. They might share a coastline and a state, but each metropolis offers a different Australia. Broome's streets do have some names that reflect Anglo culture (Dampier, Kennedy), but many also reflect the fact that multiculturalism is old news here—so many British divers died in this place that the White Australia policy was waived in order to allow Japanese divers to work alongside those of Aboriginal and Torres Strait Islander descent. So there is Wing Place, Tang Street, Matsumoto Street and Johnny Chi Lane.

As well as the descendants of all those divers and those of the Aboriginal people (and Broome people are frequently descendants of both), there are the tourists, the rich pearl buyers, and those seekers who come to Broome looking for other ways of seeing, and in turn see themselves reflected back in all these different mirrors. In Broome, pearling, pastoralism and parties were layered over the old cultures of the Orient and the cold European North, and under, through and around sits the Indigenous spirit of the land. It announces itself to the visitor, even the one who does not know how to look. The work of 'Welcoming to Country' is done by the place itself.

This was not always such a cheerfully multicultural place. Cultural and racial difference were at the heart of Broome's early history of exploitation, violence and tragedy. But places, like people, can be resilient: some places can have a history of tragedy and adversity and yet they can overcome it to such a degree that they stand as a testament to the very opposite qualities. Broome is just such a place, owning its shadow—some of Australia's ugliest racial wars occurred here—yet now Broome epitomises the kind of Australia we can have when we celebrate cultural and racial diversity.

It was 1990 when agricultural scientist Tim Wiley arrived in Broome. At twenty-nine he had left both a job and his marriage in the cooler, drier south of Western Australia to hitchhike north. At that time Broome had just started to polish itself in its quest to become a world-class tourist destination. For those of us down south, already puzzled by Broome's comfortable multiculturalism and honesty about its dark and bloody past, this new ambition to glow on the world stage made it seem even more alien than ever. To a southerner like Tim it felt not so much as if Broome belonged in another state, it was more that it belonged to another country entirely. Bali or Broome? The main difference was that he could hitchhike to Broome.

'This guy, Bob, picked me up in Carnarvon and he gave me a lift up to Broome,' says Tim. Bob knew a woman called Joan Wilson, who was happy to give newcomers to the town a feed. Tim had landed on his feet with Joan as she was a great adopter of strays. He became a frequent visitor in those first few weeks in Broome, where he knew no-one and was bewildered by this very different Australia. Joan was an Australian girl who'd married a Maori man, Tania's father. It was a very unhappy and abusive marriage. After the marriage was over Joan was supported by her strong friends. That support was something she wanted to give back, so Joan's door was kept open and her fridge full.

Joan's open-door policy was very like the one that had operated in the little wheatbelt town where Tim had grown up. 'Weekends and holidays we kids would roam everywhere. Wherever we rocked up we got fed and put to bed,' Tim says.

So he was made to feel instantly at home with Joan and her sons. The daughter of the house, seventeen-year-old Tania, wasn't there. She was living in Perth with a boyfriend, but her four little brothers missed her, her mother missed her, and so Tim heard a great deal about the big sister of the family.

'I got on well with the boys—I was missing my own sons, David and Scott. Joan's two youngest ones were the same age as my two. We did boy stuff together: they were like little brothers to me. Fishing, going down the beach ... they really enjoyed it, I enjoyed it. They all looked up to big sister—and one day she came home.'

It cannot be said that the first encounter between them was in fact a meeting or that it went well. Tania was cleaning the kitchen when Tim walked in. He did not look at her or speak to her, but kept on walking.

'My boyfriend and I had split up, and then Mum was sick. So I came back to Broome. Because of Mum's open-door policy with anybody and everybody welcome I was used to people drifting in and out. However, they usually said hello as they walked past you. Tim didn't. He walked past me, straight down to where Mum was. All I thought was, "arrogance".'

(Years later, Tim is still excusing himself for this: he was crook as a dog, too, he says, and he wasn't feeling talkative.)

Joan's health improved and Tania moved out of home. Tim remained close to Joan and slowly Tania got to know him in that swirling group of people who made up Joan's circle of friends.

'One evening there was a knock on the door, and it was Tim, he was just back from a party, drunk as anything.'

Tim had spent weeks feeling most uncomfortable about the attraction he had begun to feel towards Tania. His emotions seemed out of joint with reality: Tania was a teenager and he was now thirty. But then there was another reality: she felt like his equal. Her way of considering and then speaking her mind, her subversive sense of humour and her quick, practical compassion—in none of these ways did she seem younger than him. And life had made Tania wise beyond her years. The dark times had taught her (as they so often do) to be a moment-seizer and to laugh when she could. In addition, there were her darkly glowing good looks and her comfort with her curves: with his inhibitions lost to alcohol, Tim had been unable to resist going to see her. 'My story was the cyclone season was coming and I needed a place to camp.' He was living in a caravan park in a tent annex off Bob's caravan and working as a gardener at the Cable Beach Club. 'He'd come from a work party. In a typical fashion he showed me how this chick had bitten his bum—'

'—I was fully clothed and she just bit me,' says Tim.

'He had a large bruise on his butt,' says Tania.

So Tim arrived at her door that night and he simply never left. At first glance Tim and Tania look very different. Tania is made up of curves and glow—not olive or brown skin but dark gold. Her dark eyes are long ovals and her steep cheekbones the widest part of her oval face. Tim is muscular, with very blue eyes, sun-weathered skin and squared-off features. But there's something similar about them, too, despite the differences in colouring and features. They are robustly made, direct-gazing and energetic people with the air of being prepared to wade through absolutely anything at all to achieve what needs to be achieved.

Tim was far more worried about the age gap than any cultural gap, though.

'Tania was younger than my car, which was a classic HQ 1970 model. I was uncomfortable with that, but you don't have control over these things. It's not a rational decision, is it? If it works, it works.'

The age gap was irrelevant to Tania. In many ways, the fact that her entire family liked him so much had 'pre-qualified' Tim in Tania's eyes.

'I remember telling Mum that Tim had told me he loved me and she said, "Oh that's good, he must really love you because I don't think he would say something like that otherwise."'

Their attempts to understand each other's culture flowed in on the tide of their fascination with each other. In Australia there are many cultures, but all are in flux on a continuum between two extremes: traditional and modern Western culture. Traditional culture focuses on family, on the basics of food and surviving, and having faith in its particular social and religious beliefs. Modern Western culture emphasises independence and individualism rather than family, on pursuing interests rather than surviving and earning the money to pursue those interests rather than 'having faith'. Where Tania grew up in a multicultural setting where people were determined to hang on to their various traditional values, Tim grew up in a monoculture where traditional values were giving way to the prevailing Western ethos.

'I'm a Meckering boy. It was a great little town, but very narrow culturally. Everyone had the same history. Mostly bloody Irish convicts: and then everyone had been in the town for generations.'

Tania is Maori by birth, but like her mother and her brothers, she had benefitted from the inclusiveness of the Australian Indigenous culture.

'Because I grew up in the road camps at Fitzroy Crossing, all the people I went to school with were Aboriginal people, so I've always had that Aboriginal culture in my background,' she says. Aboriginal culture is the closest and most important culture to her, the warp through which the diverse cultural threads of Broome are weaved, whereas in Meckering the warp and weft of the cultural cloth were all made of the same thread.

'Growing up in a community where everyone's the same, you think everyone speaks like you,' says Tim. 'The first time I heard an Italian speak English was a bit of a culture shock—I had no idea that everyone didn't sound the same. And then, when you as a kid think, "Maybe we are the different ones," it's a real insight. You can't hear your own accent and I don't think you can see your own culture, you can only see it reflected in someone else's.'

From these early thoughts grew Tim's lifelong interest with what is divergent, what is new, what isn't known yet. Whereas such a gulf in culture can sever some relationships, for Tim the contrast between their backgrounds simply added to his fascination with Tania.

'Indigenous culture is very different—confusing, until you start figuring it out. I like that extended culture of belonging. We have an exclusive culture where we do things for our kids but not necessarily for our cousins' kids. It's not wrong, it's just culture. Indigenous people try to build their families and include more people. We try to exclude people from our nuclear families,' says Tim.

Even agriculture in Broome has little in common with the farms of relatives and friends Tim knew from childhood. If Tim saw a pastoralist in the south, he wasn't in town with a seeder in for repairs, but with the nose cone of his plane. Even the hats here are distinctive: down south they are worn low and dark, in the north hats are pale and high-domed.

Tim's interest in the gulf between Broome and the Australia he knew best was contagious: in short order Tania wanted to see the Australia which had produced someone so intriguingly like and unlike herself, and any other Australias that were out there, too.

'I'd barely been out of Broome or the Kimberley. Our plan was to work our way around Australia, but we had to go and see his children and family first. So we went in that direction,' says Tania.

'I wanted the family to meet the new woman—and that went great. But Dad was crook. He had cancer and he was on the way out ...'

'So we just didn't go any further,' says Tania.

'We were staying at Mum and Dad's and I wasn't working. I don't handle not working at all well, so I applied for some jobs and I ended up getting one with the Agricultural Department in Moora.'

The bewilderment Tim had felt in his first weeks in Broome, Tania felt in the inland country just north of Perth. Surely she'd left Australia! These undulating soft plains, covered in paddocks full of larger-than-she-had-expected livestock or strangely uniform heavy-headed grass—which was in fact wheat—didn't belong to the Australia she knew.

When they moved to the country town of Moora life revealed yet more cultural differences.

'We had a discussion and decided we'd have a baby. We didn't actually think beyond that. There was no intention or discussion around getting married. We just thought, "Let's have a baby,"' says Tania.

'I was keen on the baby, but I wasn't sure about the marriage bit, having had one experience that wasn't great,' says Tim. 'I was committed, I had decided that this was the woman for me, that was it, but I felt we could do without the bit of paper.'

At least, that's how he thought he'd feel. Children do hold up a mirror to their parents every bit as much as being immersed in another culture does: suddenly Tim knew that he wasn't having his child considered a bastard.

'Then I fell pregnant and I remember Tim looking at me and saying, "We'll have to get married now." I'd have done fine without the marriage bit. It was part of how he grew up and where he came from: you can't have a child out of wedlock.'

They went for a traditional country wedding: in fact, the very first wedding Tania, country girl though she was, had ever attended.

'We had the wedding my mother wanted but didn't have—I'd have been happy with a pig on a spit in the backyard,' says Tania.

Tania thought she knew what the traditional country wedding involved. It had to be a full-on rellie bash, a bang-up meal, all the trimmings and hullabaloo and she would wear a white dress and Tim a suit, and they'd drive away in the HQ ute.

'So all my aunties, uncles and cousins, everyone's there,' says Tim, who is setting the scene for me.

'My grandparents came over for it,' says Tania.

'Joan is a master chef, she and her mates have done all the cooking and the food is in the hall. We get married. Photographs have been taken. Tania's about six months pregnant and she's hungry. So we sit down and have a feed. Then we finish and Tania says, "That's it, we're going."'

Tim had one moment of utter confusion. Then he got it: the gulf between their disparate heritages had opened up again. Although Tania looked the part in her white dress, these were his traditions and not hers.

'I had to explain—at our own wedding—that you can't just walk out at that stage of proceedings. The best man's got to toast the bridesmaids, I'll give a speech, then we've got the bridal waltz.'

Tania's deep immersion experience in Tim's social mores at her own wedding is a story Tim loves to tell. He's still laughing about it twenty-five years later.

Once Tania had fallen pregnant she had known that preparation for her child's arrival was going to take her into new terrain. Her mother's abusive marriage was also her childhood, and Tania had been abused as well. As Sophie grew in her womb, nineteen-year-old Tania tried to keep pace. A brutal childhood like Tania's too often echoes down the generations, vulnerability and abuse begetting more. Knowing this, she set about creating a new story for her children, and theirs. She did this through counselling and also let-in-the-light talks with a good friend who'd travelled the same path and knew that bringing such wounds into the open was the first step in healing them and then leaving them behind. Her daughter Sophie was born in 1992 and Jade in 1993.

'Between having the two girls I went from fretting that they might experience my past life to knowing that they will be safe and Tim loved them and could be trusted. I've always been open with my girls about my past and if I had any niggles I accepted them for what they were and worked very hard not to stop the girls having a life with freedom. I gave the kids every protective skill in the world to address anything that was even suggested when it came to their bodies.'

The people best able to talk about how Tania achieved this are Sophie and Jade themselves.

'I always remember Mum being very honest. What I remember most was not the fact that this past happened, but that the same fate was never going to be an option for Sophie and me,' says Jade.

'It wasn't a one-time-only speech and leave-it-at-that deal. It was a continuous dialogue that was always open and developed alongside with us,' says Sophie.

'Mum ensured that we always had a choice and although Dad was quiet-natured in my upbringing, he always supported our decisions as well. I knew I had the freedom to do anything. Mum was very encouraging of us being able to say no if there was something we didn't want to do such as going to the shops with my nanna. This may not have been the intention of the lesson, but I think it's always stuck with me since a young age that I'm allowed to say no and that this was okay and sometimes the right answer. Not only did Mum change the cycle of abuse, she also gave us all the encouragement and support that she never got as a child,' says Jade.

'The strength my mother had to get through her childhood is something I have yet to see in anyone else and I have serious doubts I ever will,' says Sophie.

The girls are right to be proud. I don't know anyone with more resilience.

Children are powerful change agents. The directness with which the little girls shared their richly emotional lives shaped Tim and Tania's family life.

'The girls didn't tolerate that Tim couldn't make it to something that was important to them. They would just burst into tears and tell him. At first he struggled to deal with all the emotional stuff in our household, but in the end he relented and just went with the flow and lived his life around us girls,' says Tania.

At work life wasn't quite so rosy for Tim. The role of the Agricultural Department is to support farmers to make more money. Where more money has been made, more support follows. Financially this sounds reasonable, but in practical terms this means that the farmers who most need the support of innovative science attract the least investment by the government. Tim was less interested in refining an established production system to squeeze out more income—it was the frontiers that appealed to him. He was (and still is) drawn most to working with farmers and pastoralists who were trying to turn around land degradation, who were adapting to climate change, who were trying to find new industries and were frontier-thinkers themselves. Quite close to Moora was an innovative group of farmers trying to salvage some of Australia's most marginal farmland: the West Midlands.

This was sandplain country that had once been covered in low shrubs: their dense interlocking roots anchoring the sand together, their leaf litter endlessly composting and humidifying the sand, pulling moisture up towards the surface for the roots of the annual grasses to capture. Overgrazing had seen the shrubs die, the sand loosen and blow, and less and less grass every year. Cropping had only made things worse. On top of the soil it looked bad, but there was a bigger, unseen disaster occurring underneath.

Healthy soil is an enduring carbon trap, but when soil is wrecked, as this soil had been, it not only releases the carbon stored within, it doesn't sequester more. A great deal more carbon is stored below ground than above it: the ratio is for every one tonne of carbon stored above in pasture, bush or trees, there are ten tonnes of carbon below. Degraded, eroded and bare soil is unpleasant to the eye but worse still is that which can't actually be seen: the earth unwillingly releasing additional carbon into our overheating world. Under their breath industry experts were muttering the word 'basket-case' in relation to the West Midlands, and averting their eyes. Farmers were abandoning their farms—with the best will in the world, you can't make a living when one hectare of land feeds only one sheep.

Abandoning farming land has happened throughout history and it happens in waves. The emotions that go with this are often similar to those experienced on leaving a marriage. What was once loved now repels you. Farmers report feeling ill on some parts of a property—it might remind them of a particularly bad day or a tragic incident. With no hope of an income there's no reason to stay. Just such a wave of walk-offs had started in the West Midlands.

'It was going to get a lot worse. It was on the brink of collapse. The farming system fails, no-one makes money, the community fails and it all goes to pieces. It's the triple bottom line—it's got to be environmentally, financially and socially sustainable. If one doesn't work, the other two won't. The only thing I thought might work to save the West Midlands was tagasaste,' says Tim.

The question was: could the lost native perennials be replaced? If so, could that heal the land? Tagasaste is a tall perennial shrub (not native to Australia), which is also good stock food. It grows fast. Its roots snake in deep, meaning that it can survive the increasingly erratic rainfall and hot, dry summers. Tagasaste roots capture and store nitrogen. More nitrogen in the soil then helps all other plants grow. The hope was that tagasaste planting could help set off a positive chain reaction in the soil so that it would become progressively healthier over time.

Planting tagasaste was just one part of this project. How stock was managed in the West Midland farms had to be changed as well. When we acknowledge that too many animals grazing for too long is destructive—killing plants and exposing soil—we also have to acknowledge that these animals must be able to contribute to ecosystem restoration. The right number of animals grazing for the right amount of time can till the soil with their hooves, fertilise it with their manure and prune plants down to their grazing points, thus kick-starting more root growth, which then powers better leaf growth. This is what happens in nature. In switching from annual grasses back to perennial shrubs, the grazing methods also had to change to support that type of landscape.

Tim had been made manager of the Moora office. In short order he'd created an office in the coastal town of Jurien (closer to the Western Midlands). He then demoted himself to take on the tagasaste project and spend his days working alongside the West Midland farmers. Sophie and Jade were just entering primary school when the family moved to Jurien. It was at this time that Tim's sons Scott and David came to live with them. The two boys were just entering high school.

'Everyone got on great,' says Tania. 'The boys were keen to join in with everything and they loved the girls, and the girls loved their big brothers.'

It was a very happy time in the Wiley home. The beaches laid out their wealth at the children's feet. The older two cared for the younger two: books were shared, play equipment was made and pictures were drawn.

And at work the tagasaste project was soon successful—once the fertilising schedule was fine-tuned, the tagasaste grew, grass grew, soil stabilised and there was enough grass growing for the farmer to run stock profitably. Less enjoyable was the reaction from the industry experts who had felt nothing would work.

'Once we started having success, they all got upset. They all expected it to fail. That was really handy initially. Because they did not expect success, they didn't care what I did. But then some of them really gave me curry, they tried to stop the project, tried to stop me talking to farmers ...'

Where Tania had shown that the human heart can repair and grow afresh, Tim had shown that the same thing can happen with land. The revitalisation of the ecosystems, economy and community of the West Midlands, beginning with the change in the farming system, is one of the great success stories in Australian agriculture.

One long-acknowledged fact from marriage research is how very similar spouses are in terms of intelligence. At the time Tim was engaged in his world-changing radical-action research, Tania was working in the crayfish factory in Jurien or at the supermarket.

'I didn't marry my wife for her brains,' Tim says at the beginning of this story. Tania laughs. Of course, when you marry a person you marry all of them—Tania's brains cannot be separated from Tania's quick reasoning, her ability to see when change is required and from there make those changes—but I know what he means. Passion, not rationality, brought these two together.

'But there's a story that's got to be told. I'm just too old for the computer, ay? I just missed it at high school, just missed it at university and when I worked in private industry I missed it there. I'd never touched a computer. So when I joined the

Agriculture Department in Moora they gave me a room with a desk and sitting on the desk was a computer and I'd never used one before. I've got this nice young fellow in the office with me, Tom, and I said, "Okay, how do you work this thing, where's the on button?"'

Eventually convinced that Tim wasn't kidding, Tom taught him how to turn on the computer and operate it. Tim did learn to be competent in using the computer, but when it crashed, as it frequently did, he was undone. Back he would go to the young fellow, or to the nearby vet, who was also a computer nerd.

'So I could drive it—but I couldn't fix it. A bit like the stereotypical woman who learns to drive a car but has no idea what's under the bonnet. I was like that with a computer. When I escaped to Jurien I had an office at home and a computer there. Tania used to bring me a coffee in the office. It had been there a while when it crashed.

'I have no tolerance for computers. I tried a few things and got upset, went into a rage and stormed out through the kitchen. Tania said to me, "What are you doing?" I said, "Bloody computers, it won't work, I'm going to use it for an anchor." So she said, "Can I have a look at it, see if I can fix it?" I said, "Don't be stupid, you've never touched a computer, you won't know what to do." I had no idea of her talents or capabilities. She said, "Oh, go on, let me," and she went in. About ten minutes later she came out and said, "I've fixed it." I said, "What do you mean?" She said, "I've fixed it." I said, "You can't have. You've never touched a computer before, you've only watched me with it."

'So she'd just watched me use it and she'd figured it out. I couldn't believe it. I'd married a computer genius. So I went down to the pub and I was bragging to all the boys about this smart woman I'd married. And it turns out all these people had bought computers and there was no computer technician in town. She ended up fixing all their computers.'

Nothing in Tania's final years of education had prepared her for this kind of technical work—or, indeed, for work at all.

'I didn't think Broome was a racist town, but there was this racism in the institutions, this belief that black people are stupid. Coming from outside it really struck me,' says Tim.

Whereas Tim had been encouraged to go to university, no such encouragement was provided to Tania. Her concluding years of school prepared her instead for a future on the dole. And the situation hasn't changed, she says. This lack of expectation on the part of our society is not just the "absence" it is so often described as in the media. It is, instead, an active anticipation by some teachers that black children and teenagers will fail. So marked is this that sometimes a success story right in front of them does not even enter their consciousness.

Tania tells the story of a school reunion she attended with her brother.

'The principal was asking my brother next to me what he was doing. And my brother said, "Oh you should ask Tania about her work, she's working for the University of Western Australia," and the principal just wasn't interested.'

Expectations do count. Very rarely does anyone do anything without a cheer squad of family and friends who believe in them. Australian society as a whole tends to believe in the Tims of this world: the white middle-class males. Our expectations of our Tanias—the black women who are unaware of their own potential—are often actively negative. For Tania to learn that society was wrong about her, required the intervention of people powerful enough to dispel her assumptions about herself. Tim's stunned pride in her computer wizardry was the start of her journey of learning what she was capable of. For the first time Tania began to apply for technical and administrative positions.

Not one of these applications was successful.

'Everyone saw me as a checkout chick or a barmaid or someone who wrapped crayfish. When I applied for another kind of job the assumption was that I wouldn't have a clue. I found it really hard. I knew I could do the other jobs. So I had to stop work for a whole year. Then I started applying again and I got a job working at the telecentre. I messed around with lots of computers there and I really gained skills. If they asked me if I could fix it I would say, "No worries," and then I'd mess around for forty to fifty minutes and I'd finally work it out. I was pretty much self-taught with computers.'

Tim is still castigating himself for his lack of knowledge of Tania's capabilities.

'Now I think it's a form of child abuse, these low expectations ... all these guys out in the bush who can speak five languages and we call them uneducated,' he says.

'But given my history,' says Tania, 'with how I grew up, I probably didn't think I was capable myself either. It's been other people over the years who have said, "Tarn, you can do this," and who have eventually got me to the point where I believed in myself, too.'

When Tim 'discovered his wife had a brain' he was keen that she should have all the opportunities that had come his way—and the same professional experience and success he's had.

'I came from a fairly poor family because we got wiped out with the earthquake. Lots of my relatives were farmers, lots of my mates were farmers' kids, but my old man was the town mechanic and I realised that I didn't want to be a mechanic. Because I wasn't born a farmer's son I thought I could never be a farmer—that's another kind of cultural barrier—and so the way for me to be in agriculture was to go to university. And I was lucky in that there was free education and the expectation was that some of us would go, even though it wasn't that common.'

Tania had never even considered that university was something she could do—and she didn't start to consider it until she met Professor Ann Larson, who headed the Combined University Centre for Rural Health. This occurred in 2004 when Tim moved to a new job in Geraldton at the successful conclusion of the tagasaste project.

Ann's manner is warm and engaging, but you can also almost feel the air around her pulsing with thought. She holds vast data fields of people and priorities and possibilities in her head and all the time she is juggling them to find the best fit for the best result. And she cares. Her academic background is simply a tool: she never forgets that it is people away from the big cities that she serves. The job she eventually hired Tania for was one she'd never been able to fill satisfactorily.

'We asked about video-conferencing. Tania told us that she got the youth in different towns to play charades together,' says Ann. The job was Tania's from that moment. 'Right then and there I knew I wanted someone who would think of things no-one else on my team could think of—and Tania kept doing it.'

'I was told they interviewed a lot of people with academic backgrounds,' says Tania. 'I was the only one who didn't have this. But Ann saw something in me and loved my community-development experience. I thank the stars that I was able to meet people like her who gave me the support to help me grow.'

Before long Ann was urging Tania to consider studying at university herself.

'With Ann's support I started studying externally: an arts degree, majoring in community development.'

Tim had come to Geraldton hoping to find yet more new frontiers in agriculture—to be part of perceiving and taking up new opportunities to revitalise land and the farmers' profits, sustain rural communities and create a healthier planet. In short order he, along with many others in the agricultural community, had identified just such an opportunity. Five years later, in rage, in disappointment so acute he could have wept, it became the issue over which he would resign.

'It should have been a no-brainer,' he says. The opportunity he saw was for farmers to store carbon in their soil, and to be paid for doing so. More carbon in the soil means healthier soil, and less carbon in the atmosphere.

It can be difficult to understand how one molecule (and a molecule so intrinsic to the creation of organic matter) can do so much good in large quantities in the soil, and such damage in large quantities in the air. The term 'greenhouse effect' adds to the confusion. In fact, the effect of carbon in the atmosphere is far closer to being a one-way mirror. Carbon dioxide lets in short-wave heat from the sun: it also keeps in long-wave heat radiated out from the earth. The more carbon dioxide, the more heat is both allowed in and kept in. The more the earth heats up, the faster the deserts grow, the faster the deserts grow, the more carbon is released and the hotter it gets.

The carbon in Australian soils is half-gone after two centuries of European farming techniques. Reversing this would be a gift to the world: a vast contribution towards mitigating climate change. But the dollars to support the switch to the right kind of farming methods have long left the agricultural community. The famous phrase 'riding on the sheep's back' speaks directly to the flow of dollars from bush to city. The heritage buildings in our cities and their surrounding landscaping, the establishment of universities and banks, the cultural life of metropolises: all were brought into being by dollars from the bush. As well as the dollars, what was exported—without ever being replenished—was the health of our soils, our biodiversity and our nutrients.

An emissions-trading scheme that included soil-carbon sequestration would have given farmers the dollars with which to reverse this trend. This was the big opportunity Tim desperately wanted to see made real. It has never happened; indeed the chance has retreated further in recent years. But back then it teetered agonisingly close on the brink of the possible.

While Tim was struggling with barriers to success, Tania, for the very first time, was not. Study was going well. Work was engaging. Now a management position had opened up in the remote desert town of Wiluna. This was a community and country Tania had often visited in working for the university: she felt at home, she felt she could do the work. But it did mean that she would have to live away from Tim and the girls.

'Tim has never, ever held me back. He's never said you can't,' says Tania.

'It was a tough year—I wasn't a great mother—but it was Tania's chance,' says Tim.

Wiluna is a country of circles: clay pans, spinifex rings and curves interlacing across the landscape, bushes sweeping their curves on the earth, grass stalks spreading out like bouquets into the welcoming air, ants' nests raised for rain. Close to the town site are the mines: cut deep in search of gold, wide mouths howling into space, with the pastoral lands and the desert hugging up against them like a comforting blanket.

It is in that nearby desert that Australia's most famous version of Romeo and Juliet played out. Passionate romantic love is an anarchic force. It goes against all the other reasons for marriage that societies have generated throughout human history: strengthening business ties or consolidating power bases between two families, reinforcing social class or social prejudice or demonstrating support for the prevailing religion. Traditional Indigenous society was no different. Rule-breaking in the name of passion was every bit as unwelcome in the Wiluna clans.

Passion (or lust) is as distinct from the deep romantic attachment it becomes as prose is to poetry. Whereas the prose writer is engaged in constructing a world in your mind, the poet is better perceived as an electrician. She strips back the protective layer from your nerve and with deft moves wires it to a living thought or perhaps an association you'd never make. Sometimes it's a cataclysm, sometimes just a tingle of contrast. Passion is like this: mind has gone and body has gone—it is just nerves, spirit, energy, touching. It is profoundly disruptive to society.

In the 1930s many Wiluna Aboriginal people were leading their traditional nomadic lives. All the rules still held and rule-breakers earned severe punishment. Girls married older men. Boys waited until they were old men themselves. Marriages were arranged well ahead of time. Yatungka was betrothed to an older man. But she loved Warri and he loved her. Defying every tradition—and knowing they were risking death—they ran away together into the desert.

Pursuit was quick, but Warri and Yatungka found shelter with another tribe, and were protected from retribution for a time. But there's no expiry date on tribal punishment—and Warri and Yatungka remained fearful. The 1930s was also the height of the gold rush around Wiluna. Life in town was arguably easier than the boom-and-bust life of the desert, and soon Aboriginal people moved to where there was always water, and medicine to save children's lives. Warri and Yatungka, with their three children and their dogs, stayed in the desert.

Their daughter died. Still they stayed in the desert, keeping clear of tribal reprisal. Their sons left in their teen years to take up working in the towns and on stations. By the 1960s the couple had become legendary figures. Were they still out there somewhere in the Gibson Desert, or had they perished?

Mudjon was one of the original group of warriors who had tracked the pair after their elopement. He had grown up with Warri and so for him these two people were very far from legendary. He kept an eye on the sky. He felt his own loss of strength with the years. He imagined Warri and Yatungka without young people to help them, and he imagined that most vividly in the dry times.

In 1977, three years into a severe drought, he felt the time had come to go looking. Search party in tow, he headed into the desert, guided by the map unrolling in his head. They saw almost no water, and his hopes were evaporating further with every dry clay pan passed. Then, in the air, unfurling like a flag, he saw a wisp of smoke rising in the sand hills. Warri and Yatungka: emaciated, ill, weary, ready for rescue. There was no tribal punishment for these two, now celebrated as the last of the nomads.

Their family still live in Wiluna to this day, and it remains a between-two-worlds place. Aboriginal people gather here to discuss and apply the law. And every year, in suits and white cars, come the bureaucrats and the politicians for their meetings. So different are the two cultures that the perceptions of one sometimes can't even admit the perceptions of the other. But there are also the halfway places which try to bridge the two worlds: the art gallery, the ranger program. It was within these that Tania had come to work.

'The job was the Community Development Manager with the Shire of Wiluna. My role was to look after a few different departments they had: the ranger, the swimming pool, the sports and recreation centre, the art gallery and tourism.'

After years of cultural immersion in Tim's half of Australia and brimming with the skills she had gained from that time, Tania was back in the kind of Australia she'd known first. She loved the chance to work in strategic planning, networking and sharing, and to help her managers look with two sets of eyes: first, to see what it was that people wanted; next, to reconcile that as best they could with the shire's scope and strategy. She loved, too, the people and the place. The look of a town is immaterial to Tania—and Wiluna is a strange mix of battered and just-built—it is the people and the land that she inevitably falls in love with.

That it is people who are the critical asset of any place is something Tim echoes.

'I'm trained as a scientist, but I always understood—I knew from growing up in a little country town—that it is always the people that are most important. Agriculture is successful if the people know how to do it well.' Tim was missing living with Tania full-time. He was loathing watching the best opportunity in Australian agriculture being ignored by policymakers. A year after she had moved to Wiluna, he resigned from the Agriculture Department and moved to be with her. This decision took Tim into Tania's world. Wiluna was the beginning of Tim's journey into the spirituality of land and his appreciation of the indivisibility of land from the human soul.

'The spirituality of the Aboriginal culture is really strong and powerful, and strange things happen. Tania knew that already, but for me as a scientist it was a shock. Wiluna and then Marble Bar is where I started to understand the spiritual aspect of the land through Indigenous cultures.'

'Tim had just made the move and I thought I'd take him out to the places I'd explored. So we headed out to this particular area where there is a ravine. Now, I could feel one half of it was no good—I just didn't go anywhere near it—but I knew I could be on the other side of it.'

Tim was keen to explore and simply strode away, down into the guts of the ravine.

'He was gone for an hour and I was starting to think, "Where the hell is he?" Eventually he returned, shaking like a leaf. And I said, "What's wrong with you?"'

'I'd walked into the ravine and I started to feel ill. I took a step, I felt sick. I felt sicker with every step. It was like someone had a microwave pointed at my brain, as if my brain was going to explode, that's how strong it was. Eventually I twigged what was going on. I was in the wrong spot, I needed to get out of there.'

In this environment Tim was an explorer without a map or a compass. He had nothing in him to provide a footing or even bearings so that he could begin to understand what had happened. He was a scientist, but this was a radical, reality-altering and expanding experience.

'You hear some pretty weird stories, but I guess I've come to accept them, not try to deny them, because once you've had that experience you can't deny it. There are other forces in the landscape that we don't understand but the mob seem to understand. I don't believe now you can ignore the spirituality of the land.'

What underlay his experience in the ravine Tim is yet to discover, but it was enough for him to become eager to learn more of what Aboriginal people saw, felt and understood. Like all scientists, he is an information junkie. He began to be concerned that his clients—who were now pastoralists rather than farmers—were missing out on a relationship of potentially great benefit.

'We've got the story of clashes and massacres and there is no doubt that happened. But the other story is not told, of really close, cooperative relationships that lasted for generations, and in some cases still do. There's the odd pastoralist out there who is the complete redneck, but they really aren't too many and that's encouraging.'

Tim believes the evidence that this relationship was the common experience can be found in all kinds of ways.

'In the De Grey River catchment we had this massive flood with Cyclone Rusty, biggest in living memory—at its widest it was ninety kilometres wide,' he says. In fact, for most of the time the De Grey River is a large dry bed. When it is flowing it is no more than 130 metres across.

'All the old, original homesteads are built within two hundred metres of the main river channel and when you see a flood like that you think the builders would have had to be mad. From the air you could see all the original homesteads, on a strip of sand, in a ninety-kilometre-wide inland sea. The reason none of those original homesteads went under water is that they were built to be above even the biggest floods—but those first settlers wouldn't have known what a big flood could look like. The local Aboriginal people would have told them that,' says Tim. 'The early pioneers tapped into the traditional owners' knowledge, respected that knowledge and would have obeyed that knowledge, otherwise they'd probably have got a spear through them.'

Loving the same land can create a connection as profound as loving the same child. Caring, even caring in very different ways, is a forger of mutual appreciation and bonds built on a shared commitment to the wellbeing of the land. The stories of 'other forces in the landscape' that Tim mentions are found all over Australia, not just in the outback, but in cities, too. The mysterious stewardship of the traditional owners is another kind of land care. It is based on a body of knowledge, a language and a science most of us don't yet understand.

'I was talking to Chris Ward at Lake Violet outside of Wiluna—they've been there for five generations, they were the original settlers. I said, "How do you get on with the mob?" And he says, "Oh really, really well, my great-great-grandfather was best mates with these guys in town today, and we have this friendship passed down through the generations." And I asked the mob and they said, "Oh, our family were best mates with his great-great-grandfather." There's been a strong positive relationship out there for five generations on that property. No dramas at all. Chris knows a lot of the Aboriginal history for his property: he respects them and they respect him. Where it exists it works really well.'

Sadly, that mutual respect isn't found everywhere, not because of a lack of goodwill, but simply as a function of the revolving ownership of many pastoral properties. Tim identifies 1967 as a critical year: with the increase in Aboriginal stockmen's wages, the number of stockmen employed greatly decreased, and many families moved to find work in the towns. After this time, if a property changed hands, often pastoralists and traditional owners never met. Tim believes this is a loss felt deeply on both sides, yet rarely do either pastoralists or traditional owners act to re-create the relationships.

'There is a need for a "dating service" out there,' says Tim. 'Pastoralists often say to me they would like to know more about the Aboriginal history and culture of the sites on their place. They don't want to muck it up—but they don't know where those sites are, they don't know how to manage them. I say, "Why don't you talk to the traditional owners?" and they don't know who the traditional owners are. Then there's the mob in town, they don't know the pastoralists and they're too scared to go and introduce themselves.'

Their shared lives in Wiluna (and then Marble Bar, where they moved next) taught Tania and Tim that their relationship could act as a bridge between traditional owners and pastoralists.

'It was Wiluna that really taught me that this was where we fit. This is where our common links are, this is where we are strong because we have those relationships on both sides of things and are able to bring it together. That's bound what we do—we think and feel the same in our own different fields, but they connect really nicely,' says Tania.

'When Tania was working with those communities I had the opportunity to sit with very traditional cultural people and listen to them and learn from them. Without her I wouldn't have developed those relationships—I'd have just been working with the pastoralists.'

In helping Tim connect meaningfully to Aboriginal people Tania was further refining her mastery of one of the most precious and rare skill sets in Australia: cultural brokering. We tend to understand cultural brokers as intermediaries, messengers and translators between two or three different cultures. That's not quite it, though. When a message is passed from a person of one culture to a person of another, at that very moment of transmission, the broker absorbs and holds the message and very gently, in their body and their face, in their gestures, in their words, they reframe it for both people.

The broker says and conveys what was meant to be said and conveyed by one person to the other, and they help the other person hear it and convey their response in return. It all happens in a flash. It is teaching as much as translating, building trust as much as it is building knowledge, being in the moment with the people rather than doing any particular thing. Nowhere is this harder—and more important—than in brokering across the gap between any traditional culture (where it is all about cooperation, sharing, surviving and spirituality) and any modern Western culture (where it is all about specialising, owning, producing and self-expression). We have nowhere near enough of these people, simply because they are most often created when an unusual sort of person is given an unusual kind of life.

Such expertise in negotiating boundaries can only be developed when a born negotiator has had to make their way back and forth across a society's liminal spaces for a very long time. Of course, this has been Tania's story. From living under the oppression of domestic violence and low expectations to suddenly having to find her way in Australia's mainstream and finally to her apprenticeship on the frontiers of academia under Ann Larson, she's been crisscrossing Australia's cultural borders for a very long time. And she is a born negotiator. The wonder is not that she's become a cultural broker but that her marriage to Tim has taken her into a place where we have so few cultural brokers working: the interface between modern agricultural science and the oldest living culture on the planet.

If Wiluna had showed Tania that this in-between space was where she and Tim fitted, Marble Bar went one step further. It adopted them.

'The day we rocked up, someone said, "Do you need a hand unloading?" and we didn't have any tucker and Foxy the publican said, "Oh, we'd better feed you." As soon as you walk in you feel a sense of community,' says Tim.

Marble Bar is an entire community living on the borders of old Indigenous culture and the new mainstream. There are only two hundred people in Marble Bar: more of them are Indigenous than not, and everyone gets on.

'You've got people who come up with an idea, the people who say, "Yes let's do that!" and then the organisers who make it happen,' says Tania.

These are the ingredients, she says, for a lively and rich community life, no matter a town's size. Tim and Tania had a year and a half in tidy, pretty Marble Bar, then a year and a half in Port Hedland, when they spent most weekends travelling back to Marble Bar, and then they returned to Marble Bar for another two years.

In and around Marble Bar Tim and Tania played and worked, and listened and changed. Tania was managing the Commonwealth Development Employment Program (CDEP) in three communities (Warralong, Gooda Binya/Marble Bar and Irrungadji/Nullagine), while Tim worked on a range of projects, including a bio-diesel project for Ashburton Aboriginal Corporation. In both their work and leisure hours they were listening to custodians of the very oldest knowledge about what it means to be human, what it means to work together and all the ways humans, land, animals, plants and spirit interact.

The work Tania was doing is considered one of the 'impossible' jobs in outback communities. Mostly CDEP seems to not quite do what it is meant to do: that is, provide meaningful work and training to Aboriginal people and get the jobs done that need to be done. Too often a community's CDEP yard is a place where any hope of self-direction and meaningful work must be abandoned at the door, and cynicism and distrust hangs in the air. Even worse, a CDEP program can expand rifts, or even create them, between different groups in a community.

'When I left the CDEP program the numbers of people turning up for work had tripled,' says Tania. What had made the difference was the fact that Tania didn't see her role as 'organising and telling', but rather as 'facilitating and asking'.

'If there was a problem I'd say, "How are we going to fix this?" and they'd say, "Oh, we could do this, or we could do this." And I'd say, "So what do you want to do?" and they'd say, "Let's try this." At the end of projects there was complete ownership of those projects because it hadn't been me saying, "This is what you have to do." People chose what they wanted to do.

'And I didn't acknowledge any family issues between any of the mobs. If you acknowledge there's a rift you enhance it. With those that couldn't work together because of the son-in-law and mother-in-law thing, we just worked around those cultural zones. I had a whole pile of jobs that the guys said they wanted to do and I let people pick what they wanted to do and they went off and did it. They solved their issues culturally among themselves. As long as I provided the tools and resources for them to do what they wished, that was all I needed to do.'

'That's the way I work with farmers and pastoralists, you've got to treat people with a bit of respect,' says Tim. 'I say this is your place, your life, your problems, you've got a brain and you'll figure it out ... we are just here to help.'

Just as there are rifts in Indigenous groups, there are rifts between pastoralists, too.

'One of the things I did when I got there was go out to the De Grey Land Conservation District Committee and say, "Are you keen to get fired up again?" They said, "Yep," and early on what we said to the group was, "Look there's going to be disputes among neighbours, so we're going to have to have a way of dealing with it—not ignoring it, but not letting it get in the road of everything else."'

Tim sees another parallel between pastoralists and Indigenous people: over the last few generations in the pastoral country the relationship between government and pastoralists has been characterised by increasing government control and consequent increasing distrust on both sides.

'The government's been the landlord, the pastoralist the tenant. The government has treated pastoralists like naughty boys out there trying to rip them off. The pastoralists see the government as the policeman trying to beat them into submission. I found this culture a shock, having come from the wheatbelt freehold land where it doesn't exist. It's really a significant problem, that lack of trust, the lack of power for pastoralists and control by government,' Tim says.

He feels it is a far milder echo of the extreme and ongoing reluctance of government agencies to allow Indigenous people control over their own lives. Tightening government control is not just, he says, a reflection of the modern Australian trend towards tighter management and more and more documentation, but the distrust by public servants of both pastoralists and Indigenous people.

'Of course, the ultimate disempowerment has been for the Aboriginal people. In both cases we have this power imbalance and control by government that have now been in place for generations. We need to get rid of the deeply ingrained British class culture of power and control and elitism, which we so unfortunately inherited from the Poms and it is still there. That thinking is still ingrained in government. These guys are so sharp and switched on, but they don't get treated that way.

The only way to get real change is for people at the grassroots to take responsibility for their own problems and speak for themselves. That's Tania's and my job: to make sure they can speak. But I've found that with these groups when you give them the opportunity to take control, they're very scared and reluctant to take it on.'

At the heart of this reluctance is a lack of trust in the institution offering the opportunity. Both pastoralists and Indigenous people have a history of painfully discovering that opportunities presented have been illusions or have had strings attached.

'So how do we overcome that, how do we break that cycle and how do we change the relationships? Tania and I have the same view of what needs to happen: it's exactly the same with the pastoral industry as it is with Indigenous society. What I do with pastoralists, and what Tania does with the mob, is to try to create a new culture that breaks those existing power relationships and develops one of collaboration and cooperation in order to create links. You can do anything if you work together, but you have to build trust. We know it works—and when it works it is just so rewarding.'

Tim and Tania are seeing so much speaking up, collaborating and taking control all the time now in the Kimberley and the Pilbara. It's a new way which borrows from both traditional and modern Western cultures—collaborating, for example, is a strongly traditional value, but speaking up is very much a modern Western behaviour. Their favourite example of seeing this culture emerging came in the middle of a project Tim created which brought Tania's connections and work with the mob together with Tim's connections and work in agriculture.

In working with pastoralists in the De Grey River catchment in 2013 Tim had found that the scale of the properties he was working with prevented him from being able to build and hold a mental map of how they worked. Without that encompassing map of the whole catchment, Tim knew that any intervention might work on a small scale but do more damage somewhere else. The scale, coupled with the complexity of the interactions in the landscape, meant a map showing how it all worked was vital.

'I went from four hundred hectares to four hundred thousand hectares—where do you start? It was just too overwhelming.'

To help him make sense of the landscape over many hundreds of square kilometres, Tim invited Peter Andrews (a farmer who has had remarkable success in turning degraded land into fertile, healthy land again) to work with pastoralists in the De Grey River catchment.

'Early in my career I figured this out and it is really important: you can't learn anything from someone who thinks like you do, you can only learn from someone who thinks differently. So I like talking to nutcases, the thinkers with radical ideas—like Peter Andrews. He's a genius. He talks about how to read the landscape, these patterns, the water—its movement and control.'

Peter Andrews is considered a land-prophet, a water-whisperer, with a singular concentration that lets him observe, interpret and predict how land and water and plants will relate over many rains. Tim had met him several times over the years, and was convinced that he needed Peter to assist him in mapping the geomorphology of the De Grey catchment, which holds a number of pastoral properties.

'I've figured out a way to map it, based on Peter's stuff, and it's pretty new, but it's working really well.'

This map is the basis for figuring out how to interact with the landscape: to see how best to send water to an area that has been water-starved due to man-made structures such as mines or roads, or how to slow water down by such actions as altering how animals graze so more plants grow and water can sink into the earth along with the plants' roots.

Tim was aware that while Peter's thinking is cutting-edge in this time and place, Peter also knows his way of seeing land isn't unique to him. When Peter first encountered traditional 'abstract' Aboriginal art he was amazed by it. He did not see art but a map presenting detailed information about how water moved in the artist's landscape.

'All the information was presented and Peter could read the message. He was pretty keen to get out and meet some of our guys and talk to them because he'd recognised that this knowledge had been pre-existing in their culture and was expressed in their art.

'To help me learn this same thing, I was going home and using Google Earth—basically painting out what I'd learned onto Google Earth. Peter can do that from the ground—when you really understand it you don't need to see it from above. Then Tania bought me a painting from someone who lived out near the South Australian border. After my experience using Google Earth, when I saw it, I said, "Whoever painted this has painted a Peter Andrews description of how landscape and water works." Then one day I was travelling between Perth and Alice Springs and I looked out of the window of the plane from thirty thousand feet and I said, "That's our painting."'

With this in mind, Tim had lined up both pastoralists and traditional owners to meet Peter and work with him tracking the actions of water in the land, reading the subtle changes in landscape and slope. And it was then that Phillip, an Aboriginal man well into his middle years, began to speak up, to offer his knowledge in collaboration with the group.

'Phillip's reaction was amazing. There's this old fellow who doesn't normally say anything to anybody and he was speaking up in groups of all these pastoralists, talking about his knowledge,' says Tim. 'He got what Peter was all about and what he was doing and how he was doing things to heal land. He could synchronise his culture with what Peter was saying.'

Phillip's contribution was powerful, and no-one felt it more than Tim. The merging of that other, older Australia with his scientific world view, which had begun when he'd met Tania, was offering new insights from this still deeper engagement.

'Their creation story is that this land was all flat, until the snake came along. The snake is the creative spirit that moved through the landscape. And water is the creative and destructive force in this landscape.' The snake Tim is referring to is the creator deity in Aboriginal myth. It has as many names as there were tribes, but it is more popularly described as the 'Rainbow Serpent'. The Dreamtime stories—and 'Dreamtime' is not then or now or at some future time but means rather 'throughout' all times and all spaces—have the snake deity as an all-powerful water spirit, digging into the land, lifting it or levelling it, nourishing life and occasionally dealing death and destruction.

'The Dreamtime stories make complete sense in scientific terms. I've discovered situations where the Dreamtime story is exactly the story I've had to figure out through a scientific route. It's how the landscape works, what's important and what's not. Some hills don't matter and some do. Some hills have a lot of control over where the water goes and what the river does. The sacred hills in the Marble Bar, the spirit hills, are the critical hills in the landscape for the control of the water. The waterholes that are sacred are also important holes in the river. It isn't surprising these guys figured it out. They've been here for fifty thousand years.'

The wealth of Indigenous Australia was in their observations and their understanding: the rest of us are beginning to know just enough to value that wealth as we should. We have pre-existing maps for water movement in these landscapes, and this is going to be of critical importance. Time, after all, is running short.

'So when I talk with pastoralists we talk about Mother Nature—how she works, how we bugger her up, how if we understand what she's doing we can get around and help her recover the landscape. If I was talking with the mob, we'd talk about the snake. It's the same story. Where we stuff things up we stuff up the water cycles,' says Tim.

With the knowledge we now have we can reverse injuries to the water cycle and grow more plants, and thus return carbon to the soil. The massive rains in Australia's central rangelands in 2011 produced a discernible drop in the carbon dioxide in the biosphere: in fact, sixty percent of the extra carbon the world stored that year was in our outback. Unfortunately, because that storage was only in grasses (and could only be in grasses because the type of land management and rewards for carbon sequestration Tim advocates are not in place) most of that carbon is back in the atmosphere again. Yet that event has taught us that with political will on our side—and with all we can learn from our land-rehabilitation pioneers and our scientists, including those who are Indigenous—the Australian rangelands could play a central role in cooling our planet.

In 2015 Tania and Tim reluctantly left Marble Bar and moved back to Broome where it all began. Tim is continuing to work with pastoralists and Tania is working back in health. They are grandparents now: David has three children, Sophie two, and both of them are warm and caring parents. This brings

Tim real joy, and he and Tania are equally proud of the other two. Scott, with courage and patience, has achieved his goal of supporting himself despite the difficulties presented by a severe illness. Jade has just finished a degree in Speech Pathology and is looking for her first job.

All Tania's little brothers—whom Tim considers also to be his own little brothers—have had children of their own. Broome is not the same place it was when they met all those years ago, but of course, neither are they the same. When Tim met Tania two worlds collided. It happened in the slowest of slow motion, and it is still happening as I write.

They could not have been further apart when it all started: in one corner of our stratified social landscape stood the hard-nosed, well-regarded white male agricultural scientist. In the other was the black girl in tune with the land, into seeing the connections and weaving herself and others into that living fabric, who had spent religion classes learning how to fill out dole forms. Even in those first moments of attraction they both began changing. Tim's trained-in reductionism met Tania's gift for seeing how everything interacts. Tania's inculcated acceptance of low Indigenous achievement met Tim's utter irreverence for authority. Falling in love in this case was far more than an exchange of hearts. Each has opened up to the other an Australia they'd never suspected could be theirs, but more even than that, in their love for each other, in their two Australias colliding and slowly merging, in their changing, in Tania's cultural brokering, in Tim's making scientific sense of Dreamtime stories, they have been helping into life a third way of being Australian.

This new way is one where non-Indigenous people in Australia talk about the Indigenous spirit of the land, share ownership of it, believe it and feel part of it, and where, knowing that they are valued as equal, our Indigenous people again feel part of the rest of the country. The price is that we must give up our old stories and make new ones, but this is an investment which returns us far more than we ever pay. We regain a feeling of security in our better connection to place and find peace in a more intense experience of nature. In feeling more connected to the planet we also feel more connected to other people. In Tim and Tania's passionate, disruptive way of being Australian, there's just more love.

Home Again

It is now the beginning of 2016 as I bring this book to an end. The people in it feel like family to me. I have just asked everyone to choose a song that reflects their story and Bill has instead sent me a film clip of him singing that song. It's the one he sang to Cissy on her sixtieth birthday. I've been by myself for eight days—one of the great love stories in my immediate family has ended without warning and the best thing I can do to help at this tragic time is mind the homestead—and it has been lonely. Listening to Bill sing, hearing his love for Cissy in his rich warm voice, has lifted my spirits. Love *is* the heavy lifter of the outback.

Love lifts us. It gives us energy. In the outback, where there is much to be done, we need every bit of human energy and wisdom possible. These are landscapes of extraordinary complexity. Plants, water, animals, life in the soil, temperature and the length of days, disaster, the shape of the land, the spirit of the land, all we've built and changed, our stories and rules, the markets and politics a world away … the landscape might suggest rugged individualism, but here interdependence rules.

Each interaction ripples through the landscape. Lay a finger on one part and you touch it all. And yet this complexity must not frighten us out of taking action to regenerate and heal: people have been part of this landscape for a very long time. In recent times we've added too much and taken too much away for these places to heal by themselves. Our heartfelt engagement with them is more necessary than it has ever been before.

The Australian outback is facing multiple threats, some are local, some national and some global. I've only touched on a few of these in this book, but I believe the biggest threat of all is that we will not find a way for us all to work together to solve them. The processes that we have accidentally harnessed to degrade the landscape are powerful but we can as easily harness them to heal. Solutions exist. It is the working together that is so hard. The easiest thing to do would be to stay locked within our camps of opinion, ego, profession, policy or social group. It can be very hard to transcend such barriers or even to build a professional relationship with someone in another camp. But it is vital that we do so. Stories such as that of Tim and Tania—of another kind of relationship which transcends such boundaries—show us why. When love dissolves the barriers between and recreates two people from very different worlds, the rest of us are offered a remade future too, and not just a new future for us but for the interwoven-with-us wrapped-around-us world.

We work on, for and in this landscape, and in return it works on, in and for us. Rebel learned to love Michael and to be loved in turn in his home town of Lightning Ridge with its ingenious, paradoxical landscape. In her multi-faceted projects I can see echoes of the Lightning Ridge landscape. To live where they dig, the miners grow new kinds of houses: to work where she lives, Rebel grows new kinds of business. The opal miners cooperate where other mining businesses compete, and just as paradoxically, Rebel uses distance and isolation to draw women closer. Somehow, along with Michael, this landscape seems to me to have become part of Rebel's soul.

The people in this book have taught me that, when it comes to falling in love, real life outstrips fiction. The ways we meet too often rely on an absurd series of improbable coincidences that can look oddly like destiny. When we meet we might talk our way into love, or play, or laugh, or simply look. We can fall with the speed of light or make the journey over decades. Our stories are held in those of our parents and our children's love stories within ours. Love stories start before we are born and continue after we die. I've found this learning fascinating, but, after all, how we fall in love is not the most important thing. How we treat the people we love the rest of the time is the most important thing.

How we treat each other is made more visible in the outback because of the lack of distractions, of other consolations and comforts, and, frequently, the lack of any other people. You can't miss the importance of love when you live here. The people in this book are successful because of their focus on relationships—not just relationships with each other, but also with their parents, children and siblings—but also because of their ability to relate past the barriers behind which most of us hide. They are people who are comfortable navigating complexity in the world they inhabit and in the people they love. Bill has just this moment written to me again to emphasise that we can do other things in the world but our first priority *must* be to the people in our everyday lives. As evidence that Bill is right, I just have to think of Cissy, making sure that her bush camp is the very best it can be; Luke and Frances putting all else aside for Todd's farewell to Lamba; Cathy's unstinting giving of her best to her students; Mary and John's rule that a good conversation takes priority over the work on the property; and Rebel and Robina's message that to love others women must also love themselves ... this is a book about love in everyday life.

So what is love? It gives us energy, so is it energy itself? Do we make it? Does everything make it? Is it a field that simply exists, that we can allow in, and that we can both draw from and give to? Can I find in this both Cathy's God and Kath's belief that love is the only divinity? Can this explain the strange gravitational tug of love which entangles the orbits of people who would normally never meet? Can it explain the exchanges we have with the landscape itself? I ask Rebel for her opinion. She says (hesitantly) she suspects it is something 'we interpret in our different ways', and then she describes love as a feeling that is made manifest in action.

So what do I think love is? I am still thinking about this, and I suspect I will be for a long time. It is far easier for me to say what love *does*. Love connects us, and it changes us—and in doing so, it changes the world.

Jo Jackson King, 2016

Acknowledgements

First I'd like to thank the people who trusted me to tell their story: Frances and Luke Frahn, Catherine and David Jones, Robina and Aaron Meehan, Mary and John te Kloot, Kath and Steve Baird, Rebel Black and Michael Matson, Bill and Cissy Bright and Tania and Tim Wiley. I thank their families too, and I must particularly mention here Janne and Richard Warwick, Ashling Turner, Lin Baird, Vickie Bright, Jade Wiley and Sophie Wiley.

The family members with whom I live—my husband Martin King, my parents Barbara and Tom Jackson, my sons Timu, Samai and Rafael—provide the best setting I could have in which to write. Martin's subversive humour and his encyclopaedic knowledge of science and the broad sweep of history kept me glued to reality; Barb's unfettered empathy and knowledge of Australia's social history is responsible for much of the insight into people found here; and I've tried to infuse Tom's knowledge of agricultural history, his passion for healing land and his bond with places, animals and plants into these pages. My sons have wielded equal influence. Rafi is ten and any discussion of love is agony for him: but the suggestion to use love song names as chapter titles is his, as is one inspired analogy, and by following his lead in natural history I learned a great deal that has made this book richer. Following Tim and Sam's lead took me further into understanding military history, Indigenous history, social justice, politics, spirituality and community healing; and my borrowings from their written and spoken thoughts add greatly to this book's poetry, currency and clarity. In addition to this, these six people have brought me coffee and food, encouraged me to exercise, taken over my roles at home and work and forgiven me as often as has been required (which is often).

A book like this is the product of thousands of conversations on thousands of topics. Some of these conversations have been online, others many years ago and others were conversations that I wasn't present for but have influenced this book profoundly. For those conversations I would like to thank Stephanie Degens, Bradley Degens, Elizabeth Jackson, Megan Jackson, Adrian Cutler, Ann Larson, Peter Howard, Cathi Montague, Christine Plaistowe, Canda Reynolds, Cathy Gillzan, Fred Provenza, Greg Brennan, Bruce Maynard, Dean Revell, Peter Andrews, Anna Tierney, Elsa Raubenheimer, Peter Lillenfield, Lyn Hawking, Lachlan Gatti, Annette Evans, Tim Goodwin, Katie Jeffries, Des Thompson, Wanda Flanagan, Fe Waters, Shay Telfer, Emma Hawkes, Janine Binsiar, Pam Mongoo, Art Diggle, Anna Hepburn, Andrew Binsiar, Carolyn Halleen, Mark Halleen, Maggie Dent, Jenny Allen, Janette Roberts, Caroline Thomas, Simon Thomas, Donna Chapman, Rebecca Handcock, Michael O'Brien, Gina Goddard, Terry Chilvers, Sandra Norman, Deb Costello, Liz Bowyer, David Chandler, Lara Hopkins, Karen Moyle, Bevin Rose, Noelene Turner, Cindy Payne, Jo-Anne Burgemeister, Sandy MacDonald, Bridget Bongers, Noel

Ferguson, Russell Shaw, Stuart B. Hill, David Bent, Tracy Bent, David Cake, Karen McKenna, Elaine Walker, Pia Kemelle Inverarity-Stone, Kate Williams, Cath Wood, Jennifer Bailey, Deanne Blake, Robin Pensini, Marie Parsons, Debbie Dowden, Kate Hutchison, Jenny Watters, Steph Bateman-Graham, Pam Armstrong, Michael Madlener, Andrew Outhwaite, Rachel Maslen, Amanda Rowland, Elizabeth Mackay, Sally Male, Alma Dender, Tanya Brown, Susan Wilding, Jo Johnson, Tracie Blair, Chris Ward, Bridget Cameron and Ann Anderson.

I could not have written this book without confidence in the education my sons were receiving. Christine Bevans, Jenny Wilson, Stacey Keating, Pauline Winrow, Narina Christensen, Sue Thompson, Joanne Dobbs, Alwyn Cann, Quita Berry, Noemi Reynolds, Lisa Black, Cathy Jones, David Platt, Gabrielle Garratt, Ian Hardy, Tania Aveling and Karen Woods—thank you all. I was also able to keep writing knowing that I had other people I trusted caring for my sons at critical times: my parents (of course) but also Stephanie, Bradley, Elsa, Peter, Caroline, Simon, Donna and Andrew.

With no readers there might as well be no book, so I would like to thank the people who are helping me get this book out into the world: Caroline Williams who took the author photo, the cover designer Christa Moffit, the typesetters, Theresa Bray, Adam van Rooijen and all the team at Harlequin.

Finally, thank you to all my editors: Jacquie Kent, Annabel Blay, Laurie Ormond, Elsa Raubenheimer, Kate James, Alex Nahlous, Julia Knapman and Jo Mackay. Annabel's faith in the book and in my writing was vital in Jo Mackay's absence. Elsa provided the first (and most extensive) of the copy and language edits and helped me submit a manuscript far closer to being ready for publication than would have been possible otherwise. Jo commissioned this book, telepathically detected the regular wavering in my confidence, kept me writing, and then took the manuscript to a new level with her vision of stories that unfold as if taking place before the reader's eyes.

Even with all of this help, there will still be mistakes, and they will be mine.